THE LAW OF DECEIT

USA *TODAY* BESTSELLING AUTHOR

K WEBSTER

DEDICATION

To Matt—
I always have and always will love you.

From USA Today Bestselling Author K Webster comes an opposites attract, age-gap M/F small-town romance!

He's a rebellious young man with a lifelong obsession with his mom's best friend.
He always assumed she'd be nothing more than a fantasy, but he's not the only one with forbidden feelings…

I've loved her for as long as I can remember.
She's my mom's best friend and a cop.
Two reasons why I should stay far, far away
from Sloane Thurman.

It's nearly impossible to keep my distance, though.
The ache for her rare smiles and
her sweet scent is more than I can bear.
I'm more than her friend's son.
I want to show her I'm a man now and that I could be *her* man.

My wish becomes a reality when Sloane takes in her nephew. She needs help and I'm just the man to step up. Hikes, coffee dates, and game nights are just the beginning for us. Entertaining the kid in an effort to get closer to her is no hardship. Being near her is the only reward I need.

As we spend more time together, I manage to break down her rigid walls. When she's not worried about her morals and being a good cop, she realizes the two of us can have a lot of fun.

A good time isn't all I'm after. If it were up to me, I'd haul her down to the courthouse and make her mine forever. Unfortunately, neither life nor love is that easy. There's no way my family would understand our relationship. A secret romance will have to do…*for now.*

We may be able to deceive everyone we care about, but one day our shameful secrets will come to light. For Sloane's sake, I just hope I'm worth the fight…

This is a complete M/F standalone novel with a happily ever after. Tropes for this book include: older woman/ younger man age-gap romance, opposites attract, he falls first, coffee lovers, mom's best friend, romantic suspense, secret romance, and found family.

Shameful Secrets Series

1 – *The Teacher of Nothing* (Callum's Book)
2 – *The Tangle of Awful* (Hugo's Book)
3 – *The Heart of Smoke* (Jude's Book)
4 – *The Law of Deceit* (Dempsey's Book)
5 – *The Torment of Two* (Gemma's Book)

TRIGGER WARNING

This book has triggering scenes for some readers including physical and sexual assault (not by main character), past family traumas, domestic abuse (to a side character), and other potentially upsetting subject matter. Please read with caution.

THE
LAW
OF
DECEIT

CHAPTER ONE

Dempsey
Graduation Night

All hail Queen Gemma.

While I barely made it to this night considering my shitty grades, my twin sister gracefully arrived with perfect attendance and straight As, earning the adoration and praise of every single person in this auditorium.

They all cheer proudly as she takes her turn across the stage I just dragged myself across.

I just want to go home, dammit.

"Can you believe we finally did it?" she whispers once she's seated again beside me in our chairs, diploma in her dainty hand. "PMU, here we come."

Nudging her with my shoulder, I smirk at her. "You're going alone, sis. I told you. I can't do college."

Her bottom lip juts out despite us having this same conversation over and over again. No matter what I do, I'll never be as smart as my sister…or good.

Gemma is just good.

The angel to my devil.

A twin who stole all the decent genes and left me with all the genetic garbage.

"You can't live with Mom and Dad forever," she says with a frown. "And why would you want to? They suffocate us."

Her.

They suffocate her.

If she thinks they'll allow her to live on campus like she wants, she's out of her mind. Dad is overly protective of her.

"I'll figure something out," I say with a shrug.

The last person walks across the stage and then the principal is back at the microphone, speaking about following our dreams and living life to the fullest. Gemma and every other fool around me grin at him, eating up all his empowering words.

Not me.

I just want to get the hell out of here.

"Cool tattoo," Brandy, a girl sitting on my left, whispers. She points a finger at my newest tattoo on the back of my hand.

"Graduation gift to myself," I tell her. "Designed it myself."

Gemma elbows me. "Mom is going to freak when she sees you got another tattoo."

We're eighteen now. It's not like she or Dad can actually do anything about it.

"I'm so scared," I deadpan.

The principal congratulating our class and the auditorium subsequently exploding with cheers and applause drown the rest of our conversation. All the girls around me with their fancy hair and caps pinned neatly on clap happily. The guys, however, all try to see who can toss their caps highest into the air. I decide to use mine as a frisbee to try and nail my annoying-ass English teacher in his bald head.

My cap disappears and unfortunately misses. Not that I give a shit. I'm ready to get out of here and go home, hide away in my room until I'm forced to socialize with family for the graduation party Mom has planned.

The next hour is a blur as we shuffle through the crowd,

looking for our parents to hitch a ride back home with because we still don't have cars of our own. Finally, we load up in Dad's SUV and make the trek back to our property.

As Mom and Gemma chatter with way too much enthusiasm, I stare out the window, wondering what happens from here. I can't go to college. No way. I'd die from boredom. But I'm also not cut out for working with Dad or my brothers. The military can fuck off because I'm not about to be some meat shield.

It won't matter that I don't exactly have it all figured out, though. Dad will expect a plan bright and early tomorrow morning. I'll have nothing but smart-ass remarks and general disrespect. It'll end in frustration and slammed doors. I know the drill.

There's a car waiting in our driveway when we arrive. I practically fling myself out of the SUV, eager to make my escape until the party starts. In the darkness, I can't make out whose car it is, but when the person steps out, I know.

Golden blond hair flutters in the late May evening breeze, sending a hint of lavender my way. I inhale the scent, knowing it without ever having to see who it belongs to because I've memorized it—obsessed over it.

She's a gorgeous, long-legged beauty with lips that beg to be kissed.

Local cop and pillar of the community.

Twice as old as me and my mom's best friend in the whole world.

Sloane Thurman.

I'm obsessed with her, but she's completely off-limits. She was in the room when we were born, babysat us twins on occasion when my parents needed a break, and has been a part of our lives for eighteen years.

Because she's *Mom's best friend.*

I can look all I want, but I can never touch no matter how much I want to.

And, goddammit, I really, *really* want to…

"Sloane," Mom greets happily as she rushes over to her best friend. "Oh my goodness. I forget how long your hair is. You really should wear it down more."

Sloane, lovely face shimmering in the moonlight, smiles at Mom. To my mother, it's an indulgent, patient smile, but to me, I see the slight tension in her shoulders and the twitch of a muscle in her cheek.

She's uncomfortable in her own skin when she's not being Officer Do-Good. Without her job and sense of purpose, Sloane grapples with her identity. This, I understand wholeheartedly.

Dad gives Sloane a slight nod but otherwise ignores her altogether. I feel like there's beef between them, but I've yet to find out what. Sloane is always around to help our family because of her loyalty to my mother, but I don't think she exactly cares for Dad.

Mom loops her arm around Sloane's and together they walk into our house. It's decorated with red and black graduation banners, a shit ton of balloons, and red streamers everywhere looking like barfed spaghetti.

The twins only graduate from high school once. May as well go all out.

I follow them inside, suddenly not so eager to escape to my room upstairs. Sloane looks especially good tonight in a form-fitting navy-blue dress that hits just above her knees. She has a couple of wrapped gifts peeking out of the top of her purse—another unusual thing to see on her. I've seen her plenty of times not wearing her PMPD uniform, but she's usually donning jeans and a T-shirt.

Tonight, she's not plain or wearing a ponytail, trying her best to blend in.

She sparkles and shines and fucking blinds.

My fingers twitch to sketch her form in the dress that should be illegal. Even drawing her feels forbidden. And yet, I ache to know how the curve of her breasts feels simply from running my pencil over the paper, mimicking their shape.

As guests begin to arrive for Mom's party, I slink away from the people and linger in the corner of the living room, my gaze never leaving Sloane. Watching her whenever she's around feels like a gift. An indulgence in a treat I'm not supposed to sample.

Sloane is a beacon of strength and resolve, yet shrouded in an air of unapproachable mystique. When it comes to policing the fine folks of Park Mountain, Washington, she's firm and unyielding. She sticks to her morals like fucking glue.

But the real Sloane beneath her badge and place in this community?

Well, no one knows that version.

Hell, I don't think she truly does either.

It's in my nature to poke and prod, testing people's limits to see if I can get some sort of rise out of them. Though the urge is there with Sloane, I don't. I can't. There are too many factors at play.

She's been my mom's best friend since high school, so there's a lot of history involved.

There's also the fact I respect her. Something about her

personality demands it. I can be a shithead to everyone else but not Sloane. She'd put me in my place.

The most important is that I'm stupidly in love with the serious cop who's old enough to be my mother and who will never ever see anything in a guy like me.

It's wrong to keep pining after her. Stupid. Reckless. Selfish.

And yet, I can't turn my feelings off just because it's the right thing to do.

I'm drawn out of my complicated inner musings when someone sidles up next to me. Spencer lifts a brow, asking a silent question. *How are you, cuz?*

Of course we're not actual cousins.

Technically, I'm his uncle, but he's older than me, so that's fucking confusing.

Spencer, despite also being a family fuckup like myself, has finally gotten his shit together. Who knew all it'd take was becoming a dad? Rex, his adorable kid, sleeps with his head on his daddy's shoulder, drooling all over his crisp Polo.

"Everyone's so happy for Gemma," I tell him, avoiding the topic of Sloane altogether.

"You graduated too, dumbass. Even if you did have to suck off your English teacher to get a passing grade."

"Mr. Collins wishes," I say with a small chuckle. "Although, bald heads and BO really do it for me."

"Cheer up," Spencer says, reaching up to poke at my cheek. "You're depressing as fuck to be around lately. Keep it up and I'm gonna sic Tate on you."

I grimace at that thought. Not that I don't like Tate because I really, really do. Nah, it's because Tate is a therapist—our family therapist, to be exact—and my brother Jude's boyfriend. Tate has an uncanny ability to get inside your head, pull out all the shit you don't want to discuss, and force you to inspect it under a microscope with him so he can fix you.

Hard pass.

I don't need fixing.

I just need a distraction. A new direction in life. Somewhere else to look besides the always magnetic and alluring Sloane Thurman.

Thankfully, before Spencer can pick inside my brain any more, the rest of our family and friends arrive. Mom turns into Party Planning Princess, magically greeting everyone, urging them toward the refreshments, and making sure everyone is having a good time.

They are.

As for me, if I didn't have Sloane for eye candy, I'd have bailed as soon as no one was looking.

I watch Sloane as she hands Gemma one of the gifts from her bulky-and-so-not-her purse. Gemma opens it, grins widely, and then hugs Sloane. From my vantage point, it's a white box. Probably a mirror. Gemma loves mirrors.

I smirk at my internal barb at my perfect sister when Sloane searches the small crowd of people. For a brief moment, I wish it were me she's looking for. What would it even feel like to be Sloane's man?

Before I can dream about such a scenario, her blue eyes lock onto mine. Her smile is small, but it feels fucking huge pointed my way.

Why the hell is she smiling at me?

Fuck, she's coming over.

My shoulder muscles tighten as she ambles across the room. I force my gaze to remain on her face and not focus on how her nice tits jiggle and bounce as she approaches. Staring at her tits won't win me any brownie points.

"Troublemaker," Sloane says, hugging her massive purse to her. "Looking kind of lonely over here all by yourself."

The first time she called me "troublemaker" was when I drove Mom's car into a telephone pole when I was thirteen. She wasn't Sloane, my sometimes babysitter. That day she was an angry cop. The nickname sort of stuck since then, and I hate that it makes my skin crawl.

I don't want to make trouble for her.

I want to make it all go away.

"Officer Do-Good." I grin at her, wide and fucking fake as hell. "They let you out of the donut shop—er, police station—long enough to socialize with the Park scum?"

Her brows knit together and her smile falters. "You okay?"

Hell no, I'm not okay.

The woman of my dreams has always seen me as a little shit stirring up drama in this town. If she knew I crushed over her so madly, she'd probably laugh in my face.

"Peachy. Just counting down until this shit is over," I admit with a huff.

"Same."

I jerk my eyes back over to her, surprised to find humor dancing in her beautiful eyes. "Sloane Thurman," I say, mock horror in my tone. "Don't let your bestie know you'd rather be anywhere than here. She might die of a broken heart."

She smirks at me. "Jamie knows how I feel about stuff like this." After she plucks the wrapped present from her purse, she meets my stare. "You and Gemma are special, which is the *only* reason why I'm here."

We're *special*.

Fuck, I feel thirteen again and not at all like the adult I now am.

Rather than cringing at her well-meant words, I take the horribly wrapped gift from her. She watches me, nervously nibbling on one corner of her bottom lip. I save her the trouble of the suspense and rip off the paper.

An iPad.

"Uh, thanks?"

Her shoulders stiffen and she lifts her chin. "It's more than just an iPad, Dempsey. You'll have to excuse that it's been opened, but I added some apps to it."

Curiosity has me plucking off the lid and retrieving the lightweight device. I have my phone for all my socials and a laptop I used for school, but I've never had a use for much more than that. Once I have the iPad out, I flip open the cover and hit the button to turn it on.

"The passcode is your birthday, but you'll want to change that to something more secure," she says, stepping closer—so close I can smell her fruity perfume that makes my mouth water.

Knowing she was there when I was born, hence how she knows my birthday, is a bit of a buzzkill when it comes to my crush on her. I mean, she saw my naked, screaming crybaby ass, for fuck's sake. She will *never* see me as a romantic interest. And I will *forever* be bitter over that fact.

The iPad shines brightly and I look over the apps, most of them I know well. She points an unpainted, filed-down fingernail at the Procreate app.

"It's for drawing. I know you do a lot of sketching in your drawing pads and notebooks, but I thought you might like to try your hand at digital art." She digs into her purse and retrieves another item, this one not wrapped. "This came today and I didn't have time to wrap it up. It's an Apple pencil. You use it to draw with."

Her thoughtfulness for my gift pushes away all my previous awkward feelings. Warmth blooms inside my chest and that familiar longing aches.

"I love it, Sloane." I love *you.* "Thank you."

She grins at me, relief shining in her eyes. "Good. I can't wait to see what you come up with. You're really talented."

I blink at her, soaking up her words. She thinks I'm talented?

"You want to see what I draw?" I ask, sounding dumb as fuck. "I, uh, sure. Yeah, I'll text you."

Carefully, I close the iPad and tuck it back inside the box, stacking the Apple pencil box on top. The paper I'd ripped off litters the floor in front of me. As if we both come to the conclusion that it needs picking up at the same time, we kneel, faces inches from each other.

Amusement dances on Sloane's usually stoic face and I can't look away.

She's so fucking beautiful.

"I guess you got this," she says, reaching over to ruffle my hair. "Stay out of trouble, kid."

And just like that, I'm reminded again of what I am to Sloane Thurman.

Her best friend's son.

That's all I'll ever be.

CHAPTER TWO

Sloane

Astifled yawn manages to escape and earn me a chuff of laughter from one of the detectives who's taken up residence at the coffee machine.

"Late night, Thurman?"

Detective Ethan Montgomery spends more time yapping his jaws than doing actual police work. I give him a tight smile, pushing past him to make my own cup of sludge.

"Aww," Montgomery teases, "I see how it is. Ignore your best friend in the whole world then."

As if I'd ever willingly hang out with that douchebag outside of work.

Andre Bishop, another detective, playfully punches Montgomery in his side and saves me from a response. "You wound me, bro. I thought I was your bestie."

I leave the two knuckleheads to sort out their bromance once my coffee is filled to the brim with enough cream and sugar to mask the tarry taste. One of these days, I'm going to spend my hard-earned money and buy this department a real coffee machine. Maybe even one that wasn't born in the late '70s.

The station is filled with the usual crew this morning. Even our new chief of police, Hiroshi Tanaka, is hard at it already in a meeting with what looks like the mayor. Tanaka is your typical COP—a suit-wearing top brass who schmoozes with the upper echelon of Park Mountain, Washington. We snagged him from Seattle and supposedly, he's the best of the best.

If he was so great, why'd he leave his cushy job in a big city then?

"You know, Sloane, if you keep glaring at the chief all the time like that, he's going to give you one of the shitty shifts," my friend and patrol partner, Aisha Patel, says with amusement. "What's your beef with Tanaka anyway? He's kind of cute."

I grimace at the realization I'm so transparent. If only I could learn to control this resting bitch face I have. "He's married."

Aisha shrugs. "So am I. Can't blame a girl for looking."

Bringing my steamy paper cup to my lips, I swallow down some of the bitter excuse for coffee, needing caffeine to jump-start my internal engine. You'd think someone like me, who grew up in the diner my mom worked at, drinking their own version of shit coffee, I'd not be so particular.

But I am.

I'm a snob who knows all the great local spots to grab the best coffee.

"Are you finished?" I ask, setting my cup down on my tiny desk. "I'd like to hit the streets early today. Being here in the station is making my skin crawl."

Aisha sighs heavily before plopping down in her seat across from me. In the mornings, we spend about a half hour catching up on paperwork before we cruise around, doing our part to keep the streets safe.

Since it's been fairly quiet this week, my report

completion goes quickly. In record time, I'm hustling Aisha along so we can get out of the station that reeks of chauvinism and Old Spice.

Once I'm behind the wheel of my cruiser, I finally relax. Patrolling the town of Park Mountain eases something that's always been locked up inside of me. I like being able to do my part to clean the delinquents off our streets.

People like my dad.

Aisha fiddles with the dials of the air conditioner while I take us to Main Street. My thoughts drift to when I was ten years old, living in the run-down, crime-ridden neighborhood of Walter Oaks. It was when I really began to realize my family sucked and I didn't want anything to do with them. It's also the year I met Jamie Park—Booker before she married—and discovered there were other people like me.

Good people.

Nice people.

People who didn't scam the system, get into whatever trouble they could find, or hurt others because they could.

"We're getting out of here one day. I promise."

Me and Jamie had a pact. As soon as we were old enough, we'd run away to some better town and start a new, happy life together as roommates. It was a solid plan until she got involved with the Parks.

Aisha rambles about her toddlers and how they can't keep out of the dirt of her potted plants. This is the norm for her. She tells me all about her wonderful husband and kids to fill the silent squad car and I listen, wondering how I came to be almost forty and never having thought of marriage or kids.

My mind drifts back to my best friend. Though we're worlds apart these days—me, a cop who makes mediocre pay, and Jamie, a stay-at-home wife and mother who's treated like a queen—we're still as close as two women can be.

"How did the graduation party go anyway?" Aisha asks, done talking about kids for two seconds to mention something else.

I shrug as I turn down Cedar, curious to see if there are any vagrants taking up residence in the blue house that's had a "for sale" sign in the yard for as long as I can remember. "It was fine. The kids like their gifts."

"What kid wouldn't?" Aisha says with a chuckle. "I mean, you got them both iPads. That makes you like the best auntie ever."

Auntie.

It's pretty bad I'm a better "auntie" to Dempsey and Gemma than I am to my own nieces and nephews. Guilt niggles at me, but I attempt to squash it. My older sisters, Nevaeh and Rhiannon, had a mess of kids each. Nevaeh and her five still live with Mom in the old house I grew up in. Rhiannon is shacked up with some loser, Lenny, who's playing stepdad to her three kids. I hate Lenny because he's a drunk like Dad was and causing chaos. If he keeps it up with the drunk and disorderly conduct, he's going to earn his ass a spot in prison beside Dad too.

My silence urges Aisha to continue babbling about anything and everything. Sometimes, I think if we weren't partners, Aisha would never in a million years waste her breath on someone like me.

I'm not exactly friendly, nor am I that great of a friend.

I care about my job and the found family I have in Jamie and the kids, but other than that, I'm not fun to be around.

Because you saw what fun brings. Your parents had fun all the time and look where that got them…

Honestly, I can't remember the last time I had fun. Maybe when I finally beat the super hard level on Candy Crush? Yeah, that's the kind of fun I have.

"Whoa," Aisha says, flinging her finger up to point ahead. "That idiot just flew through the stop sign and narrowly missed two cars!"

My heart rate speeds up as I flip on the sirens and lights to go after the rule breaker. We typically respond to calls around town, both emergency and non-emergency, but we've made our fair share of traffic stops when someone blatantly breaks the law in front of us.

The car—a dented-up Dodge Caravan from the early 2000s—continues to cruise without a care in the world. It could be an elderly person who didn't see the stop sign or even a distracted mother dealing with crying kids.

Or it could be something darker and more sinister.

That's what always keeps me on my toes with this job. You never know which way things will go. If you're always ready, nothing will surprise you.

"They're pulling over," Aisha grunts, already unbuckling her belt. "There's a carful. I'll signal you if I need you."

As soon as we've stopped, she gets out while I run the tags on the vehicle. It's registered to a man named Michael Dennison—nineteen years old. I keep an eye on Aisha, who's speaking to the driver. She sets her hand on top of the vehicle, which is my cue.

Quickly, I climb out of the cruiser and make my way to the other side of the vehicle. The woman in the passenger's seat is young—maybe seventeen or eighteen—and pregnant.

There's a person in the back. When I rap on her window with my knuckle, a pregnant woman rolls it down.

"Mr. Dennison here says he's just taking his girlfriend and neighbor to Nadine's Diner," Aisha says over the top of the car to me. "Didn't see the stop sign."

I cringe at the thought of Nadine's—a greasy spoon that I practically grew up in. Only the sketchy locals step foot in that place and it's a known place to go eat after a night of drinking or to cure a hangover. All the normal folks of Park Mountain choose to take their business to the upscale places that litter Main Street.

A gust of wind blows through the vehicle and the distinct smell of liquor washes over me. There are two Yetis in the cupholders, and five bucks says one of them has alcohol in it.

"What's in the cup?" I ask, nodding to the drinks.

Someone curses in the back of the vehicle.

"Pepsi," Dennison grumbles. "Can we go now?"

Aisha continues to talk to the man and I take a step back to see the person in the back of the van. A kid with shaggy dirty-blond hair buries his face in his hands and shakes his head. He's younger than the two up front and clearly frustrated by the turn of events.

I rap on the side of the van. "Open this door, please, so we can talk."

The kid tenses and then does as instructed. When I lock eyes with the familiar blues, my heart sinks.

"Hey, Aunt Sloane."

Jerking my head from my nephew to Aisha, I see her eyes widen in response. She gives me a nod to let me know she has things handled.

"Kaden," I grit out. "Come on. Let's take a walk."

He groans but obeys. Even though I don't see my family much, I still keep up with them. Kaden is Rhiannon's youngest boy. At thirteen, he's already falling in with the wrong crowd.

Once we're several feet away from the van and out of earshot, I put my hands on my hips and frown down at the scrawny kid.

"What are you doing, Kaden?"

He crosses his skinny arms over his chest and shrugs. "Going for pancakes."

"You should be at home with your mom, not riding around with a guy who's clearly been drinking," I hiss, pissed at both him and his mother. "This is dangerous."

"Mom doesn't care," he mutters, not making eye contact with me. "You don't either."

The guilt I feel when it comes to my sisters' kids once again punches me in the gut. I want to be the aunt he needs by pulling him to me and hugging him, but I'm on duty and he's in trouble.

"I'm going to call her to come pick you up," I tell him. "And we both care. You know that."

His lip curls up and he gapes at me as though I've lost my mind. "Do you know when the last time she bought groceries was? Me neither. Mikey and June, our neighbors, feed me more than she does."

Anger chases away any lingering guilt. He looks a little bony, but I thought maybe it's the age. Is Rhiannon really so far up Lenny's ass that she's letting her youngest starve?

"Where are Lucy and Trevor?" I ask. "Why aren't they making sure you eat?"

"Lucy moved in with Grandma and Aunt Nevaeh. She's been with them since Christmas. Trevor is never home and always off with his stupid friends." Kaden scowls at me. "You'd know this if you cared."

I don't let the guilt trip work this time. I'm not his aunt right now. I'm the law. And right now, Aisha is giving Dennison a breathalyzer test. If he's been drinking and driving with a minor in the car, the law will have to intervene.

"Once we sort out what's going on here," I tell him, my eyes darting back over to Aisha and Dennison, "I'm taking you back home."

Kaden winces and a flicker of fear shines in his blue eyes. "Whatever."

Taking a step closer, I study him. He smells like he hasn't bathed in some time. There are dark circles around his eyes from apparent lack of sleep and his hair is greasy. The kid looks exhausted and tired.

Exactly like I did at thirteen.

When all I wanted was for someone to rescue me from my shitty home life.

I had no one, but he does.

He has me.

"Are you safe?" I ask, eyes locking with his. "Tell me the truth, kiddo."

His eyes water and he stares down at my feet. "I hate him, Aunt Sloane. I fucking hate Lenny."

I'm not sure what's going on, but until I get to the bottom of it, I'm not letting my nephew go back to that man who's been nothing but an anchor weighing my already fragile sister down.

"You're coming with me. We'll get you some food and talk about what's going on. Maybe you can stay with me a couple of nights or something."

He searches my gaze, hope brimming in his eyes so bright I'm nearly blinded. "Really? I can stay with you?"

Before I can confirm, he launches himself at me, hugging me tight. My eyes sting with emotion, but I quickly blink it away.

Rhiannon needs to get her shit together and quick.

I'm tired as hell that our family keeps repeating the same mistakes, making each new generation of children suffer from the choices and consequences made by those who were supposed to love and care for them.

I'll be there for Kaden because no one was there for me.

CHAPTER THREE

Dempsey

"THERE'S COFFEE AND THEN THERE'S *COFFEE*," TATE says, emphasizing the second time he uses the word. "Coffee is the same everywhere. McDonald's is closer. Why not just grab your iced coffee from there?"

We stop at a red light and he looks over at me, shaking his head in mock frustration.

"Coffee is not the same everywhere. If you'd actually try it, you might like it, and then we could be better friends."

I snort out a laugh. "I tried it once. It was fucking sick."

"You got the wrong kind obviously. I'll make you a connoisseur yet. Just wait."

I'm amused that he's driving us to the other side of town just to get iced coffee from a place he and Willa deemed *the best* of Park Mountain. I never agreed to get coffee for myself. I'm along for the ride and in desperate need to escape my prison.

It's technically not a prison, but Dad still refuses to get me and Gemma a car. We're eighteen and getting ready to start our adult lives. It's ridiculous at this point. He's just being spiteful if you ask me.

Someone cuts Tate off and he bitches at them like a little Chihuahua even though the driver isn't looking at him and certainly can't hear him.

"Is Jude selling this thing?" I ask as I bump the roof with my fist. "I bet I have enough in savings for this piece of junk."

"Junk?" Tate scoffs at me. "This Jeep is a classic. She purrs like a kitten too." Then, to the damn car, he says, "Dempsey didn't mean it. He's just hangry."

Hey, I *was* promised pastries on this outing…

"I obviously don't think it's that big of a junk bucket if I want to buy it," I say, backtracking. "Seriously, tell your boyfriend I want it."

Tate rolls to a stop at another red light. He glances over at me, seeing straight through my words and getting to the heart of the matter. His uncanny way of doing that is super annoying. "Nathan still hasn't mentioned anything more on the car situation? I thought you were going to have a talk with him about it."

Gritting my teeth, I shake my head. "Every talk with Dad ends with disappointment and anger."

For the past month since graduation, he's been putting pressure on me to go to college in the fall. I refuse to do any more school. He then refuses to buy me a car or even co-sign for one. By the end of the conversation, we're both so pissed we can't even speak without yelling.

A car honks behind us, signaling the light has changed. Tate gasses it but not before shooting me a concerned look.

"We're not done discussing this," Tate says as he pulls into the parking lot of the coffee shop. "But no talky until after coffee."

I chuckle as we climb out of Jude's Jeep. Even though Jude can drive and the vehicle belongs to him, Tate always drives them everywhere. It's weird to see my brother out of the house and without a mask.

The coffee shop—Park Peak Brew—is rustic and has a bear sipping from a mug painted on the front window. It has an unobstructed view of Park Mountain in the distance. Naturally, idiots on their laptops who aren't even appreciating the beauty of the view took all the window seats.

Inside, the place smells like caramel and coffee, a scent I admit is enticing. Gemma loves her iced coffees, so I think I hate them on principle. Not that I hate my sister, because I don't, but I do love to be her polar opposite as often as I can.

"I think a caramel macchiato is what I'll get for you," Tate tells me as we stand in line behind a small woman in a PMU hoodie that swallows her. "It's sweet but still has coffee in it. Plus, before you graduate to iced coffee, you need to learn to love the warm, cozy stuff first."

I'm amused that Tate is making this whole coffee thing a *thing*. I like that he's joined our family. I mean, not technically like Willa did on a random Tuesday this past March when my brother Callum dragged her to the courthouse, but it'll only be a matter of time. Jude's so fucking obsessed with him. Tate's a cool dude, though. He's one of the few good friends I have who aren't related to me.

Yet.

"They have chocolate milk just in case," I tease, gesturing to the kids' section of the menu.

Tate gives me a withering glare that makes me crack up laughing. The PMU girl who's wearing a hoodie in the June heat turns to look over her shoulder at us in disdain.

"What?" I ask, grinning at her. "No talky before coffee?"

This makes her smirk and she faces front again. Tate gives me the side-eye, playfully nudging me with his elbow. That's his thing anytime we go out. He tries to point me in the direction of girls who look interested or laugh at my jokes. Problem is, I don't want any of them.

"Get her number," he mouths, discreetly pointing at the girl.

I shake my head, choosing to look out the big windows instead. The mountain gleams in the morning sunlight. It's pretty. Maybe I could come here some time alone, drink my coffee or at least pretend to, and steal one of the window seats to draw on my iPad.

Thoughts of my iPad bring thoughts of Sloane. After all, everything I've done digitally so far has been of her. I took her advice and changed the password on my device because if anyone saw just how obsessed I was with drawing her, they'd have me committed. The only reason I haven't drawn her naked is because it feels like a violation, especially since my illustrations are delving more into realism with my new digital capabilities.

Tate's chipper voice starts telling the barista our order. I remain standing in place, admiring the view, when a police cruiser pulls into a parking spot next to the Jeep. The same tight feeling I get inside my chest whenever I draw her forms in the hope it might actually be her.

Stupidly, I look for her in every cop car I see.

Always.

The police officer climbs out of the vehicle, dressed in a crisp navy-blue uniform. Immediately, I recognize the familiar, gorgeous face and my heart stutters. Somehow with no makeup and her blond hair pulled into a severe bun, she's more beautiful than ever.

Maybe it's the mountain behind her.

Maybe it's because she's doing what she loves.

Whatever it is, I feel lucky as fuck to witness it.

Someone gets out on the other side, but it's not her usual partner she's with. It's a kid—maybe thirteen or fourteen—who climbs out and follows after her.

They're coming into the coffee shop.

The door opens and Sloane steps inside. Even when she's frowning and in police mode, she still turns heads wherever she goes. Does she realize she has such magnetism? What would she do if she knew how twisted up I am over her?

Like the good cop she is, she scans the small coffee shop, looking for threats and familiar faces in one quick sweep. When her gaze finds mine, her features soften and a smile tugs at her lips. I don't know how I managed to earn it, but I'm thankful as fuck to see it nonetheless.

"Officer Do-Good," I say, sauntering over to her. "Sorry, but they're fresh out of donuts."

The kid beside her sniggers. "Aunt Sloane hates donut jokes."

Aunt Sloane?

"Hey," I say to the kid. "I'm Dempsey, your aunt's favorite delinquent."

She rolls her eyes at me, making her seem closer to PMU hoodie girl's age than my mom's. "Dempsey's trouble," she whispers to her nephew. "Avoid it whenever you can."

He grins and I shrug like being a troublemaker is all I know. She steps closer, filling my nostrils with her fruity scent, and squeezes my shoulder. "Keep an eye on Kaden while I order our drinks?"

For a brief moment, I see us as equals. I'm a friend helping a friend. A man looking after another woman's family.

Not a kid.

Not a troublemaker.

Someone worthy of someone like her.

"Oh, hey," Tate greets, handing me my caramel macchiato. "There's a table opening up by the window. It's a four-seater. You guys can sit with us."

This earns us a wide, thankful grin from Sloane. Suddenly, I'm really fucking happy I'm in a coffee shop. If Sloane comes here a lot, you better believe it I'll figure out a way to like the stuff if only to get to see her more often than I currently do.

Tate snags the table and quickly cleans if off with a paper napkin. He takes one of the comfy armchairs. I decide to sit on the love seat, wondering if Sloane will choose to sit by me or not. Kaden sits in the other armchair, making my heart rate kick up with anticipation of where she'll be forced to sit.

"PMU girl looked around your age," Tate says as he sips his iced coffee. "Oh my God. Heaven."

I laugh at his orgasmic expression as I sample my own drink. I'm stealing a peek at Sloane's ass in her tight work pants as I sip. "Heaven indeed."

"You love it? I knew it!" Tate sets his drink down to clap. "I knew I'd make a believer out of you!"

The drink actually does taste okay. I could definitely drink the whole thing. My appreciation isn't for the coffee, though. It's for Sloane Thurman's perfect, smooth curves.

"What about if we have a session?" Tate asks. "Just me, you, and Nathan. I could act as mediator."

Buzzkill, man. Fucking buzzkill.

"Why would you want to torture yourself?" I take another sip of the sweet drink and shake my head.

"Helping people is not torture," he says with a huff. "It makes me happy."

Before we can dive deeper into the conversation, Sloane arrives. She eyes the only open seat and then sits beside me. My spine straightens as I'm quickly aware of her proximity. She leans forward to hand over a jug of chocolate milk and a pastry to Kaden.

"Where's my pastry?" I ask Tate, arching a brow.

"Drink your coffee and you can have dessert after."

Sloane laughs, soft and breathily. "Is he always this bossy?"

"Always," I say as Tate says, "Never."

This causes Kaden to cackle with laughter, clearly finding his new coffee friends amusing.

"You working today?" I ask Sloane, casually letting my arm stretch out over the sofa behind her.

"Headed that way after." She sips on her drink that looks just like mine. When she notices my staring, she holds her mug out. "Cheers to liking the same coffee. Is that a caramel macchiato?"

"Yeah. I'm a virgin."

Kaden and Tate both erupt with laughter that causes several people—including PMU girl—to glance over at us with curiosity.

"Wait," I start, feeling fucking stupid right about now.

Sloane shakes her head, smirking, and holds up her hand. "Stop. It'll only get worse." She takes another sip of her coffee and motions at me. "How's the iPad? I keep waiting to get a picture to see your work. Have you even used it yet?"

Used it?

I've drawn countless portraits of this perfect woman.

Once, I even beat off to them.

To fucking art.

Shame curdles my stomach. I hate that I'm this way around this woman. I lose all cool and sense of who I am, stumbling over my words and acting like a general idiot.

"I use it a lot," I assure her, unable to meet her eyes. "I just can't show you anything yet. Not until I'm better."

She reaches over and touches my forearm, sending a thrill shooting through me. "I'm looking forward to seeing what you come up with. Text me soon and show me."

I find the backbone to meet her stare. She's being genuine and really wants to see my art. This settles something deep inside of me. I'll draw her something she'll love. Something really special.

Kaden burps from his chair, earning everyone's attention. He's wearing a chocolate mustache and a goofy grin. I burn the image into my head, knowing exactly what I'll draw for Sloane.

And then I'll have an excuse to text her.

All shitty thoughts of Dad and my future and a stupid car vanish.

Everything vanishes whenever Sloane is around.

She's magical as fuck.

CHAPTER FOUR

Sloane

KADEN IS BORED OUT OF HIS SKULL AND I CAN'T BLAME him. I don't have any other choice, though, but to bring him here with me. The department receptionist, Tara O'Connor, has been nice enough to help me keep an eye on him whenever I've had to go out on a call or patrol.

Why won't Rhiannon call me back?

It's been a month and she obviously knows her son hasn't come back home. I'm not exactly adjusting to having a kid in the house, but at least he's safe, fed, and somewhat happy.

Since they're my family, I'm not about to involve social services. From experience, I know they'll just put him back in the apartment with Rhiannon and Lenny, which is clearly not where he wants to be. My gut churns thinking that I may have to visit Mom and Nevaeh to see if they have a way of getting a hold of her.

"Can we do something fun tonight, Aunt Sloane?" Kaden asks, plopping down in the chair across from my desk. "All you do is work and when you get home, we watch boring cop shows."

I remember being in his shoes—when I finally escaped hell—and learning that when you weren't always in a state of distress, life was actually kind of boring. As it is for him, I found it difficult to adjust.

My phone buzzes on the desk and I hold up a finger, letting him know we'll get back to this conversation in a minute.

Dempsey: It's not my best work but I hope you like it.

I open the picture he's attached and find my nephew staring back at me. He's cheesing for the camera and has a chocolate milk mustache. In the illustration, you don't see the heartache and pain he's gone through. All you see is pure joy—the kind a child should have at his age.

It's beautiful.

My eyes burn and a lump forms in my throat. I knew Dempsey was artistic, but the level of skill he possesses is unreal. He didn't just draw my nephew. He took a perfect moment and transformed it into something everlasting. Something special and wonderful.

Me: Wow. I have no words. This is phenomenal. Thank you.

He sends me several smirking emojis that make me chuckle. I show Kaden and his eyes bug out of his head.

"Dempsey drew that?"

"Yeah. He's pretty amazing." I grin and look down to see he's texted me again.

Dempsey: You and Cayden should come over for dinner tonight. Mom likes seeing you and I could teach him to play pool. Might be fun.

Me: Kaden is how you spell it. I'll ask him.

My stomach twists in an unnatural way and I wonder if I'm getting sick. Probably all the stupid sludge coffee I have to drink when I don't have time to pop into Park Peak Brew.

"He wants to know if we want to come over for dinner tonight and—"

"Hell yeah!" Kaden hollers, jumping up from his seat before I can finish my statement.

I laugh at his antics, ignoring a few sour glares from some of the older officers at our precinct. It may not be cool to bring your nephew to work, but I did get Tanaka to authorize it. They can kiss my ass if they have an issue with it.

"Who wants to earn a king-sized Snickers?" Tara asks as she shuffles over to my desk. "I have some files that need putting away ASAP or they're going to topple over and bury me in my chair one day."

Kaden, who loves food and anything to take away the boredom, nods eagerly at Tara. I give her a thankful smile.

As my nephew walks away with her, I try my sister for the millionth time.

No answer.

Surprise, surprise.

◎

"Holy shit," Kaden says, whistling. "These people are loaded."

"Don't say shit," I grumble. "And please be on your best behavior. Dempsey's dad can be a bit of a dick sometimes."

Kaden frowns and I hate that I've taken away his excitement. He of all people knows about being around a dickhead. Lenny is the absolute worst.

"Come on. Jamie's a way better cook than I am. She'll fatten you up like a tick."

Kaden laughs as he climbs out of my car. "Anyone is a better cook than you, Aunt Sloane. Your specialty is frozen lasagna and pizza rolls."

"They're good, though, am I right?"

He cracks up laughing again. I know he agrees. The kid was catching a ride with his drunk neighbors just to be able to eat. Store-bought lasagna and pizza rolls are probably heaven to him.

I ruffle his blond hair and we walk up to the front door. My knock is sharp and no-nonsense, making me cringe. I even knock on doors like a cop.

Thankfully, it's not Nathan who answers but my best friend.

"Oh my gosh, Sloane," Jamie says with a squeal before launching herself at me. "What a surprise!"

A surprise?

What the hell, Dempsey?

"I, uh, I…" I trail off, feeling stupid as she hugs me.

"I invited them, Mom," Dempsey calls out from inside. "I knew you'd be happy."

Jamie pulls back and stares at me as though she can't believe I'm here. I come here sometimes. Okay, so maybe only on special occasions or when the Parks have trouble they need help with. But still, it's not that much of a shock.

"And who is this guy?" Jamie asks, turning her attention to Kaden. "He looks like you when we first met."

"I'm her nephew, Kaden." He offers her his hand, standing tall and smiling wide. "Nice to meet you."

Kaden is a good kid, but this is different. It's then I realize he thinks Jamie is hot. Ugh, boys are so weird sometimes.

After Jamie introduces herself, she ushers us inside. Kaden's crush on Jamie is squashed the second he sees Gemma.

"Oh shit," he mutters under his breath. "Oh shit."

I glance down at my panicked nephew. "Don't say shit and what's wrong?"

His face turns beet red and he stares unabashedly at Gemma. "It's Gemma."

"You know her?"

I mean, it's possible he knew her from school maybe. Except, I'm pretty sure he's in middle school which means they wouldn't have seen each other. Actually, I don't even know what grade Kaden is in. Crap, another thing to figure out before school starts back up in the fall.

"GemmaParkLovesUx2."

I wait for him to elaborate, staring at him in confusion.

"She's an influencer," he hisses. "She legit has almost a million followers."

Ahhh.

I still don't know exactly what an influencer is, but apparently, Kaden does. And it's a big deal to a thirteen-year-old.

"So basically a celebrity?" I ask, clarifying before I put my foot in my mouth.

"Yes. Oh my God, she's so pretty in real life."

Gemma, face buried in her phone, finally realizes she has guests. When she sees us, she grins happily. Kaden withers where he stands, clearly at a loss for what to do.

"This is my nephew, Kaden, and he's a huge fan," I tell her, motioning at him. "He's in shock."

If looks could kill, I'd be dead. Kaden glowers at me, humiliation turning his cheeks even redder. I've seen the same look on his mother's face a time or two. Well, crap. I really am sucky at this kid stuff.

Dempsey swoops in and saves the day, thankfully.

"Want to see my pool table?" he asks Kaden, ignoring

his sister and my faux pas altogether. "We have a mini fridge in the game room and like a million different kinds of snacks."

Kaden practically bolts out of the room on Dempsey's heels. Gemma chews thoughtfully on her bottom lip while Jamie runs her fingers through her daughter's long, dark hair.

"He's adorable, Sloane. Is he visiting for the summer?"

I like that answer. Why didn't I think of that? It's a lot better than his mother abandoned him and he needed rescuing.

"Yup," I lie. "I really am sorry for popping in unannounced. Dempsey texted and asked us over."

Jamie's smile falters. "I didn't know you and Dempsey text."

Something about the way she says those words has my blood turning to oil. It clogs every cell and makes me feel dirty inside.

She's not thinking…

Oh. No.

Absolutely not.

"The iPad," I choke out, eager to explain myself. "He showed me something he drew of Kaden. We, uh, ran into him and Tate at the coffee shop. Then he invited us over."

The tension in Jamie's body releases and her warm smile is back. She and Gemma chatter about PMU in the fall. How they're trying to talk Nathan into letting her live on campus. Gemma's major. Etc. Etc. I'm still processing the fact she thought something gross was happening between me and Dempsey.

Hell no.

He's a kid.

Well, not exactly a kid anymore considering he's eighteen

and has more tattoos than I can count, but he'll always be the little troublemaker to me.

"I was going to text you today," Jamie reveals as she motions for me to follow her into the kitchen. "One of Hugo's colleagues, Oliver, just went through a divorce. He's been dating a bunch of women who are only interested in him for his money. Oliver is pretty cute and has a great personality. How do you feel about me setting up a blind date for you two?"

The thought of going on a date with some rich lawyer sounds nauseating. But what's worse is having Jamie think I have the hots for her son.

"Really? Oh, uh, yeah. I'd like that." I force a smile. "Truly. Thank you."

I can think of a million other things I'd rather be doing than going on a date with this guy, but I walked myself into that trap. And who knows, maybe I might connect with the guy. The few dates I've been on over the years have fallen flat. Most guys get bored with my no-nonsense personality and want to skip straight to the sex. I'm not interested in having sex with someone I have zero connection with. Disappointment on all fronts for everyone involved.

Sorry, Oliver, but you're going to have to really be something special or this will be another dud date.

Jamie puts Gemma to work on chopping veggies for a salad. I excuse myself to go check on Kaden. When I make my way to the game room, I find Kaden listening, a Coke in hand, to everything Dempsey says. It's cute how taken he is with Dempsey.

Dempsey grabs a cue stick from the wall and then hands it to Kaden, exchanging it for Kaden's Coke. "Hold it like I showed you."

I sneak into the game room and watch them interact. Dempsey is patient with Kaden, showing him little tips and tricks. Compared to Kaden, Dempsey isn't a boy any longer. I'm realizing he's tall, lean with muscle, and carries himself like a man.

No wonder Jamie was worried.

Dempsey grew up overnight and he's turning into one of the Park men who turn all the heads in this town. This family ate up all the good genes, that's for sure.

He must feel me staring because he glances my way. The small smile he shares with me feels private and just for me.

Why?

Why does it feel that way?

I try to think about this Oliver guy and what he looks like. Jamie wouldn't lie to me and set me up with a toad or some weirdo. I've always trusted her, especially with something like this.

But thinking of someone I don't know doesn't work. I'm fixated again on the way Dempsey's black T-shirt stretches across his back and shoulders, revealing sculpted muscles underneath. Probably tattooed muscles. Just when the hell did he get muscles?

Stop.

Dempsey's electric blue eyes land on me once more, but all playfulness is gone. He searches my gaze like one might size up their prey. As if he's just now realizing he's not a cub but a grown-ass lion and I'm the gazelle just standing there waiting to get eaten.

His lips curl into a devilish grin that makes me break into a sweat.

What the hell, Sloane?

This weird thing between us ends now.

Bad decisions are for my parents and my sisters. Allowing myself to think of Dempsey as a man rather than the trouble-maker kid I've known all his life is dangerous. It's reckless and something my family would do.

I am not like them.

I. Am. Not. Like. Them.

CHAPTER FIVE

Dempsey

"A RE YOU READY, HONEY?" MOM ASKS FROM THE doorway of my bedroom. "You know your father doesn't like to be kept waiting."

Ever since last night, I've been trying to sketch the expression on Sloane's face. It was something different—unlike anything I've ever seen on her pretty face.

Surprise? Anger? Embarrassment?

"Do I have to go?" I grumble, snapping my iPad shut. "He already knows how I feel about this."

She gives me a sympathetic smile, but it doesn't make me feel any better. When it comes to Dad, she always, always chooses his side. It's so fucking annoying.

"You're going. Put on something presentable and preferably without holes in it."

Drawing Sloane will have to wait. Apparently, I've been summoned to go with my parents and sister for a private tour of Park Mountain University. It's like they still don't get the fact I'm not going. No matter how much they try, it's not happening.

As soon as Mom leaves me alone, I slide off the bed, grumbling about having to do this stupid shit. My holey Metallica shirt looks cool and was pretty expensive. But heaven forbid Dad's bougie friends at the college see what a delinquent his son is.

I snatch my standard black Polo for events such as these and yank it on over my T-shirt. The combat boots will have to do because I'm not wearing any lame-ass shoes. That's where I draw the line.

Stalking out of my room, I nearly plow over my sister. She, of course, looks like your typical college student, already wearing a PMU T-shirt and an eager-as-fuck smile.

Gemma sees college as an escape.

To me, it's a prison.

"You know," Gemma says, looping her arm through mine and grinning at me, "they have art classes there. Why don't you just take those?"

Everything I've learned is through observation and re-al-time research via the internet. Some antiquated professor isn't going to be able to teach me about any art I'll be interested in. Screw that. Sounds boring as hell.

When we make it downstairs, Mom smiles at seeing us. Sometimes I feel like I'm five and we're being paraded around town as the adorable Park twins. I don't feel adorable, goddammit.

"Your dad's already outside," Mom says, practically bouncing on her heels. "We have something exciting for you both. Come on."

Gemma shoots me a wide-eyed, gaping-mouthed look. Did they really get us cars? Finally? I find my mood lifting. Maybe this tour won't be so bad if we have the freedom to leave whenever we want.

My sister practically drags me out of the house behind Mom. It reminds me of Christmas morning when we were kids, so damn eager to see what Santa had brought us.

As soon as we're outside, I see a brand-freaking-new Chevy

Tahoe with a custom glittery black-colored paint job. All the doors and hatch are open, inviting us to come take a look.

It's nice as hell, but where's the other one?

I detach from my twin and stride to the back of the vehicle to see if Dad's hiding an Audi or something for my sister. Nothing.

Oh fuck.

He's not going to let her drive.

Her squeals of excitement make my ears ring. I'll let Dad rain on her parade. I'm sure as hell not telling her she's going to be stuck hitching rides from our parents forever.

Dad climbs out of the driver's seat to hug Gemma. She's talking a hundred miles per second, telling him how beautiful the car is and how excited she is. Mom simply grins so wide she's showing off every one of her shiny veneered teeth.

"Well," Dad says, turning his attention to me. "What do you think, Son? You like it?"

I scratch at my temple, feeling awkward as hell. He's being so blatant about it. Is he going to break my sister's heart right here in the driveway?

"It's nice," I murmur, breaking his gaze to run my eyes along the sleek SUV. "Really nice."

Gemma pulls from Dad's hug to dazzle me with a bright smile. "I'm so in love with it, Dad. Thank you!"

Dad nods, not correcting her. Wait. Is this car hers? Am I the one who's not getting one? Shock, outrage, and mostly hurt burn hot through my veins. I can feel my face turning red and I hate it.

Am I some joke to him?

The loser, worthless kid?

"As you kids can see," Dad says, voice gruff and firm. "There's one car here."

Here it comes.

Favoritism at its finest.

"There are some rules that go along with this vehicle," he continues. "You're not allowed to drive it alone."

Gemma frowns while I clench my teeth, staring vacantly at my sister's car.

"What do you mean?" Gemma asks. "Like with you or Mom? We're eighteen and can drive alone."

Dad grunts. "I know the law, but these are your mother's and my rules. If you drive anywhere, you must take Dempsey with you."

I scoff but secretly revel in her shocked expression that quickly morphs into anger.

"Because I'm a girl? Dad, that's so unfair!" Her big eyes fill with tears as she looks at our mother for aid. Fat chance, Sis. Mom's always on Dad's side.

Technically, with all her paid sponsorships on social media, she probably has enough to buy her own vehicle, not that Dad would let her.

"It's not because you're a girl," Dad explains, huffing in frustration. "Same with Dempsey. It's your shared car, but I want him to take you if he drives it anywhere."

Wait.

Shared?

Seriously?

We've literally shared every-fucking-thing since being in the womb and now we're sharing a car, too. Annoying but not all that surprising.

"Am I being punished because I don't want to go to college?"

I grit out, crossing my arms over my chest and glaring at Dad. "Because, if so, that's a mindfuck, Dad."

Dad stiffens and his nostrils flare. "I knew I had spoiled children, but I didn't realize they were both going to be such brats. I bought you a ninety-five-thousand-dollar car and it's not good enough? Unbelievable."

I guess he has a point.

We're not being very grateful. But it's his fault. He made us this way. It's not like he doesn't have the money to get each of us a car. He could have bought two cheaper cars for the price of this one.

"Whatever," I mutter. "Fine. Thanks, Mom, Dad. Car is cool. We'll drive together. All is good."

Gemma's shoulders hunch and she nods. "We do love it. Thank you. I just didn't expect to have to ride everywhere with Dempsey." She glances my way. "What about if he doesn't go to college? How will I get there?"

Dad glowers my way. "He's going. Now, if we're done with all this, I'd like to head over to PMU for our appointment."

He climbs back into the driver's seat and slams the door shut. Mom pats Gemma's back and then joins our father up front. Despite this being our car now, me and Gemma climb into the back like usual. I can tell my sister is trying hard not to cry. I'm pretty over this whole day myself.

While we drive and Dad prattles on about the features of the vehicle, I stare out the window as my mind drifts back to last night. Teaching Kaden to play pool was pretty fun. After the weird moment with Sloane, she bolted and left me with her nephew. I learned a lot of shit from that kid. His mom's boyfriend is a meth head and drives him crazy. There's never any food and sometimes the boyfriend knocks Kaden around.

No wonder Sloane has him. She's not exactly one to sit around while there's injustice going on.

My fingers twitch to sketch her face again. I feel like I'm almost to where I can recreate the look she gave me. It was warm. No, it was hot.

Hot?

Or is that wishful thinking on my part?

Maybe it was just happiness that someone was entertaining the kid for her. Whatever the look was, I'm curious to see it again.

I open up our messages and stare at our conversation. This morning, I asked her if they had fun last night and she never responded. Sloane stays busy at the police station, but it still hurts not to get a response.

This day fucking sucks.

Needing someone to talk to, I shoot a text to Tate.

Me: Dad got us a car.

He responds immediately as though he was waiting for this moment.

Tate: WHAT?! NO WAY! CONGRATS!

Me: To share. With Gemma. Yay.

Tate: Ohhh. Well, I mean, it's not uncommon for families to have their children share a car. It's not a personal attack, Demps.

Me: She can't drive without me and I can't drive without her.

The dots move and stop several times before he finally responds.

Tate: Yikes. Okay. We're definitely going to need to unpack that one. You free for coffee?

Me: Nope. On the way to PMU to check out my new prison. Fun!

Tate: Come over after. We'll sneak away and chat. Hang in there. Your dad loves you.

I give him a thumbs-up and then shove my phone into my pocket. Gemma, over her disappointment of having to share a car with me, happily talks about how beautiful it is and how excited she is for this campus tour.

My mind is back to last night as I follow my family aimlessly out of the car and toward the admin building where Dad is meeting his friend, who's the dean. I'll get through this stupid thing even if I have to pretend to be a robot.

The administration building smells like cheese and I curl my lip up. I already hate this place. Dad asks us to wait in the hallway while he fetches his buddy. Mom and Gemma walk over to the enclosed glass case filled with college memorabilia and trophies. Needing to escape them, I make my way over to a bulletin board that's littered with fliers.

Several are for people seeking roommates to share rent with. A few are offers for various odd jobs like dog walking or house sitting. Some are job ads for on-campus positions like admin assistant or cafeteria cashier. A cream-colored one with shimmery gold writing catches my eye.

PMU Art Expo - Looking for Artists

I quickly read through the flier. Essentially, the college is having an art expo to display different pieces in varying mediums. They even have a category for digital realism. The event will happen in a few weeks and influential artsy people all over the Pacific Northwest will be invited to attend. You can even opt to have your art available for purchase. It then provides an email and contact number.

The only requirement. You must be enrolled as a PMU student.

As much as I don't want to go to college, this art expo sounds interesting to me. Maybe I could supply a really awesome piece and get noticed. Would Dad take my passion seriously then?

He might…

"Ready?" Dad calls out.

I glance over to see him, an older man, my mom, and Gemma all staring at me. "Yup."

They turn to walk down the hallway. I start to follow, but my feet don't want to budge. Without second-guessing myself, I rip the flier off the bulletin board and cram it into my pocket.

I probably won't do it.

It's not like I'm a professional or anything.

But what if?

What if I made it all the way to Seattle and earned money from my art? Dad would have to see me as someone with hopes and dreams and talent. Not some loser, lazy ass. Plus, if I made money, I could buy my own damn car with zero rules attached. If Gemma can make money "influencing," then I can do it with my art.

That's pretty enticing.

Ahh, fuck it. I'm doing it. There's no harm in trying.

CHAPTER SIX

Sloane

THE GHIRARD CASE IS CLOSED.

Accidental explosion. No foul play.

I stare at my computer, confused as to how the case is done already. It's literally the biggest thing to hit our police department in the fifteen years I've been here. There was evidence of an arsonist and several disgruntled employees went on the record about how much they hated the Ghirards. Yet, after a few weeks of investigation, it's suddenly ruled out as an accident.

How?

I certainly don't buy it.

Our detectives are clearly sleeping on the job around here.

"Did you see this?" I ask Aisha, who's swiveling in her chair, waiting for me to get my ass moving this morning.

"If it involves work, probably not." She laughs at her own joke, but it fizzles when she realizes I'm not in the mood. "Oh geez. What is it?"

"The Ghirard case," I grumble, looking over the monitor to meet her stare. "It's closed. Accident. No foul play."

She smiles. "Ummm, that's good, dork."

But it's not good. This case wasn't something that should have been open and shut so quickly. It's the same with most every case since Tanaka took office. What if he's making all this happen to look good in his new position? That's plausible.

I glance over at Tanaka, who's on the phone in his office. His features are sharp and serious as he listens to whomever is speaking. Is it the mayor? Someone far more sinister like Harvey Ghirard?

"Come on," Aisha says, leaning forward. "There were six people killed in the Ghirard explosion. It probably gives the families peace of mind knowing it wasn't their boss responsible. Let it rest."

Prickles of unease stab along every surface of my skin. I can't let it rest. Something's not right and I can feel it. I might let it rest if it were the only thing to have happened, but recently, there're just too many "odd" things to count. I'm suspicious, that's for damn sure.

Or maybe you're looking for a distraction…

Thoughts of Dempsey infiltrate my mind and my gut sours. Ever since last week when me and Kaden went over there, I've been having these intrusive thoughts about him. It makes no sense because he's just Dempsey. Jamie's baby boy.

Maybe I should be the one investigated around here.

Ugh.

I need to get out of here. Stat.

"Whatever, I'm not going to worry about it any longer," I lie as I stand. "Let me go tell Kaden bye and we can hit the road."

Aisha playfully cheers. She hates desk work and suffers when I take my time doing it. While she gathers her stuff, I locate Kaden at Tara's desk. She's put him to work with a label maker and made him label files over the messy handwriting of certain officers. It's a good job for him and will keep him busy for hours until I grab him for lunch.

"Where do you want to go eat when I get back?" I lean against Tara's desk and peer down at him. "I can't handle fast food again. My stomach hates me."

He sniggers. "Your farts are worse than mine."

"Doubtful," I say with a smirk. "Yours make my eyes water."

His gaze falls back to his file and his shoulders go stiff. "What about Nadine's?"

I freeze at the mention of that place. Mom still works shifts there and we're not exactly on good terms. But maybe he's missing his family. Just because I'm estranged doesn't mean he wants to be. It'd be selfish to deny him this no matter how much I will hate my life.

"Lucy's working there this summer," Kaden says. "I miss her."

Like I can say no to that. Ugh. Kids. They're great at knowing exactly which buttons to push to get what they want—or in this case, need.

"Yeah, bud. We can go there. But when my farts out-stink yours, I don't want to hear any complaining."

Tara winks at me, letting me know she's proud of how I handled it. It's definitely relieving since I feel like I'm flying blind with this. Tara has a couple of teenagers, so she knows better than anyone.

Aisha comes running to me while talking into her radio. She motions for me to move my ass. I give Kaden a quick wave and then we race out to the car as she fills me in on our call.

Three-vehicle accident on Main Street.

As we rush to the squad car, I pass by a shiny red Porsche

that's parked in the chief's spot. I make a note to have it towed later if it's still here when we get back. The police station is near Park Mountain Bank & Trust and we often have people park in our lot if the bank's is full. It's an annoying pet peeve of mine and I take satisfaction in having them towed if they outstay their welcome.

"How much do you think they pay him anyway?" Aisha asks as we get settled in the car. "I mean, they're not paying us that well."

I drive past the parked Porsche with the new paper tags on the back. "That's Tanaka's?"

"Yup. Saw him drive up in it this morning."

"Hmm," I utter under my breath.

Something is up with our chief and I'm not crazy for thinking it. Perhaps I'll have a little investigation of my own.

Today has been a day from hell for car accidents. You'd think the people of Washington had never seen rain before. Tara texted to let me know she'd take care of feeding Kaden since I never made it back to the station. I feel like a terrible aunt making promises I can't keep.

When I clock out for the day, dead on my feet, Kaden waits by the front door, eyebrows furrowed. I can tell he wants to ask about going to Nadine's but must see the look of pure exhaustion on my face.

"Still up for our diner date?" I ask while stifling a yawn.

His lips curl into a grin. "Yup. Tara made me a peanut butter and jelly sandwich for lunch. Not exactly filling."

Teen boys and their bottomless pit stomachs.

"At least you got lunch," I tease, elbowing him. "I ate

some peanut butter crackers Aisha had stowed away in the glovebox. I'd kill for some onion rings about now."

We chat about how his day went for the fifteen minutes or so it takes to get to Nadine's Diner. It's always busy morning, noon, or night. Cheap, decent food within walking distance of two apartment complexes and three neighborhoods. I haven't been here in years, so when we pull into the parking lot, I'm hit with a sudden bout of nostalgia.

So many days I used to sit in one of the empty booths, working on homework and dreaming of a better future for myself. I finally got where I wanted to be, but until I made it, I wanted to give up so many times.

Unlike Jamie, I didn't have a knight in shining armor to swoop me off my feet and save the day. I had to earn it myself, fighting tooth and nail along the way.

Before I can psyche myself up to go inside, Kaden flings himself out and all but runs to the front door. I groan at his enthusiasm and quickly follow after. The bell chimes when I push through. Kaden is already sitting at the counter and picking up the menu. Lucy is on the phone, taking an order, but is grinning at her younger brother.

When did she get so grown?

Rhiannon made beautiful babies, that's for sure. It may have been the only good thing she's done in her life.

Lucy ends her call and then lets out a yelp of excitement at seeing us. She hugs her brother and then hugs me before I sit down. Her golden tresses are pulled back into a high ponytail that looks cute on her.

"Long time, no see, Aunt Sloane," Lucy says, smiling so wide her jaw has to ache. "Grandma said you were looking after my brother. Thank you."

At least I know Mom got my messages. It would have been nice to get a response.

"You guys must be cramped living in Grandma's house," I say as I sit next to Kaden on a barstool. "Where do you sleep?"

She winces at my question and I know I've already screwed up. I sound like a suspicious cop and not like a caring aunt. Lucy presses her lips into a firm line and pushes a menu at me.

"We all manage. What'll you be having?"

Kaden orders enough food to feed an army, which makes Lucy glance at me with a questioning look. I nod to let her know it's fine and then add in a cheeseburger, onion rings, and root beer for myself. She slips away to pass our order on to the cook and to make our drinks.

"You're cool once you spend time with you," Kaden assures me as he gives me the side-eye. "Lucy will come around."

I relax at his words. I'm a terrible aunt, I know, but at least Kaden is learning that I'm at least trying to be a good one.

Lucy does return and is once again smiling. I let the siblings do all the talking in an attempt to keep from screwing up again. Questions pile up in my mind, but I refrain from asking every single one of them. Thankfully, once our food has been delivered much later, Kaden asks her what I want to know.

"Have you talked to Trevor?"

Lucy scowls as if her older brother is standing right in front of her. "No, but I'm surprised you haven't." She glances my way, but then the anger quickly turns to guilt. "I'm sorry. He's just too much like Lenny for his own good."

That makes my hackles rise.

Lenny is a piece of shit.

"Is he using?" Kaden asks, voice soft. "Is that why he's been being a dick?"

"I'm guessing so." Lucy frowns as she absently scrapes a glob of ketchup off the countertop with her thumbnail. "I was tired of them all. Grandma may not be perfect, but at least it's peaceful at her house."

Peaceful?

Growing up, my house was far from peaceful. Dad was a cruel drunk. Mom drank to put up with him. Together, mixed with their on-again, off-again long-time lover, Jim Beam, they'd nearly bring the house down with their fights.

Nothing was peaceful.

Dad still lived at home with Mom when I got out of there at eighteen. It was constant chaos even then. He eventually went to jail and his violent tendencies landed him a long, cushy sentence in a penitentiary upstate. He's been serving time ever since and won't be up for parole for another few years.

Is Mom happy now or does she miss the forever drama?

As curious as I am to know those answers, it's not the most important thing at the moment. Right now, I'm more worried about Trevor.

"Should I visit Trevor?" I ask, hating that I'm back to cop mode. "If he's using or even dealing, he's setting himself up for trouble."

"You would do that?" Lucy asks, hope brimming in her eyes. "I mean, he would hate me for wanting you to check on him, but I'm worried about him."

She's not pissed?

I glance at Kaden, who wears a matching expression. For

once, I don't have to be the bad cop. Maybe I can be the good one plus a good aunt too.

"Of course," I promise. "Do you have any idea where he's been staying or who his friends are?"

"He's been hanging with some uppity kids. A couple of them work at Park Mountain Lodge. They party nonstop but spend time 'working' at the lodge when they need money." Lucy sighs when a customer walks in. "Dinner rush is about to hit. Thank you, Aunt Sloane."

"For what?"

"For caring."

That's something I'll never stop doing with these kids. I will keep caring about them even when they don't want me to. I have a feeling Trevor definitely doesn't want me to.

Tough luck for him.

CHAPTER SEVEN

Dempsey

"COFFEE?" I GRUMBLE FOR THE FIFTEENTH TIME AS I lace up my combat boots. "You woke me up for coffee? Isn't that like an oxymoron or something?"

Gemma smooths out her long dark hair before wriggling her pointy cat claws at me. "Don't pretend you didn't sleep through English and actually know what an oxymoron is."

Ignoring her, I make a pass through the bathroom to fix my hair and brush my teeth. She stands sentry by my door with her giant Louis Vuitton handbag that matches her fingernails so precisely it's scary. Knowing my sister, she probably did that on purpose to show her followers how stylish she is. That influencer shit she does seems exhausting.

"I'm driving," I tell her as I snag my chain wallet and hook it to my belt. "If I'm being forced out of bed to get coffee with you, then I at least get to drive the damn car."

Gemma, with her model-runway face already made up with lash extensions and whatever else bullshit makeup that probably took her three hours to apply, glowers at me. With a frustrated huff, she lobs the keys at me, nearly taking out my fucking eye.

"Mean," I say with a grin. "Always so mean."

She softens and shrugs. "You bring out the best in me. What can I say?"

The thing with Gemma and me is that no matter how different we are or how much I resent her place in our family over mine, we always will be friends. She's been my go-to person since before we could speak. If there was trouble to get into, we did it together. When we became teenagers, that all changed because Dad watches her like a hawk, but we still manage to maintain that friendship okay.

Mom is cleaning all the old silver at the dining room table when we make our way downstairs. Her hair is pulled back in a messy bun and she's not wearing a stitch of makeup. She's also wearing her messy housecleaning clothes. We have a house cleaner, but she likes to clean it first so it isn't so dirty for the maid. Again, I think that's an oxymoron, but according to Gemma, I may have that confused because she's right, I did sleep in English.

"You two are up bright and early," Mom chirps, grinning over at us. "My sweet babies are driving now."

I bite back the fact we should've been driving two years ago, but it's not necessary to start wreaking havoc this early in the morning. Plus, my beef is mainly with Dad, not Mom. I'll save my smart-ass comments for him.

"We're going for coffee. I'm bringing stuff back for Willa and Tate. You want anything?" Gemma asks as she digs around in her purse for something. "I'll need your credit card, though."

I snort out a laugh and Mom smirks at me. Gemma always has an excuse to use our parents' credit cards. I'm pretty sure the purse she's wearing was one of those times.

"Nah," Mom says with a chuckle. "Just use your account. If you need more money, text Dad."

Texting Dad to refill our accounts between allowance time usually comes with a lecture about money management and responsibility. I would rather cut off my own foot with a pocket knife than have to sit through one of those. Apparently, Gemma feels the same.

"It's fine," Gemma grumbles. "I'm getting paid tomorrow for that ad I did for Sparkles Gems and Fine Jewelry."

Gemma makes money, she just doesn't like spending it.

"I've got you," I assure my sister, even though we both know she's got a shit ton more money than I do. "Since you're letting me drive and all."

Her grin is vibrant and blinding. "That's why you're my favorite brother!"

Mom waves at us as we head into the garage. Her Mercedes rarely sees the light of day since she's mostly a homebody and rides everywhere in Dad's car. I wonder if I can talk her into giving Gemma her car and I can keep the Tahoe for myself.

The twin connection must be buzzing with electricity because Gemma looks over at Mom's car like it's an aging minivan and says, "Ew, no. Never. It's a mom car."

We both crack up laughing as we climb into the vehicle. Dad pisses me off with this whole car shit, but this vehicle is nice. I'd love being able to drive it around all by myself and go wherever the hell I please. Maybe one day.

He's been more bearable once I agreed to enroll at PMU. Of course he doesn't know my reasons for doing it, but he was pleased nonetheless, which got him off my back.

The drive to town isn't quiet. Gemma, the passenger princess, has already hooked her phone up to the stereo and is playing something obnoxious from her playlist. I'm able to tune it out because I have something better to think about.

Sloane.

Always Sloane.

That woman is never far from my mind. Last night, I drew what I thought she might look like with her shirt hanging down just low enough to expose her nipple. It was so fucking hot that I immediately jerked off, making a huge-ass mess. Shame had me deleting that artwork so fast off my device, though.

Who the hell does that?

Before I can make myself feel any worse than I already do, we're pulling into the coffee shop that apparently the whole damn town loves. We decide to hit the drive-through rather than go in since it's madness inside. When we reach the speaker to order, Gemma climbs across the console to yell out her three orders.

"Anything for you?"

A sudden impulsive thought comes to mind.

"Two caramel macchiatos," I blurt out. "Please."

Gemma frowns at me in confusion as she settles back into her seat. A nervous buzz of energy pulsates through me. I just ordered Sloane a drink. What now? I'm just going to show up and bring it to her?

Fuck.

And now Gemma is watching me with narrowed eyes, trying to use her twin powers to read my mind.

"It's for Sloane," I say to put us out of both our misery. "She likes the same thing as me."

Gemma's sculpted eyebrow hikes up her forehead. "Since when do we bring Mom's bestie a coffee?"

I shift in my seat, avoiding her stare. "Since now. It's called being nice."

"Nice," she repeats. "Interesting. You do remember she's a cop, right?"

"Yeah, smart-ass. And I haven't done anything wrong. We'll drop it off on the way back home. Stop making it a big deal. It's not a big deal."

Oh, it's a big fucking deal.

"None of my business," she says, waving her manicured hand at me. "Carry on, Romeo."

Heat creeps up my neck, but I don't satisfy her with an answer. She can assume I'm crushing on Sloane all she wants. It's not like she'll ever be validated with the truth. I'm not telling a fucking soul about this. Even Tate has tried to pry the information out of me and I won't budge.

We pull up to the window where I pay and then fetch our crazy amounts of coffee. The girl at the window flirts with me, making sure to lean out the window to give me a nice view of her cleavage. I'm sure this works on most guys. Not this one. This one is still obsessing over the tits he drew last night.

Gemma observes everything quietly, which makes my skin crawl. Ignoring her scrutiny, I drive toward the police department. I'm jittery, even without the coffee, wondering just how bad of an idea this is.

The station is jam-packed with cars, but I find a spot up front. It's marked "Chief," but it won't matter since this'll take a second.

"Wait here," I instruct, shooting my sister a death glare. "This will go faster without you."

She sticks her tongue out at me. "What if she's not there? What then?"

I don't reward her with an answer as I climb out with Sloane's coffee in hand. If she's not here, I'll toss it in the trash. Actually, that's preferable since I don't want to humiliate myself.

"Dempsey?"

As I walk inside, I see a familiar face behind the front desk. Kaden grins at me, as though happy to see me. This, at least, doesn't make me feel like a total tool visiting one of the places I hate the most. I saunter over to him and offer my fist for him to bump. He returns the gesture before nodding at the coffee.

"For Aunt Sloane?"

My cheeks heat. "Yup. She probably doesn't want it—"

"Are you kidding?" he hisses. "She's a witch when she has to drink the coffee in the breakroom."

The other woman behind the desk sniggers along with Kaden. "You're a lifesaver today, hon."

She points to where Sloane sits at her desk, head bowed and brows furled together in concentration. A tendril of blond hair has slipped from her immaculate bun and teases along her jawline. My fingers itch to stroke it back into place for her.

"I heard you were in need of saving," I say in a forced, easy greeting. "Your savior has arrived."

Sloane jerks her head up, confusion marring her pretty features when she sees me. Then, her eyes skate over to the coffee. A huge grin curls up her tempting lips and she lets out a girly squeak of delight.

"Oh my God! Dempsey, I love you!"

Several men in suits—probably detectives—glance our way. Meanwhile, I'm trying hard not to pull her words deep into my soul and take them as truth—as everything. Sloane rises from her chair and accepts the coffee from me. Our fingers touch, sending thrills of pleasure rippling through me.

"We were already there and this place was on the way," I explain, my tongue tangling in knots. "I just thought it would be nice."

Her eyes close as she inhales the aroma. Then she takes a sip before giving me the most rewarding groan of pleasure. My mind immediately goes to scenarios where my tongue has her making those sounds.

Fuck.

I'm losing control.

"Sit for a second," she says, pointing at the seat across from the desk. "How is everyone?"

Right. Mom's bestie. She wants the obligatory family checkup.

"Mom's cleaning silver, Dad's working, me and Gemma are all signed up for college."

Her eyebrows lift in surprise. "You're going to college?"

Her words strike me, feeling every bit like the loser I am. A flare of anger spikes in my chest. Anger at me, at Dad, at her. Mostly just me, though.

"Yup," I clip out, irritation in my tone. "Shocker, I know."

"Oh," she mutters and then curses under her breath. "I'm so sorry. Sometimes things come out worse than I mean them. I just didn't realize you liked school. I thought maybe you'd do something with your art, is all."

Her explanation soothes my embarrassment. Maybe she doesn't think I'm a total tool bag.

"Students can enter this art expo they're doing," I tell her with a genuine smile. "So maybe I can kill two birds with one stone."

Blue eyes bore into me, studying me closely and more intensely than ever before. I want to squirm under her gaze, but despite feeling awkward, I like being here. I like any part of her on me, even if it's only her eyes.

"I'm really proud of you," she says and then sips her coffee. "You always had way more potential than you let on."

"Gee, thanks," I deadpan.

"Well," she teases, "it's the truth. You know I'll always be straight with you, kid."

Kid.

Fuck my life.

Clearing my throat, I start to stand, deciding I've had enough emotional torture for one morning. Panic glimmers in her gaze and she holds up a hand to stop me.

"Wait, Dempsey, please." She sighs heavily and rubs at the tension on one side of her neck. I'd love to put my fingers there instead. "You know I never say the right thing. I appreciate you and I know you're a good guy. Look how well you've done with Kaden. He worships you." She bites on her bottom lip and then looks at me with slightly hooded eyes. "I was wondering if I could ask a favor."

Oh great.

She wants me to babysit.

"It'll cost you," I grit out, not giving a shit about the money. I'll find something else to trade for. "My services don't come for free."

Sloane chuffs and shakes her head. "That Park blood runs thick in those veins, huh?"

I shrug. "I am what I am."

She glances around the station before lowering her voice. "My nephew is in trouble."

All teasing evaporates as I stiffen at her words. "Kaden?"

"No, Trevor. He's around your age."

I only know of one Trevor who hangs out at the lodge and can be a major prick.

"What's going on?"

"He's been hanging out at your uncle's place with some guys who work there," she says, confirming that this guy may be the one I know. "Lucy and Kaden are worried he's using or even dealing. I just wondered if maybe you could help me locate him. I'm not sure if he'll talk to me, but I have to try. And, I can't exactly use police resources or be on the clock when I'm doing it."

Help Sloane?

Fuck yeah.

"Text me later and we'll discuss it more?"

She winces ever so slightly like she's just agreed to a deal with the devil but nods in agreement. "Tonight. After work."

"It'll still cost you," I say with a teasing grin. "I'll figure out my payment later."

Her eyes narrow, clearly sensing bullshit from me, but her love for her nephew prevails. "Deal."

Holy shit.

Me and the gorgeous, out-of-my-league, older, forbidden woman cop have a deal.

I'm going to make it worth it for both of us.

Trevor, here I fucking come.

CHAPTER EIGHT

Sloane

H E BROUGHT ME COFFEE THIS MORNING.

A sweet, simple gesture that brought me immense joy.

So why does it feel wrong?

I look up from the book I'm pretending to read and watch Kaden take out other players with scary precision on his video game. Maybe he'll be a cop one day too and use his powers for good.

As he continues to annihilate the competition, I ponder this new, strange dynamic in my relationship with Dempsey. He's always just been Jamie's kid. Now he's inviting me over for dinner, befriending my nephew, bringing me coffee at work, and helping with my other nephew.

My phone buzzes on the sofa cushion beside me with an incoming text.

We can add texting as something me and Dempsey do now too.

This whole thing doesn't feel right. I know that if Jamie were to find out, she'd be angry. I mean, she kind of freaked out on me when she learned we'd been texting.

It's not like that, though.

Dempsey is just being helpful and kind. It's nothing more.

With a frustrated sigh, I pick up my phone and prepare myself to read whatever Dempsey has sent me while trying not to *read into it*. But it's not Dempsey.

Jamie: I heard the news.

I stiffen at her text. What the hell does that even mean? Is she about to bitch me out for talking to her son?

Jamie: That you blew off Oliver. Ring any bells?

She sends some bell emojis to emphasize her words. It takes me several seconds to realize we're not talking about Dempsey.

Me: I didn't blow him off, Jame. I just told him I don't have time to date right now. With Kaden being here, that's the truth.

Jamie: It was a total blow-off and you know it. Oliver is a great guy. He's even friends with your new chief, too. That should tell you something.

It tells me something all right.
If Oliver is friends with Tanaka, he might be sketchy too. I put a pin in that thought to unravel later when I'm not having an existential crisis over this blossoming friendship I'm having with Dempsey.

Jamie: I think you should text him back and set up a date. Do it now.

I'm reminded of when we were twelve years old, running the streets together. She was bossy back then as well. Relentless, too.

Me: You're not going to let me out of this are you?

Jamie: Nope. Text me back once you've set a date.

Grimacing, I open the text messages between me and Oliver. He was nice and friendly when he reached out a few days ago to ask me out. We talked back and forth a little bit to get to know each other. And, while he seemed like a decent guy, I just wasn't in the mood to go on a date. Especially with all that's going on with my family.

Me: Hey, Oliver. I might have some time this weekend if you want to meet up for lunch or something. It's kind of last minute, so no big deal.

The dots move for a few seconds and then he immediately responds.

Oliver: I can't do lunch, but what about dinner on Saturday? There's this cool little pizza place I've been wanting to try. Pick you up at 7?

The last thing I want to do is go to dinner with this man, but it'll get Jamie off my back and hopefully distract me from thinking strange things about Dempsey.

Me: I'll meet you there. 7 is great.

I send him a thumbs-up emoji to end the conversation. At least I hope it's a conversation ender. Then I flip back over to Jamie and reply.

Me: We're having dinner on Saturday night. Happy?

She sends me dozens of heart-eyed emojis and then offers to help me with my makeup, which I vehemently refuse. I finally get her off my case when I promise we can have brunch Sunday morning so I can fill her in on how it went.

My phone starts ringing and I brace myself for Jamie's

excitement but freeze when Dempsey's name flashes across the screen.

Why is he calling?

Panicking, I send it to voicemail before shooting him a text.

Me: What's up? I'm a little tied up at the moment.

He sends me a bunch of big eyes emojis that I'm unable to interpret.

Dempsey: When you get a chance, call me back. I've already been collecting intel on your nephew.

My stomach twists, making me regret eating more fast food tonight for dinner. I'm going to have to start cooking or something because I can't take much more of Kaden's food choices. He sure as hell hates my microwavable dinners. We're going to have to meet in the middle.

I start drafting a long text, but before I can complete it, Dempsey calls again. This time, I hop up from the sofa and slip out onto the back patio to privately take the call.

"Hello?"

A deep voice chuckles from the other end. "I knew you weren't too busy to talk to me."

Why does he sound so much older on the phone?

"What do you have for me?" I ask with a huff. "Is he okay?"

He clears his throat and launches into what he called for, saving me from my awkwardness. "Trevor is friends with a dipshit named Charlie, who works at the lodge. My friend Omar says Trevor is always up there with Charlie and some other kid, Alex. They hang out during their breaks behind the main building. Could be smoke breaks, but it's kind of strange Trevor goes up there if he doesn't even work there."

My thoughts exactly.

"I'm going to go scope it out tonight," he says, voice matter-of-fact. "See what I can find out while I'm there."

"Wait," I blurt out. "I just wanted information. What you've told me helps, but you don't need to physically involve yourself over my problems."

"Our deal is for me to *locate* him, not confirm your suspicions." He sighs heavily into the phone as though he's decades older and dealing with my drama is exhausting him. "Let me find him, Sloane. For *you*."

Butterflies flutter in my lower belly and I don't know what to make of it. Clearly, I'm confusing who in the hell I'm talking to right now. This isn't Jamie's pick for me, Oliver. This is her damn son.

"I…" I trail off, unable to find the right words. "I don't know what to say."

"Most people just say thank you," he deadpans.

I crack a smile and shake my head. "Thank you. But seriously, Demps, your mother may not approve of…*this*."

This being the coffee, the texts, the butterflies.

He snorts out a laugh. "Believe it or not, Mom doesn't know about everything I do. This can be our little secret if it makes you feel better."

Does it?

No.

The entire thing makes me feel like total and utter shit. However, Dempsey has grown on me lately. I'm discovering there's more to him than the bad boy who's always giving his parents trouble. Behind that front, he's thoughtful and caring.

And handsome.

Seriously, Sloane?

"Oh yeah," he says, humor in his voice. "Are you ready to hold up your end of the deal?"

What could he possibly want from me?

It's a desperate act, but I force myself not to think about the answer to that question.

"What is it?" I ask, exasperation in my tone. "It better not be anything embarrassing."

"Nah, I'd never embarrass you." His words are murmured and so soft they almost tickle my ears. "I only want to see you happy."

My stomach dips dangerously at his words. God, I really do need to go out on a date because Dempsey's smooth talking is going to be the death of me.

"I'll be happy when I know what my nephew is up to and can help him," I say tightly, trying hard to steer the conversation back to a safer territory.

"You may as well consider it done already," he says with a smugness that makes me roll my eyes. "Let's go hiking Saturday."

Hiking?

Of all the things that could come out of this man's—er, guy's—mouth, I didn't expect him to throw something outdoorsy at me.

"And here I thought you were going to ask for a get-out-of-jail-free card or unlimited speeding ticket removals."

"You make me want to behave, so I won't be needing any of that." He laughs, husky and deep. "Come on. What do you say?"

I grin because all this banter between us feels good. And

I like his laugh. A lot. I'm about to agree when I come off my cloud of fantasy, stumbling right back into bitter reality.

"Oh, shit," I grumble. "I can't on Saturday. I have a date."

"This date will be better."

"Dempsey." I pace the back patio, feeling jittery with nerves. "We can't go on a date. Ever."

He's silent for a beat and then he laughs, though this time it feels forced. "Yeah, I know, Officer Do-Good. I'm just messing with you. It's not a date if Gemma and Kaden come along anyway. As much as you'd like to get me alone in the woods, I'm going to have to ask you to get your head out of the gutter. It'll be a group hike."

Oh.

Oh.

Now I feel like a complete idiot. I also feel like a bitch too because I know Kaden would die of happiness to get to hang out with those two and I'm preventing him from his fun because I agreed to a stupid date with Oliver.

"The, uh, date is not until seven," I rush out. "If we went in the morning for a few hours, maybe that would be okay. I think Kaden would like that."

I would really like that.

"Fine. Me and Gem will pick you two up at nine. Dress appropriately. Leave the cop outfit at home. I'll bring all the stuff we'll need."

I smirk at his bossiness. "Have you ever even hiked before? We're not all about to get ourselves eaten by a bear or something, are we?"

"There's a lot you don't know about me, Sloane, but I'm looking forward to showing you more."

Again with the stupid butterflies.

This is bad news.

He's bad news for *me*.

⊙

Tap.

Scrape.

Tap-Tap.

I jolt upright in bed, blinking away the dregs of sleep, confused as to whether the sound was in my dream or in real life.

Tap.

Sucking in a sharp breath, I reach over to mash in the code for my bedside gun safe. Once I've removed my Glock, put a round in the chamber, and flipped the safety, I slip out of bed and creep over to the window.

Tap.

I freeze mid-step and squint my eyes. I can barely make out a shadowed form standing on the other side of the window beyond my curtains.

What sort of intruder announces their presence?

Now that I'm not half asleep, I realize they wouldn't. I push aside the curtain to reveal my nighttime stalker.

Dempsey Park's teeth flash brilliantly in the dim moonlight. I eject the bullet from the chamber and then set both the bullet and the Glock on my dresser before opening the window. It's warm this evening but breezy. I can smell pine mixed with something spicy and pure male.

"What are you doing here?" I hiss as soon as I've lifted the window. "Most people knock on the door like a normal person. I almost shot you."

He laughs softly, unperturbed by my admonishment. I

step out of his way and then switch on my bedside lamp. By the time I turn back around, he's standing in my bedroom, sharp gaze pinning me in place.

Maybe I should have thrown on more clothes.

A T-shirt and a skimpy pair of shorts are hardly visitor appropriate.

Dempsey bites down on the inside corner of his bottom lip, his icy blue eyes raking down my bare legs. By the time his stare is back on mine, I'm feeling flushed and way out of my depth.

"Answer the question," I demand, instilling my harshest cop tone. "Is my nephew okay?"

Why else would he show up at my house in the middle of the night?

He nods before sauntering over to my bed. I watch him sit, ignoring the prickling sensation that washes over me. There hasn't been a man in my bed, well, ever. And now I have Dempsey in it. Great.

Also, he's not a man.

He's a kid.

Jamie's kid.

It'd do you some good to remember that, girl!

Leaning back on his elbows on the mattress, he continues to stare at me. I don't understand how he can show up here, wake me up, and then have the audacity to eye fuck me.

Heat floods south.

Is that what he's doing?

Eye fucking me?

"Trevor's fine, I guess. A little bitch, but fine."

Relief has air swooshing out of my lungs. I approach

Dempsey, needing the information about Trevor more than my next breath. Dempsey's jaw muscle ticks when I get closer.

"Explain," I demand. "What happened?"

"Nothing," he says with a grunt. "Thought I'd go hang with my buddy, Omar, and see if I could get the skinny on what Trevor's up to. I had a run-in with him."

"At the lodge?" I clarify.

"Yup."

"What was he doing? Stop making me beg for answers."

Dempsey's expression darkens and it sends a shiver down my spine. "You never have to beg with me."

Right.

So we are getting way off track here.

Focus.

I kick at his boot with my bare foot. "Out with it. Now."

His grin is wolfish. "Do the detectives ever let you in to interrogate the bad guys?"

"Dempsey…"

"Yeah, yeah." He snorts out a laugh. "So I went outside to have a smoke—"

"You shouldn't be smoking," I hiss. "Does your mother know?"

"I thought you wanted answers, Officer Do-Good."

I wave him on to continue.

"And your nephew and his friends show up. At first, they were cool and shit, but then he asked if I wanted to get high. Of course I agreed. I thought he meant weed, but no, his dumbass friend, Charlie, legit tosses a bag of dirty meth at me."

The cop in me wants to arrest everyone, including Dempsey. "You didn't…"

His lip curls up. "No. I'm not into that shit."

"So what happened?"

I swear to God, Dempsey should have gone into theater because he certainly likes drawing out the drama of his stories. It's maddening when I'm dying to get to the point.

"I asked him if it was a sample or if he was selling." He scowls at me. "He was selling."

"What did Trevor do?" I ask, voice shaking with a mix of fear and anger. "Please tell me he wasn't involved."

Dempsey sits up and then rises to his feet. So close to him, I have to crane my neck up to see him. Intensity rolls off him in powerful waves, threatening to drown me in them.

"Tell me."

"He didn't do much until I told Charlie I wasn't interested in buying. Trevor seemed agitated and all it took was one look from Charlie before he lost it. Threw a punch at me, the fucker."

It's then I realize the slight redness on his cheek.

I did this.

I put him in harm's way.

My family did this to him.

Some cop I am.

"Dempsey," I rasp out, reaching up to touch his cheek. "I'm sorry."

He grips my wrist before I can reach his face. His blue eyes smolder with fiery heat and anger. I don't know if he's mad at me or Trevor or the situation I put him in, but it's well-deserved.

"Don't apologize for him," he growls, voice so low it vibrates my skin and every cell beneath it. "Besides, I punched him back."

I open my mouth, unsure what I want to say to him

exactly, but he dips his head until our noses nearly touch. This has whatever words I wanted to say dying on my lips. Staring at him this close has fried my brain.

"You can't touch me, Sloane. I can't…I won't be able to handle it."

He releases my hand, letting it drop, and then sidesteps me to head for the window. I'm left reeling from his words.

You can't touch me, Sloane. I can't…I won't be able to handle it.

Not because he's angry at me or Trevor. Not because I'm some cop and he's the town bad boy. Not because I'm his mom's best friend.

No, he can't handle it because it would be torture.

He glances over his shoulder at me. Pain is written all over his handsome face, tugging his full lips into a sad frown that breaks my heart.

Why is he hurt?

Why do I feel like I'm responsible for his anguish?

"Dempsey," I whisper. "I…I'm…"

"It's fine. It's nothing. Forget it ever happened." He shakes his head, teeth grinding together. "See you Saturday."

But I can't forget.

It *did* happen.

Dempsey likes me. His joke about a date wasn't a joke at all. He really actually likes me—so much, in fact, that my mere touch would have done something to him. What? I have no idea, but I do know he was worried about the outcome.

Holy shit. This is an actual problem.

A big one.

One that I'm going to have to deal with before it escalates any further.

CHAPTER NINE

Dempsey

FUCK, I'M GOING INSANE.

Sloane is slowly driving me to madness and I don't know what to do about it. Several days have passed since the weird admission of her effect on me while in her bedroom and I'm still obsessing over it.

I shouldn't have said anything.

I should have let her comfort me.

But I was barely hanging on by a thread. Seeing her in her pajamas, her pert nipples peeking through the nearly transparent fabric of her shirt, killed me. I was thinking of everyone and everything just to keep my boner at bay.

If she'd have touched me, I might have touched her back.

Fuck.

It would have been heaven, but it also would have meant risking this budding thing between us. At least, as it stands now, she's opening up to me and agreeing to spend more time with me.

"You're so quiet and it's kind of freaking me out."

Jerking my head to my right, I meet Gemma's concerned stare. "What?"

"You're in la-la land. Maybe I should drive."

I scoff at that. She's in charge of the shitty music and

directions while I'm in charge of getting us there in one piece. "I'm fine."

"Is it because we're going hiking with your crush?"

I nearly swerve off the road at her question. "What the hell are you talking about?"

My voice is high-pitched, and I sound guilty as fuck.

"Oh, give me a break, dummy. First, you invited her for dinner, then you brought her coffee, and now we're going on a hike with her. What exactly am I supposed to think?"

Not this.

Not the actual truth.

"Gemma," I growl in warning, gassing it to get us through a yellow light in a hurry. "Back off. You don't know what you're talking about."

Her vicious black fingernail stabs in my direction. "Do not gaslight me. It's so obvious!"

"I'm not gaslighting you—whatever the fuck that means," I bark out in frustration. "I'm just saying mind your own damn business."

"No." She crosses her arms over her chest, scowling my way. "You *will* tell me. I won't let it go until you admit you like Sloane."

I don't make it to the next light in time and end up having to slam on the brakes as it turns red. While we wait, I shoot my twin a withering glare. "Enough."

"Okay, *Dad*," she snips back. "You say it's enough and I'll back off." She snorts out a laugh. "Seriously, you don't get to do that to me and it works. Try again."

Unbelievable.

How is it that I'm so obvious?

Do I walk around with fucking hearts in my eyes for all to see?

"You like her," Gemma accuses, "because she's hot and it'll piss Mom off if you sleep with her!"

The light turns green and someone honks at me to go. I peel out, grinding my teeth to hold in mean words, but eventually, they burst out anyway.

"Fuck off. You and everyone else always think I'm out to ruin the world. Fuck you and fuck them."

Gemma huffs and then starts rapid firing texts to someone. Probably Mom or Willa. Whatever. It's not like I care if she tattles. Boo-fucking-hoo. I stood up for myself. I'm tired of everyone treating me like I'm rotten trash. My sister doesn't get to demand to know my life and then throw a tantrum when I don't tell her.

We drive the rest of the way to Sloane's in pissed-off silence. When we reach her neighborhood, I start to panic. Will Sloane feel the tension between me and Gemma? Will she think it's because of her?

Fuck.

I pull over just inside the neighborhood and put the vehicle in park. Turning in my seat, I try to meet my sister's furious stare.

"Hey. Yo. Womb mate."

Her lips twitch at one side. "Don't call me that. Sounds incestuous."

I do know what that word means. "Hardy har har."

"I'm not trying to be a bitch, you know," she says softly, not looking at me. "I just care about you. What I said was mean and uncalled for. I'm sorry."

The tension in my shoulders eases up. "She is hot," I

admit with a stupid grin, "but I'm not going to sleep with her to make Mom mad. I would never do that to Sloane."

She snaps her head my way, big blue eyes darting all over my face. Then she frowns at whatever she sees. "Oh, Dempsey. You don't like her. You're in love with her."

My heart aches at her words. "Stupid and pointless. I know."

She reaches one of her clawed hands my way and clutches my forearm. "I'm guessing she doesn't know how much you like her?"

"Nope."

"And you don't want to tell her?"

"Fuck no," I growl. "It's humiliating enough that you know."

"Unrequited love. Such a tragedy."

"I don't know what the hell unrequited means, but a tragedy seems fitting."

"I'm going to find you someone sweet and perfect when we start PMU this fall," she assures me. "Someone who's going to love you right back."

I have no doubt that Gemma will do her best to make that happen.

Unfortunately, I won't be interested.

The thing about love is you can't just wish it away even if you know you'll never have a chance with the other person. No matter how much you want to deny it, it just won't fucking go away.

Now that my secret is out, I continue driving us through Sloane's neighborhood and park in her driveway. It's hard to believe just a few days ago I was climbing into her bedroom window, craving a helluva lot more than just one sweet touch that would've been the death of me.

"I won't say anything to anyone," Gemma assures me. "Promise."

I give her a nod of thanks before climbing out to face the woman I'm all in knots over. Before I reach the porch, the front door opens and Kaden races out.

"Duuuude, this is going to be awesome!"

I grin at him and we fist-bump before he heads for the car. Sloane turns her back to me as she locks the front door. She's wearing jeans that hug her ass, showing off each and every sinful curve. Fuck, this is going to be difficult.

"Ready to get hot and sweaty?"

She swivels around, revealing her owlishly round eyes. "W-What?"

"Hiking," I tease. "In the summer. We're basically going to die."

Her body relaxes and she laughs. "Just be thankful I forced that kid to put on deodorant. He actually tried to get out of it."

"Thank God for women. Us males would be so fucked without you."

She rolls her eyes at me. I'd expected things to be cringy as fuck after our last encounter, but she's pretending it didn't happen. I can definitely play along with her.

When we reach the car, Gemma climbs out of the front seat. "I'm going to sit in the back with Kaden."

Sloane doesn't argue or beg to sit with her nephew, so I take it as a good sign. I wait for Sloane to take Gemma's vacated seat and then shut her inside. Gemma discreetly gives me a thumbs-up as I pass by her window. My sister is an idiot.

Everyone's chattering by the time I get back into the driver's seat. Sloane sitting next to me feels good. Really damn good. Like I could almost pretend we're a couple and going on a real date.

Nah, she's doing that later.

With someone else.

The ache inside my chest hurts so fucking badly.

Will it ever stop hurting?

"Keep going," I bark out to the three people trailing behind me. "We're almost to Park's Peak."

"The coffee shop?" Sloane asks hopefully.

"Later, princess. I'll reward you for your efforts later."

She flips me off and this sets both Kaden and Gemma into a fit of giggles. When Sloane kneels to tie her boot, I motion for my sister and Kaden to keep going while I wait.

"I've never seen you exercise or run or anything," she grumbles. "How are you not out of breath right now?"

"Like I said, woman, I'm full of mysteries. Be a good girl and I'll tell you all my secrets."

"You're relentless, Demps."

I hold out my hand for her to take. Surprisingly, she does. The small touch of her sweaty hand in mine sends jolts of awareness down my spine and straight to my dick. She releases my hand once she's standing upright, but I don't miss the pink on her cheeks.

"Water break?" I don't wait for an answer and instead

fish out a new bottle from my backpack. "It's hot. You need to stay hydrated."

"I need a shower and a nap."

"Definitely both if you plan on enjoying your date."

She laughs as we continue our hike. "Enjoy? Your mother damn near forced me into it."

The tightness in my chest eases at knowing she's not exactly eager for her date.

"Come on, Officer Do-Good. I bet the dweeb will take one look at you and fall in love. Free food and a fan for life. Sounds like a good time if you ask me."

Before she can respond, Kaden yelps up ahead. I pick up speed and make my way to a rocky landing where Gemma looms over where he's seated.

"What happened?" I demand.

Sloane squats down next to him, eyes flickering with worry. "Are you injured?"

"I'm fine," he utters, a clear lie considering the slight quaver in his voice. "We can keep going."

I notice the blood dotting his jeans at his knee and realize he must've tripped. On his other side, I drop down next to him and fish out a small first aid kit from my backpack. Sloane watches me with interest and allows me to do my thing. Carefully, I roll up Kaden's pant leg to reveal his scraped-up knee.

"Let's get this cleaned up first and then we can go," I assure him. "I've fallen more times than I can count on this trail. Sucks ass when you hit this gravelly patch."

"Totally sucks ass," Kaden agrees.

"Don't say ass," Sloane adds with a smirk my way.

I grin at her and then set to cleaning up Kaden's scrape

with my supplies in the kit. After putting on some antibiotic ointment and a giant Band-Aid, I roll his pant leg back down and offer my fist.

"Thanks," he says as he bumps my fist. "I'll try not to fall again."

"We've got five more Band-Aids, so we're good." I shake the first aid kit and the contents rattle inside the plastic case. "If you fall after that, I'm just going to feed you to a bear. You'll be beyond help at that point."

"Come on," Gemma says, offering her arm to Kaden. "I'll make sure you don't fall. Let's keep going."

They continue along, once again leaving me with Sloane. I can feel her curious stare on me as we walk. When I find my balls, I glance back over at her.

"What?"

She shrugs. "You."

"What about me?"

"You're really good with Kaden. That means a lot to me."

"He's a cool kid."

"And you're a good man, Dempsey."

Her words, though plain and simple, have life and joy racing through my veins. She called me a man. Not a boy or kid or troublemaker. A man.

"You've seen my record," I joke, voice gruff. "I'm anything but good."

"I see a lot more than you think I do," she agrees, side-eyeing me. "I'm surprised, honestly. Pleasantly so."

As we make it the rest of the way to Park's Peak, I mull over her words and let them replay in my head over and over again.

You're a good man, Dempsey.

But she's wrong. Good men don't obsess over their mom's best friend. They certainly don't con them into dates and draw the object of their affection's tits every damn night.

This *man* is anything but good.

And a woman like Sloane deserves all the goodness in the world.

I hate that I'll never be a part of her world.

CHAPTER TEN

Sloane

F I'M GOING TO BE EXPECTED TO GO ON MORE DATES, I'LL
need another dress. This same boring blue one is going to
be obvious if I wear it to every special event.

Is that what this date is?

It certainly feels monumental considering I never date.
I'm nervous, which is probably normal. I feel like Jamie would
save me if he looked like a toad, so he's probably good-looking on top of being successful. Better yet, he's around my age.

Unlike Dempsey.

This morning was fun. I felt awkward after how we left
things the other night, but today nothing was amiss. In fact,
I really enjoyed myself. Dempsey is easygoing and makes me
laugh. His smile is pretty too.

Ugh.

Don't think stuff like that, Sloane.

He can grin his alluring movie star smile at me all he
wants. I can't get caught up in it, though. I won't ever hurt
Jamie like that. Plus, despite my confusing attraction toward
Dempsey, he'll always be the little turkey I watched grow up.

Gross.

I feel like some kind of pervert.

That's how Jamie would see it if I ever allowed anything
to happen.

Which I won't. *I won't.*

"Sloane Thurman?"

A deep voice from the parking lot at the pizza place jerks me from my inner turmoil. A gorgeous man in his late thirties with dirty-blond hair and a dashing grin strides over to me. He's dressed in dark gray slacks that hug his muscular form and wears a white button-down that he's rolled up to his elbows. He's cut in a way that says he spends an insane amount of his free time in the gym. Green eyes flicker with appreciation as he approaches.

"Oliver Howell." He offers a hand for me to shake. "Pleased to meet you."

I shake his hand and offer a smile. So far, he's nice, handsome, and appropriate for someone my age. "So you know Nathan?"

"I see him sometimes at the country club, but I actually work with Hugo. All the Parks are pretty much carbon copies of each other, though, am I right?" He winks at me as he ushers me to the front door. "You know one and you know them all."

I force a smile to be polite, but it's not true. The Parks are all different. Yes, they're all maddening in the same sort of way but definitely all different.

"So, lawyer, huh?" I ask, changing the subject as we seat ourselves at a booth near the window. "You like your job?"

"Sometimes," he says with a chuckle. "Sometimes it's a total pain in the ass."

"Sounds like mine."

"Park Mountain PD. I hear you're a tough cookie in this town."

"Just doing my job," I mutter and dart my gaze to the menu. "Jamie said you're recently divorced?"

He chuckles. "Damn, and I thought the interrogation skills of dating other attorneys were intense. I've never dated a cop before."

Just answer the damn question.

His smile vanishes when he realizes I won't be blown off. Wrinkles form at the corners of his eyes as he narrows them at me.

"We weren't compatible any longer." He sighs and rubs at the back of his neck. "Neither of us wanted kids. Our careers were our babies. Then, two years ago, she changed her mind. Put the pressure on me ever since. We both grew resentful and ultimately, it's what split us apart. Nothing exciting like torrid affairs if that's what you're thinking."

Defensive.

"I'm sorry to hear that," I utter as the waitress comes to our table. "I'll have Pepsi and a large deep dish meat mountain. Oh, and a side of garlic knots."

The woman then turns her attention to Oliver, who is watching me with slightly widened eyes. "Uh, I'll have water. Add a side salad for me and we'll share the rest."

We'll share?

A shroud of awkwardness cloaks around me. This is another reason why I don't date. I don't know what's proper or what's expected of me. I'd planned on getting a big pizza so I could bring the rest back to Kaden later. I even planned on paying for dinner tonight.

"Not hungry?" I ask when the waitress leaves to put in our order.

He tilts his head to the side, studying me again as though I'm an endangered animal behind glass that needs figuring out. "I figured there was enough for both of us."

"I suppose," I say tightly. "I was going to bring the rest back home, but I can always order it to-go. Don't worry. Dinner is on me tonight."

"What? Oh, shit. I just thought you were one of those women who liked to take charge and order. I was being nice. I think I already fucked this date up." He shoots me a pleading look. "This is the first real date I've had since the split. You're different than the others. I apologize if I'm screwing this up."

I can understand being nervous and uncomfortable. I'll let it slide this time. Jamie always thinks I'm too quick to cut people out, so I'll try harder not to do that when this guy is clearly doing his best here.

God, I can be such a bitch sometimes.

You weren't a bitch with Dempsey.

The abrupt thought has my cheeks growing warm. Thankfully, the waitress brings us our drinks. I chug the Pepsi, deciding I must be dehydrated from my hike earlier.

"It's fine," I assure him. "I'm just on edge, I think. I haven't dated in so long that I forgot what it even looks like."

He pretends to wipe sweat off his brow and grins. "Thank God. This shit is hard, let me tell you. Dating in your thirties should come with a manual. It seemed much easier in college."

"Tell me about yourself. That's a start."

Luckily, Oliver likes talking about himself. He loves his job, works out like he's addicted to it, and enjoys boating on Park Lake. Unfortunately, my eyes begin to glaze over about five minutes in. I can hear him talking, but I'm not comprehending anything. Just staring, smiling, and nodding. My brain is back to this afternoon once we finished our hike.

Dempsey packed a cooler full of food for lunch. I'd assumed we'd go out to eat after or something on the way home.

Instead, me and Kaden were treated to fancy cold cut sand-wiches with rich cheeses, savory sauces, and all the fruit and veggies one could eat on the side. He even made sweet tea, which Kaden had never had, but learned he was a big fan of.

It was all so unexpected. Thoughtful and sweet.

I remember just staring at Dempsey as I tried to figure out the man I only thought I knew. Turns out, I know noth-ing just like he said.

Why do I want to start picking apart those clues to learn about the man beneath the bad boy exterior?

"Hey, Sloane," Oliver says, clearing his throat. "She asked if you wanted marinara to dip your knots in. I wasn't sure."

I give her a nod and then shoot him an apologetic look when she walks away again. "Sorry. Kind of spaced out there for a second."

His shoulders slump slightly and I feel like a total mon-ster for admitting that out loud. I'm always putting my foot in my mouth.

"I was thinking about a case," I blurt out, lying through my teeth. "It's been keeping me up at night."

His smile returns and he gestures at me. "Tell me about you now. I'll try to stay awake."

I laugh at his teasing and then busy myself with the garlic knots when they arrive soon after. Finally, when I've stalled long enough, I tell him all he needs to know.

"I love coffee, hate rom-coms, and enjoy being out-doors. If I had a job where I was chained to a desk, I'd die of boredom."

"What woman hates rom-coms?" His eyes bug out play-fully. "Kidding. They're corny. I get it. Any pets?"

Does Kaden count?

He eats me out of the house and home, farts like a gassy dog sometimes, and has to be forced to shower and brush his teeth. Even though it's on the tip of my tongue to joke about him, I bite it back. I don't know this guy really and I'm not about to tell him—Mr. I Don't Want Kids—that I have one at home.

It's not like it's a permanent situation or anything.

At least, I hope not.

Nothing against Kaden, but a boy needs his mother.

He needs his brother too, but Trevor is getting into major trouble, according to Dempsey. I'm going to get to the bottom of it and do my best to help him. If he'll let me. Rhiannon never did.

My mood once again sours and I opt not to say anything stupid by stuffing bread into my mouth. The garlic knots are crazy delicious, and I know I'll definitely be bringing Kaden back here soon. Sure beats fast food.

"Damn," Oliver says over a mouthful of food. "This is some good shit."

I give him a thumbs-up and continue to stuff my face. Eating is better than talking. I can't screw up eating. I'm actually pretty good at that.

He continues to tell me more things about himself until the waitress arrives with our pizza. It, too, looks delicious. This place was a great idea.

We're just finishing up when a man strides into the pizza parlor. Like at the station, he's too business-like. Doesn't fit in here either.

"Chief," I greet, nodding when Tanaka's eyes land on mine.

Tanaka stops mid-stride and walks over to our table. When he sees Oliver, he grins.

"Oliver," Tanaka says with a chuckle. "When you told me you were going on a date, I didn't know it was with one of PMPD's finest. Good call, brother."

The familiarity between these two strikes me. Oliver slides out of the booth to shake Tanaka's hand and then pulls him in for a fierce man hug.

"Hiroshi was the one who recommended this place," Oliver tells me, elbowing his *brother*. "Back in Seattle, he knew all the good places to eat. How's the new job and town treating you anyway, man? It's a far cry from big-city life."

The two friends chatter animatedly. The fact that Oliver is so chummy with him has an oily feeling slicking over me. Tanaka is sketchy in my opinion. There's a lot about him that doesn't add up. Oliver is clearly loaded and comes from money. These two shouldn't even be running in the same circles. Tanaka was a beat cop who worked his way up the ranks.

"The Ghirards sure are pleased," Oliver says, clutching Tanaka's shoulder. "Your ability to get these cases closed without dramatic fanfare is admirable."

The Ghirards?

Scratch the oily feeling. I'm feeling completely sick to my stomach and grossed out. The garlic knots are souring in my gut. Are these two running some sort of scheme?

"You represented the Ghirards?" I blurt out, frowning at Oliver.

Tanaka's eyes narrow as he studies me, but I don't let him intimidate me. Oliver slowly nods, confusion marring his features.

"You know them?" Oliver asks.

I force a smile and wave him off. "Just knew about the case from work, is all. The name was familiar."

The men continue to talk, but their conversation feels more guarded now that I've been caught listening. Finally, Tanaka tells us goodbye and goes to retrieve his takeout order.

"So where were we?" Oliver digs back into his now cooling pizza and continues to chatter about mundane things like golf frisbee.

I'm done talking and done with this date.

I knew something was off with Tanaka and him knowing the Ghirards' attorney, who's obviously more than a good friend, feels like there was a conflict of interest we should have known about.

I'm starting to believe Tanaka isn't as squeaky clean as he outwardly portrays.

I think we may have ourselves more than a dirty cop.

We have a corrupt chief.

CHAPTER ELEVEN

Dempsey

"I'M GOING TO HAVE TO BEAT SOME ASS," I GRUMBLE under my breath to Tate. "If that frat boy bumps into my sister one more time and cops a feel, he's going to get a knee to his nuts."

Tate chuckles and shakes his head. "Gemma can handle herself."

Despite being in a pool hall with its fair share of sketchy characters, Gemma does hold her own well. The dude bro sidesteps her when she bares her teeth and hisses like a cat, swiping her razor-like pointy fingernails at him. His buddies laugh as his face turns red and then they all saunter away from our table.

Gemma, no longer being harassed by the douchebag, takes her shot and sinks it into the side pocket. She makes a squeal of delight and then misses her next shot. She huffs as she shoves my stick back at me. "Your turn, sucker."

"Watch out," Jude mumbles when he returns from the restroom. "He's about to mop the floor with you, little girl."

She rolls her eyes at him, but we know it's the truth. Even on her best day, Gemma could never outplay me. Tate, perhaps. But Gemma? Never.

"I think those guys in the corner are watching," Tate says, voice low as I consider my next shot. "They've been playing all night for money. They're sizing up how you play. I wouldn't be surprised if they challenge you to a game."

Usually, I know the guys who haunt this particular pool hall. We sometimes have tournaments and bet on our games. The group of men observing our game, though, are unfamiliar to me.

"They any good?" I ask as I bend over and knock one of my balls into the corner pocket.

"They're all decent except for the older man. He's really good."

I continue knocking each of my balls into the pockets and miss the last one so Gemma will have another chance to shoot.

"You did that on purpose," she says with a pout.

"Don't complain when I give you a chance to catch up."

More people enter through the front door of the pool hall. One couple, dressed way too nice for the likes of this place, catches my eye.

Navy-blue dress.

Blond hair.

Woman of my dreams.

I'm vaguely aware of Gemma missing her shot, but my attention is on Sloane. Seeing her here, of all places when she's supposed to be on a date, is an interesting turn of events. The date in question is someone around Callum's or Jude's age, but he dresses like Hugo. I hate him already whether he deserves it or not.

Sloane's eyes meet mine and relief shines in them. Relief to see me here? The thought is a warm and cozy one that settles in the pit of my belly. I flash her a wicked smile before taking a risky shot that quickly ends the game with my sister.

Sloane makes her way over to me, her goober date trailing behind.

"What are you guys up to?" she asks, taking in the four of us as we loom near the pool table.

"Just trying to see who wants to give me all their money," I say with a devilish smirk.

Her date grunts at that. "You two must be Jamie's twins."

The hairs on my neck prickle. Sloane did say Mom forced her into this date, but it still doesn't sit right that this dude knows who we are.

While Sloane introduces us, I ignore the guy to rack the balls. It's then I see one of the big guys—one with a bright red beard—from the corner sauntering my way. He gestures for me to come back over to his table. Leaving my group, I make my way over to him, chin high and shoulders relaxed. Every damn one of these men with their leather cuts and inked flesh is intimidating, but I'm not going to let them know that.

"Sup?"

"Prez thinks we should play a game with you and the princess."

I follow his stare to our group that's watching us with interest. "My sister kind of sucks. Are you sure you—"

Red Beard snorts. "No. The other princess. The one who can play based on how he watches everyone. That is, if his guard dog will let him."

Tate.

He thinks Tate is a princess?

I almost burst into laughter. Tate's an annoying shark when it comes to pool—with teeth, talent, and some serious shit-talking skills.

"What are we playing for?" I ask, leveling Red Beard with an apathetic look. "Your bike?"

His eyes narrow and anger flickers in them. "You even touch—"

"Of course we'll play for the bike," the older man, aka Prez, rumbles as he pulls out a cigarette from his pack. "But if *we* win…" He trails off as he fiddles with his lighter. Once he's lit the cherry, he takes a second to inhale the smoke. Then he exhales, a wolfish grin curling his lips up. "If we win, I get to take the kitty cat for a ride on my bike."

He wants to take Gemma for a ride?

Over my dead body. Fury gushes through my veins like hot lava and I'm seconds from telling this fucker where to shove it. Before I get the chance, Prez points two fingers at me, his cigarette held between the two.

"We're not exactly asking. You'll play for those terms." He takes another drag, watching me like a cat with a canary trapped under his paw.

He's fucking serious.

"Or what?" I demand, unable to keep the venom out of my tone.

"Or we'll pay the pretty policewoman a visit later tonight."

"Excuse me?" I curl my fingers into a fist, aching to knock this asshole's teeth out. "Just who the fuck do you think you are?"

His guys crowd closer, but they don't scare me. Prez finds my attitude amusing based on the wide grin he flashes me.

"Perhaps I should be asking you that very same question." He steps closer, blowing another plume of smoke at me. "How'd you get the bruise?"

Slowly, the dots begin to connect. Those shitheads from

last night must have tattled on me. Does that mean Trevor knows this brute? Is he selling for this ingrate?

"You see," Prez says, waving his cigarette at me again. "I make it my business to know everyone in this town. You Parks weren't a problem until you were."

"You're pissed I didn't want to buy your dirty meth?" I bark out a scornful laugh. "Sorry, dude, but I'm not interested in that shit. I don't see what the big fucking deal is."

Prez glowers at me, the vein in his thick neck pulsating with anger. "The big fucking deal is you went straight to that cop's house to report what happened. Now my business is in trouble because of you."

Trevor or Charlie must've followed me back to Sloane's house. I've put her in danger, and my sister too because somehow trouble always finds me.

"I'm no narc," I spit out. "This is bullshit."

"Put it to rest then," Prez says with a one-shouldered shrug. "Play me and Bozo. First to rack up three wins will take home their prize."

My sister isn't a goddamn prize. But non-compliance means stepping aside for them to make good on their threat to mess with Sloane.

I have to play them.

And I have to fucking win.

"Let me grab my guy," I bite out. "We're getting this shit over with."

The men in his little asshole gang all crack up laughing. I storm back over to my group, ignoring the concerned looks Sloane throws my way. Gemma bites on her bottom lip, eyebrows pinched. Jude and Tate both stand nearby, bodies tense, while Sloane's date smiles goofily at me, completely unaware of the shit storm about to go down.

"It's you and me, Tate," I grit out, patting him on the arm. "Stakes are high. We can't lose."

Sloane breaks free from her loser guy and strides over to me. "What's wrong?"

I flash her an easy smile. "Nothing, Officer Do-Good. Just a friendly game of Kill the Bikers at Pool."

Her lips tug into a frown, disappointment etching her pretty face. I'm not about to get into this with her in front of everyone. Right now, I have to make sure these pricks don't harass either of these two women.

Jude's hand curls around Tate's and I wonder if he'll let him play. If he doesn't, I'm fucked. We're all fucked. These guys are itching to put me in my place. If I'm going to get out of this, I have to make sure we beat them fair and square.

"Good luck," Jude grunts, releasing Tate. "I'll be watching your every move."

"Dempsey," Sloane starts, lifting her hand as though to stop me.

"Make sure everyone stays here." I meet her stare with a warning glare that brooks no argument. "Do this for me, Sloane."

I grab my stick and storm off before she can interrogate me. Tate settles into step beside me, shooting me a questioning look.

"We win, we get a motorcycle," I say with a forced grin. "Just what I always wanted. Dad'll be so proud."

"And if they win?"

"They can't." I clench my teeth and shake my head. "They're trouble with eyes for my sister."

Tate sucks in a sharp breath. "What the hell? Why are we *leaving* the cop behind when she could be helping us get out of this?"

"Because they've threatened her too, Tate."

By the time we reach the corner table the bikers have infested like creepy cockroaches, me and Tate have our game faces on. Red Beard, or Bozo, I presume, starts racking the balls.

"We flip for break," Prez states, fishing a coin out of his pocket. "Heads or tails?"

"Heads," I grunt out.

Prez flicks the silver coin into the air with practiced precision and catches it swiftly before slapping it down onto his tattooed forearm.

Tails.

Fuck.

He grins at me before pocketing the coin. "Me and the kid'll go first round. Bozo wants the princess for round two. Any problems?"

Tate raises his hand. "It's Prince. Not princess."

"My apologies, your highness," Prez sneers as he chalks up the tip of his stick. Then, to me, he says, "Watch how it's done, you little shit."

Prez leans across the table to line up his first shot. His initial shot scatters the balls in all different directions. He lands a solid in the side pocket with the break, earning cheers from his group of Neanderthals.

Then, like the arrogant prick he is, Prez starts calling his shots before dropping them in easily one by one. I begin to lose hope when I realize this game will be a run out. He's going to bag a win without ever giving me a chance to play.

"Game," Bozo calls out cheerfully when Prez drops the last one. "Aww, the toddler looks like he might cry."

Tate starts pulling balls out of the pockets and then racks them for the next game. Bozo looms over him, muttering harassing shit at him, but Tate remains focused. He starts their game with a skilled break that sinks three solids. The next several go in easily, but when he tries a trickier move, he scratches.

"Good run," I tell him, squeezing his shoulder when he comes to stand beside me.

Bozo makes a combination shot, but his hand slips when he goes for his next shot. He curses and slams the butt of his stick hard on the floor. Tate circles the table, calculating each and every angle before setting himself up for his shot. He smoothly knocks in another ball, repeating his actions until he wins the match.

One to one. Tie.

Prez makes a gesture at the table, smirking at me. I fish out all the balls and rack them. My mind is reeling over all the stupid shit he said. I may have agreed to this, but if we lose, I'll fight my way out of this. I'll be damned if Gemma is going anywhere on the back of his bike.

My hands shake with rage. I'm in no shape to play such a high-stakes game, yet here I am.

Focus.

Breathe.

I close my eyes for a second and then break. Tuning out everyone around me, I easily sink the balls as I run out the table.

Take that, asshole.

Prez's arrogant expression is gone. His eyes flicker with

anger. Good. I'm not some stupid, useless kid. And I'm sure as hell not going to let them fuck with Gemma or Sloane.

Two to one, our favor.

Bozo breaks and carries on making shot after shot but misses the last one. He cracks his neck, clearly pissed at not taking the win. Tate effortlessly runs the table but misses when he sneezes mid-shot.

Unbelievable.

Bozo barks out a laugh and then pops his last shot in.

Two to two. Tie.

This is it. Prez is going to run out. I want to ram my stick through his goddamn eyeball.

Gemma chooses to materialize beside me. As much as I don't need her here, she does serve as a distraction. Prez can't keep his eyes off her tits and only sinks two stripes with his break. He scratches on his next shot. Then his pervert eyes are staring shamelessly at Gemma's chest.

One of his balls is in front of mine, so I line up my stick at a steep angle, going for a tricky jump shot. The cue ball lobs over his ball and slams into mine, sending it straight into the side pocket. Gemma and Tate both scream happily. Prez unglues his stare from Gemma to watch what I'm doing.

I circle the table, eyeing all my options. One of my balls is in a difficult position, but I calculate the angles, sending the cue ball knocking into two different rails before it hits my ball. Then, magically, it drops into a pocket.

The rest are easy bank shots, sending more of my balls into pockets until I'm left with one last shot. It's a fairly straightforward shot. All I have to do is hit it in. Nothing fancy.

But because this guy has pissed me off, I decide to fuck with him.

I set up my shot, angling my stick up at a steep curve. Everyone is silent as they wait for me to make my move. With a crack, I send the cue ball on its way. Masse shots aren't easy and certainly not something you bank everything on, but I'm not some pool novice. I'm a fucking professional. It makes a wide arcing curve, almost like I've miscalculated or made a mistake, before swooping in at the last second to slam into the ball for the win.

Three to two. Our win.

"Holy shit!" Tate yells, grabbing hold of my arms and shaking me hard. "You fucking did it, man!"

The relief rushing through me is dizzying. We won and my girls are safe. Bozo stomps over to me and drops a keyring to the floor at our feet.

"Lucky break," he sneers, kicking the keys so they skitter halfway across the room.

Prez stands beside him and narrows his eyes at me. "Keep her locked up or someone might steal her."

I don't know if he's talking about the bike or my sister. Either way, I'm going to heed his warning.

"Good game," I say, offering my hand for a shake. "I trust you'll stay out of my way."

He grips my hand, squeezing it so hard the bones ache. "And you better stay out of mine."

Don't fucking worry, stupid prick.

I'm hoping I never have to see your face again.

CHAPTER TWELVE

Sloane

S OMETHING HAPPENED TONIGHT.

Something scary.

And Dempsey shielded it from me.

I'm pissed and confused.

Don't text him.

Don't freaking text him.

With a huff, I sit up in bed and turn on the bedside lamp to unplug my phone from the charger.

Me: What happened tonight?

The dots move and then stop. He leaves me on read. I have a good mind to drive my ass over to his house and demand answers. I'm sure Jamie would love that. Sighing, I try another tactic.

Me: Come over.

This time, he responds.

Dempsey: Did your date leave you unsatisfied?

He can joke all he wants, but I'm not letting this go.

Me: Either talk to me now or come over so we can do this face to face. I need to know what happened tonight.

Dempsey: Can't. Almost asleep.

I hit the FaceTime button on his contact before I can stop myself. He answers on the third ring. At least he wasn't lying. His eyes are closed and his lips are in a lazy curve of a smile.

"You bailed on that guy's bike after the game without saying a word to anyone. Did you not hear me calling after you?"

He groans and releases a heavy sigh. "Wasn't in a talking mood. Kind of like now."

"You're being a dick, Dempsey."

His eyes pop open and he frowns at me. "Sorry. I'm just…I've had a bad fucking day, okay?"

Hurt needles its way into my heart. Considering I was a huge part of his day, I'm feeling stung. As though I'm responsible for his sour mood.

"Because I went on a date? Because I showed up at the pool hall?"

"What? No." He curses under his breath. "Sloane, can we talk about this tomorrow, babe?"

Babe?

A shiver tickles its way down my spine, settling in my pelvis.

"No," I bite out. "We're talking about this now. Tell me what happened. Did you get into trouble with those guys?"

His blue eyes turn electric with fury. "I handled it."

"Handled *what*?"

"Is this going to go on for fucking ever?"

"Yup."

"Fine. You want to know what has my panties yanked all the way up my ass crack?" He sits up in bed and glowers at me through the tiny screen. "They wanted to play for my fucking sister."

"They *what*? And you *agreed* to it? Just for the possibility to win a stupid bike? Those guys were most likely criminals! My God, Dempsey, you're a child playing dangerous adult games!"

He flinches as though I've slapped him across his beautiful face. "Fuck all the way off."

The phone beeps and I realize he's hung up on me. Wow. That was…intense. I can't believe I just yelled at him. I feel like a total bitch for it, too, even though he was wrong for putting Gemma's safety on the line.

Kaden peeks his head in my door. "You okay, Aunt Sloane?"

"Yeah, bud. I'm fine. Just yelling at Dempsey for being stupid."

He walks over and sits down next to me. "I'm sure it was an accident. Dempsey's actually really smart. I like him. You're not going to break up with him, are you?"

His words have me jolting.

Break up with him?

"We," I choke out in exasperation, "are *not* together. He's not my…*boyfriend*. I went on a date with Oliver, for Pete's sake."

Kaden pats my knee and shrugs. "You don't have to lie. Gemma told me we were tagalongs on a date for you and Dempsey."

She did what?!

"She was wrong," I hiss. "So very wrong. I'm fine. Just go to bed."

He slinks out of my bedroom and I feel horrible once again. I'm always saying and doing the wrong things. I sometimes think I'm an alien in a human world—not like anyone around me. Guilt at pissing Dempsey off has me firing off another text.

Me: I'm sorry I lashed out and said what I said.

Nothing.

He doesn't even read my message.

My heart sinks. I'll let him cool off—let us both cool off—and then I'll apologize in person. He can tell me what really happened without being a smart-ass and I'll feel better knowing all the facts. Then we can go back to normal.

What exactly *is* normal?

Hikes, picnic lunches, coffee dates, and late-night conversations?

Maybe normal isn't normal at all. Maybe this stupid fight is exactly what we need.

Dempsey Park is getting under my skin.

I need to pick him out before he burrows too far.

I'm miserable.

These stuffy, fancy restaurants are so not my thing. They used to not be Jamie's thing either, but then she went and hitched herself to the richest man in town.

I should have canceled this brunch.

Kaden had the right idea by sleeping in all morning. He'll roll out of bed eventually and feast on cereal. I'd much rather be doing that.

A white Mercedes pulls into the restaurant parking lot and my best friend climbs out. I'm wearing jeans and a T-shirt, but Jamie looks magazine spread ready with her floral dress, dainty wedges, and perfectly coifed hair.

"Sorry I'm late," she says, waving at me. "Nathan was being frisky this morning."

Gross.

I still remember when she admitted to me that she'd been sleeping with her boyfriend's dad. I was horrified and completely disgusted. Nathan was old. Now he's really old. I've never understood their relationship or why they fell so completely in love.

"Can he still get it up at that age?" I tease, smirking at her.

She smacks my arm. "Jerk. Yes, he's got excellent stamina if you must know."

"I mustn't. Please stop."

We both giggle and she hugs me. I inhale her familiar scent. Sometimes, when I'm not wound up by work and my own stressful life, we make time to have fun. Sure, brunches aren't exactly my thing, but being with her is always nice.

"You will never believe what Dempsey came home with last night," she says as we walk inside and wait to be seated. "A Harley. Nathan had a fit."

"Why? He's eighteen."

She cuts her eyes over to me. "Nathan is protective over the kids. Remember in the hospital when they were born? He wouldn't let anyone hold them. Not even you."

I wither inside at the reminder of being present for Dempsey's birth. If anything can kill an attraction, it's that.

"I still don't get what the big deal is. He's old enough to drive."

"Ladies," a man says in greeting. "Just two? Right this way."

"It's more than that," Jamie says as we follow the host. "It's that he always does something outrageous. His father bought him a car and had restrictions. So what does Dempsey do? He buys his own vehicle just to piss him off. It's an act of rebellion. I really wish those two could get along."

I'm surprised Dempsey told them he bought it rather than won it from a pool game. But maybe he thought it was the better of the two options. If Nathan knew he won it in a bet where Gemma was at stake, he might have done a lot more than have *a fit.*

Jamie pauses to ask our waiter if he'll bring mimosas. Once he's gone, she fiddles with her napkin and grins at me. "Enough about my family drama. Tell me about Oliver. Was he good in bed?"

I snort out a laugh that earns us a couple of annoyed looks. "I didn't sleep with him."

"Ugh," she complains, still smiling. "Did you at least kiss him? Come on. Spill the beans, girl. I'm dying to know everything."

Should I start first with our awkward dinner where I discovered he's chummy with my corrupt boss? Maybe I should just launch right into how Oliver took me to a pool hall where we ran into her children and Dempsey almost lost one of her beloved twins over a bet.

"He dresses nice," I say instead, grimacing. "He's very proud of his accomplishments."

She scrunches her nose. "Ew. Really? Was he bragging or something?"

"Let's just say his favorite subject to talk about is himself."

"Well, damn." She sighs heavily. "And here I thought maybe he could be the perfect one for you."

Oliver was okay but far from perfect.

"I'm starting to think a relationship isn't in the cards for me, Jame. You have to let it go. I already have."

We get distracted when we're brought our drinks and then place our order. Once we're sipping on our tangy mimosas, Jamie continues trying to unpack my love life…or lack thereof.

"So there was no spark? No spine tingling when he touched you?"

The only spine tingling I've felt lately is when I'm around your son.

"No," I say, clearing my throat and hoping my cheeks aren't blazing crimson. "It was just meh."

She downs her mimosa and shakes her head. "Life's too short for 'just meh.'"

"He's been blowing up my phone asking for another date," I grumble. "See what you started?"

"Maybe you just need to give him another chance. You're rusty on the whole dating scene. If he's trying to get you to go on another date, it wasn't so meh for him."

"Maybe you're right."

Lies. I know going on another date with Oliver will be just as awkward as the first one. Sure, he looks like a good match for me on paper, but there just wasn't a life-altering connection.

"You and Nathan had the spark right out of the gate, though, right?" I ask, studying my beautiful friend.

She flashes me a mischievous grin that reminds me of Dempsey. "Well, since I was dating Callum, I was trying desperately not to feel those budding feelings for his father. No matter how hard I tried, though, I couldn't fight my attraction to him. It was forbidden and wrong, but it didn't stop us."

My stomach twists into complicated knots at her words. Her love story sounds like a fairy tale *now*. At the time, however, their shocking love destroyed Callum. Jamie always felt horrible for doing that to him, but it didn't prevent her from living her happily ever after with his dad. I assume she'd feel equally betrayed if she knew her best friend was thinking unsavory thoughts about her precious baby boy.

He called me *babe.*

I *liked* it.

I can pretend all I want that nothing is happening between me and Dempsey, but my own nephew and Gemma might disagree with that. I may not want anything to happen between us, but our relationship has morphed into something different lately. I'm seeing him as a friend and an attractive grown man, not Jamie's young son. Dempsey is entertaining and fun to be around. I just have to keep him at arm's length because I have a feeling he's the kind of guy a woman could easily get swept up in.

I have enough drama in my life right now.

Definitely no time for *that.*

"I saw Lucy the other day," I say, changing the subject so I'll stop thinking about her son. "She's working at the diner."

Jamie tenses and her expression sours. "Nadine's?"

"Still the greasy place we remember. Mom wasn't there, though I hear she still works a few shifts."

"How is Lucy doing?"

"Moved in with Mom because Lenny's a dick. I still haven't spoken to Rhiannon. I'm going to have to bite the bullet and go see her."

She grimaces. "I know you're thrilled."

"I have no choice," I say with a shrug. "Kaden is doing

great, but he'll have to go to school soon. I need to know why she's abandoned her children."

"Is Trevor still there?"

"He's a whole other problem. I've heard he's dealing and most likely using too."

"Oh, honey," Jamie says, reaching across the table to clutch onto my hand. "I am so sorry. Is there anything I can do? If you want to get him in a rehab facility, you know I'll lend you the money if you need it. You don't even have to ask."

"Honestly, I don't know if we're there yet. I'm just taking it day by day. If I can pin him down and talk with him, I'll have a better idea of what to do next."

She nods, smiling sadly at me. "I'm here for you always. You know I love you and would do anything for you, Sloane. Anything."

Guilt smacks me in the face and my cheeks burn hot.

If I get too involved with her son, I'm not sure that statement will stand any longer. As much as the idea of hanging out with Dempsey appeals to me, I know I have to put a stop to it. I can't lose my best friend from childhood. We've endured too much in our lives to break apart over something like this.

I can't do that to her.

Ever.

CHAPTER THIRTEEN

Dempsey

I HAVE TO TELL HER.

Even though I don't want to, it's the right thing to do. Not only does she need to know her nephew is involved with some fucked-up guys, but she also needs to know they followed me to her house.

If anyone will know what to do, it's Sloane. She's a cop, for fuck's sake. As much as I want to pull her to me and protect her from the likes of Trevor's lowlife friends, I know she can protect herself.

"You can deny it all you want, Dempsey," Gemma says from the passenger seat as she reapplies lipstick. "You bet those assholes for that bike just to piss Dad off."

I take a sip of my caramel macchiato and shrug my shoulders. "Pissing off Dad is just so fun."

Only Tate and Sloane know Gemma was on the menu Saturday night. I sure as hell am not going to freak my sister out for no reason. Luckily, between me having to be with her every waking minute if we leave the house and Dad hovering over his little girl nonstop, she should be safe from those guys.

It's Sloane I'm more worried about.

I pull into the police station, once again taking the

chief's empty spot. Gemma smirks at me, a knowing glint in her gaze as I grab Sloane's coffee and climb out.

"Lock the doors and behave while I'm gone."

I shut the door and don't move until I hear the locks engage. Then I start for the police station entrance. A red Porsche slowly drives past me and the dude glares at me. I flip him off for the fun of it.

Once inside, I wave at Kaden and Tara at the reception area and then make a beeline over to Sloane's desk. She doesn't seem to notice my approach and scowls at her open file as she spins her ink pen around and around her fingers.

"Coffee break," I say, laughing when she jolts in surprise.

Shock registers in her gaze and then she gives me a small smile. "Just what I needed."

I know she's talking about the coffee, but I'd like to think it's *me* she needs.

"Can we talk?" I ask, sitting on the edge of her desk.

She motions for the chair across from her. One of the detectives watches us with interest.

"In private?"

"Are you going to tell me about Saturday night?"

"I have no other choice." I shrug one shoulder and skim my eyes over her desk. "You could take me to one of the interrogation rooms. Handcuff me to the desk and torture me until I squeal."

She cracks a smile at that. "I think the break room will suffice."

Once she has her coffee in hand, she stands and starts for the break room. I follow after, not so subtly checking out her cute bubble butt in her police uniform. The outfit should be banned because it's criminal how good she looks in it. One of the detectives leaving the break room notices me checking out her ass and then gives me the stink eye.

I bet every damn one of these men around here are dying to get into her pants.

Sloane's a good girl, though. A model policewoman who follows all the rules. Fraternizing with her coworkers would be a big no-no. Thank fuck for that because I wouldn't be able to stomach the thought of her getting with any of them.

Saturday night, seeing her with her date, was bad enough.

However, when she called me later that evening, I was relieved to discover she hadn't spent the night with that douchebag she went to dinner with.

Small victories.

Once we're alone in the break room, she leans her beautiful ass against the countertop, sips her coffee, and lifts a blond brow in question.

Right.

Time to talk.

I cross my arms over my chest and try to work out how and what to tell her. Her eyes dip from my face down to my tattooed biceps that strain against the sleeves of my black T-shirt. Crimson creeps up her neck and paints her cheeks before she forces her gaze back to mine.

Naughty cop likes what she sees.

My *naughty dick* likes that thought, but this isn't the time nor the place to flirt with this angel.

"I should have told you what happened that night, but I

needed time to process," I admit truthfully. "It wasn't to piss you off, I swear."

Her eyebrows pinch and her pouty lips press into a firm line. Since she's not yelling at me like she did the other night, I take it as my cue to continue.

"Those guys…they were bad news." I spear my fingers into my overgrown hair, messing up the style I worked so hard on this morning. "I think they were in a motorcycle club. Not the crotchety-but-still-cool dudes from the local VFW either. The kind of guys who should be in prison just for existing."

Hard blue eyes bore into me. It's precisely this moment when she goes from Sloane, *my friend or whatever the fuck we are*, to Officer Do-Good. She sets her coffee down on the counter before saying, "Go on."

"They'd been eyeing Gemma all night and watching our group play. Challenged me and Tate to a game. If we lost, they got to take my fucking sister for a ride on their bike. I knew if I let that happen, she'd never come back." Blood boils beneath the surface of my skin and I fist both hands, wishing I could turn back time so I could pummel them like they deserved.

"Why would you ever agree to that?" she demands, her own anger making a quick appearance.

I hold up a hand, stopping her. "Don't call me a child again. Please. That shit's annoying."

She nods but doesn't seem too happy about it. I can tell she's barely containing the urge to rip my head off about that.

"That Prez guy forced my hand." I drop my gaze to the floor. "I think Trevor's working for him."

"Wait, what?" She sucks in a sharp breath and approaches. "Dempsey, what are you even saying?"

Her small hands reach up and she grips my shoulders as though that will make me focus. It has the opposite effect. All I can think about is how good her hands feel on me. I lean into her, inhaling her sweet caramel-scented mouth.

"Explain," she rasps out, voice breathy and uneven. "Now."

I study her supple lips for a beat before meeting her eyes again. "Either Trevor or Charlie followed me to your house the night they tried to sell to me." Clenching my teeth, I force out my next words. "They told Prez I was ratting them out to a cop."

"How did they know I was a cop?"

"Come on, Sloane, you're smarter than that. Don't make me say it."

"Trevor." She frowns, sadness glimmering in her eyes. "Wow. That's low."

"Believe me, babe, I want to punch him in the fucking face all over again."

Her lips twitch with amusement. "You called me babe. That's twice now."

Fuck.

She freezes as if she suddenly realizes our proximity and drops her hands by her sides. Once again, her cheeks turn a pretty shade of red. When she starts to back away, I crowd her personal space, my hands finding her waist so I can keep her from retreating too far.

"I, uh, I still don't understand what made you decide to bet with them, Demps."

I tighten my fingers around her body through her

clothes, desperately trying to memorize the feel of her in case it's my only opportunity to touch her. "They threatened to pay you a visit."

Her eyes widen and her lips part. "Me?"

Reluctantly, I remove one hand from her waist to touch her cheek instead. Her lashes flutter at my touch, giving me stupid hope that she might feel one iota of the way I do. "I couldn't fucking let that happen."

"Wow. Okay." She exhales heavily, her breath tickling over my chest. "You do remember I'm a cop, right? I can handle myself."

My thumb greedily slides along her warm flesh close to her mouth I dream about on repeat. "I know. That's why I'm here now. That night, though, I wasn't thinking straight. I was scared shitless."

She softens at my vulnerable admission and then surprises me by stepping toward me, enveloping me in a hug. I wrap my arms around her lithe body and squeeze her to me, burying my nose in her hair that smells like sweet sunshine.

"I'm sorry I said those mean things to you," she whispers against my chest. "That was uncalled for. Sometimes I just blurt out all the wrong things."

Someone clears their throat as they enter the break room and Sloane jerks away from me like she's been caught doing something bad.

It's me.

I'm the bad thing.

"Is that your vehicle in my spot?" a man asks. "I should have you ticketed and towed."

I wheel around and come face to face with the Porsche prick. "*You're* the chief?"

"And you're illegally parked."

Sloane steps between us. Maybe she can sense the testosterone rolling off each of us in waves. He's baiting me. It's a goddamn parking spot, not a fire lane, for fuck's sake.

"He's leaving," Sloane assures the man. "No need to give him a ticket."

The chief, in his fancy suit with his slicked black hair, sneers at me. "Don't park there again, kid."

I bristle at his words and am about to tell him to fuck off when Sloane interjects.

"We'll discuss this later. Please just go."

I smirk at the chief and then tip my head at Sloane before stalking out of the break room. Several cops watch me as I pass, clearly curious as hell as to what I could possibly be doing with Sloane Thurman. Let them think whatever they want. It's not like it's true.

Kaden stops me on my way out. "Hey, Dempsey?"

"Yeah, man, what's up?"

He glances toward the break room and then back at me. "Want to come over tonight? We could order takeout and play games. Gemma could come too."

Excuse to go to Sloane's? I'll take it.

"Sure thing. See you later."

His grin helps soothe the irritation from dealing with Sloane's dick of a boss. I give him a two-finger salute and head outside. Gemma is holding up her phone and I can see her lips moving. When our eyes lock, she gives me a warning look.

She's making a video for her fans.

I take off in a sprint toward the car and yank on the handle, eager to embarrass her, but it's locked. She starts talking faster, clearly trying to quickly wrap up. Finally, she drops her phone and hits the unlock button.

"Must you do that every time I'm recording?" she demands with a huff when I climb in. "It's so annoying."

"Hey," I say with a devilish grin. "Which video has the most views again? Oh yeah, that's right. The one where I photobombed you in the background. People went bananas over that shit. You even have that video pinned. I basically made you famous-er."

"Not a word, Dempsey. Gah, you're so obnoxious."

"I'm right, though." I crack up laughing, taking great joy in her misery. "Tonight we've got plans, so keep your calendar open."

She groans. "You know, Dad thinks he's punishing you, but I'm the only one being punished. We go wherever you want to go, whenever you want to go, and you always drive. It's really not fair. You're insufferable. Google it if you don't know what it means. Your face will be the first image."

"All I heard was, 'wha, wha, whaaaaaaa,'" I tease. "Kaden invited us over tonight to hang."

She goes from being pissy to excited in a flash. "He did? Are you going to put the moves on Sloane? You saw that dork she was with Saturday night? Is that why you were being such a dick?"

I'm not about to go into all that drama again.

Unlike Sloane, Gemma can't protect herself. The less she knows, the better.

"Sloane's just a friend," I lie. "A really fucking hot one."

Gemma punches me hard in the arm. "Don't be stupid. If you're so in love with her like I think you are, don't screw it up by acting like an asshole."

"But I *am* an asshole."

"I'm actually rooting for you even though you drive me crazy." She smirks at me. "Maybe if you start fucking Sloane, our parents will be so pissed they'll forget about being so overprotective over me. You can ride off into the sunset on your stupid motorcycle with Mom's best friend. Then I can actually have a life of my own."

As much as we'd both like those things to happen, I know they won't.

Sloane's morals will keep us apart.

And Dad's fear of the unknown will keep Gemma forever locked in her cage.

Sucks to be the Park twins.

CHAPTER FOURTEEN

Sloane

THIS TIME WHEN I WALK BACK THROUGH THE BULLPEN with Tanaka hot on my heels, everyone averts their gaze. No one wants to get their ass handed to them by the boss. After that bizarre moment in the break room, I feel I'm suddenly under Tanaka's radar.

Montgomery smirks as I pass, probably thrilled by the drama of it all. He's worse than a teenage girl with his nose in all the station gossip. At least Bishop has the courtesy to give me a sympathetic smile.

"My office, please," Tanaka says from behind me. "This will only take a minute."

Great.

Is he going to chew me out for hugging *my friend* while on the clock?

Or am I in trouble because *my friend* parked where his expensive Porsche was supposed to go?

Maybe it's not about *my friend* at all. Maybe it's something else entirely.

I'm annoyed because rather than getting to simmer in the information I learned from Dempsey, I'm about to get reamed. I can just feel it.

He shuts the door behind us and motions for me to sit in the chair across from his desk. Since the old chief left, Tanaka has decluttered and updated the new space. Expensive, modern wood furniture adorns the office—a far cry from the '70s crap that was here before.

Did the department pay for this excessive upgrade?

His office walls are lined with his accolades from Seattle. When he ran out of those near his desk, he decorated the rest with colorful abstract art canvases that remind me of Dempsey.

"I see you've been busy lately," Tanaka says when he takes a seat in his squeaky leather chair. He adjusts the knot of his sleek slate-colored tie and pins me with a probing stare. "I heard you've been digging around in some recently closed case files."

A chill races down my spine at his words. His features are sharp and birdlike. He watches me as though he can see the thoughts skittering around in my head, ready to pounce on the one he wants when the time is right.

"Just doing my job," I say lightly. "Following up on cases I responded to."

"I see." He crosses his arms over his chest and studies me. "You're more thorough than our detectives around here."

No surprise there.

The PMPD detectives are comfortable in their positions, and frankly, lazy. It's a boys' club I want no part of. Most of the day, they shoot the shit and stroke each other's egos. Hard pass.

"The Ghirard case was checked out to you," he rumbles, stern disappointment crossing over his features. "Wasn't checked back in. Still dotting Is and crossing Ts of your colleagues' work?"

I try not to fidget, but I feel like I'm being put on trial

for asking questions someone—anyone—should have been asking.

"Is there a problem with that?" I ask, lifting my chin and meeting his gaze with a hard one of my own.

We're interrupted when Tara knocks on the door. She peeks her head in and says, "Chief, the mayor's here to see you."

Tanaka glances down at his shiny Rolex and sighs heavily. "I'll be with him in two minutes."

She leaves us be and closes the door. We continue our staring game for what feels like a lot longer than two minutes.

"I'm going to ask you to stick to your patrolling and normal reporting duties. No need to go above and beyond. We have a whole department that goes over files to make sure everything is above par."

It's on the tip of my tongue to ask him why? Why does he want me to back off? What's he hiding? Too many files are coasting on by without much effort since he took office.

"You're excused." He rises from his seat and continues his intimidating stare-off. "Also, tell your little friend to park in the visitors' lot. I won't ask nicely next time."

Gritting my teeth, I resist the urge to say more. In the end, I give him a clipped nod. "Yes, sir."

I'm boiling by the time I exit his office. The mayor and a couple of other suits strut past me to greet Tanaka. They all laugh like they're buddies who're eager to catch up. Does the mayor know his perfect new chief is shady?

Bishop lifts a brow at me in question and I shake my head. Not exactly something I want to discuss. But there is one thing I'd like to ask him about.

"Hey," I say as I approach his desk that faces

Montgomery's. "What do you know about the local motorcycle clubs around here?"

Montgomery lifts his head and frowns at me. "Why?"

"I'm just curious, is all." I cross my arms over my chest and dart my gaze between them. "Ran into a few sketchy guys at the pool hall the other day—"

"Hold the phone," Montgomery interrupts. "You actually do something on your time off besides obsess over police work?" He mock gasps. "Color me shocked, Thurman."

I roll my eyes, turning to Bishop. "Anything you can tell me?"

Bishop rubs at his beard as he thinks. "I mean, there're all the old geezers up the road, but I think they're pretty harmless aside from a DUI here and there. And then there's the Park Mountain Shadows MC. They mostly keep to themselves and don't cause trouble. Only two clubs I know of."

PMS MC.

Sounds like the guys who harassed Dempsey.

"You know where I can find them?"

Before Bishop can answer, Montgomery interjects. "Just leave it be, woman. You're turning over stones and one of these days a snake's gonna up and bite you."

Unbelievable and useless.

I'll figure out who these assholes are and what their problem is on my own.

"I have a surprise for you," Kaden says as we pull into my neighborhood.

"Oh yeah? What is it?"

He grins at me. "If I told you, it wouldn't be a surprise."

I'm not sure what Kaden has done, but my mind won't let me ponder it. I keep drifting back to Dempsey's revelation and Tanaka's subsequent warning. When I pull into the driveway, Dempsey and Gemma's Tahoe sits right in the middle.

"You invited them over?" I ask in confusion.

"Yeah," he says with a grin. "To play video games and eat dinner with us. You're welcome."

I frown as he climbs out of the vehicle. He's acting like he did me the favor when he's the one who craves hanging out with anyone but his dorky aunt. I follow after him. Dempsey steps out of the vehicle, dressed all in black like earlier and wearing a crooked smile that feels just for me.

We hugged.

He touched my hips and then my face.

His closeness had consumed me until Tanaka burst the lusty bubble I was in.

Now, he's here and we're away from all the prying eyes of my coworkers. This could mean trouble.

Kaden leads the way with Gemma on his heels. I shoot Dempsey a questioning look to which he shrugs. We go inside my house where Kaden takes Gemma to the game console straight away.

"Order something good, Aunt Sloane," Kaden instructs from the living room.

I groan as I pull out the food delivery app. Dempsey takes my phone out of my hand and then sets to ordering all the food. I'm actually okay with it because I get damn tired of figuring out what to feed my nephew all the time.

Dempsey sprawls out on the couch while I slip away to my bedroom. I quickly shed my uniform and change into something more comfortable—a pair of yoga pants and a baggy T-shirt. Not exactly my best outfit, but I'm going for comfort, not style.

I tug at the hairband keeping my bun in place and let all my blond tresses loose. After scratching the achiness out of my scalp, I walk back into the living room barefoot.

Dempsey, who's taking up most of the couch like it's his throne and he's the king, drags his ravenous stare up my frame. He must like what he sees—despite it being frumpy and boring—because he bites on the inside corner of his bottom lip, appreciation glimmering in his gaze.

"What?" I ask, crossing my arms over my chest.

"Nothing. Want to sit outside while we wait on the food?"

I give him a nod and then head for the back door. My back patio is one of my favorite places on earth. It has a breathtaking view of Park's Peak and backs up to a thickly wooded area. I have neighbors on either side, but they're both elderly and keep to themselves. It's about as private as someone on my salary could hope for.

Dempsey makes himself comfortable on my porch swing. Many weekends I sit out here, unwinding from a busy workweek. I'll just swing and drink iced tea or I'll piddle in the flower beds. Sometimes I get a wild hair to hack away at firewood for the winter.

"Come sit," he murmurs, voice deep and husky.

A thrill shoots through me, making my skin flush. Being here alone with Dempsey probably isn't the smartest idea, but I'm not exactly saying no either. Truth is, I'm beginning to enjoy his presence. I really like being around him.

I plop next to him, our thighs touching. He stretches an arm behind me, resting it on the back of the swing. I have a sudden urge to curl up against him and close my eyes. Of course I don't do that and instead remain stiff and awkward. I am Sloane Thurman after all.

He shifts and then his fingers are toying with a lock of my hair. I should tell him not to do it, but the truth is, it feels nice. We gently rock as he plays with my hair, neither of us saying anything. It's peaceful and I do find myself relaxing in his presence. Each muscle slowly loses its tension as my mind clears itself of all the scattered thoughts I've been having.

Then his other hand curls around my bicep closest to him. He rubs his thumb over my arm, through my T-shirt. His touch is intimate and promising. I have no business letting him do this.

Yet do I stop him?

Hell no.

The tenderness is a balm to my stressed-out brain.

He leans closer, his hot breath tickling my hair near my ear. "You're so fucking beautiful, Sloane."

His words shock me, unable to speak or react. His nose nuzzles the shell of my ear. I shiver and lean closer to him rather than pull away.

Bad decision.

Pull away, girl.

"It drives me crazy that you're so goddamn gorgeous and there's nothing I can do about it except stare, marvel, and attempt to recreate on my iPad."

He draws me?

I turn my head so I can see his eyes. The brilliant blue in his gaze is electric. As if he flicks on a switch, I'm soon all too aware of his delicious scent, manly size beside me, and the undercurrent of need rippling through him.

"Why can't you do anything about it?" I ask, voice soft as I taunt him.

"Don't play with me, babe. I almost think you're asking for something I'm too willing to give."

It's a warning.

One last chance for me to be the behaved, responsible adult here.

She's had a rough week, though, and this girl just wants—no, needs—this man.

"In case it's not clear, Dempsey, I'm not asking. I'm telling. *Do* something about it."

His eyes flicker with fire and then his fingers slip into my hair, curling around the strands to grip them tight. I gasp at how he devours me with just his gaze. A small groan escapes me when he tugs my head back. He follows my lips with his own, barely hovering over mine.

I'm not sure what sort of kiss to expect from him, but the sweet little peck he gives me nearly makes my heart explode.

Is that it?

He's just going to tease me with a brush of his lips?

A growl of need rumbles from him and then his lips crash to mine. Not sweet or soft now. Hungry. No, starved. He kisses me like he wants to eat me alive. Each lash of his slick tongue against mine makes me grow dizzy and weak. He nips at my bottom lip here and there before sucking away the sting each time.

I'm kissing Dempsey Park.

Not just kissing but making out with him.

His lips leave mine, despite my pleading whine, and then he's trailing wet, open-mouthed kisses along my cheek to my jaw. When his mouth latches on to my neck just under my ear, I nearly cry out with the sheer pleasure of it. I ache—everywhere—for him and wonder what he'd do if I straddled his lap to get closer. I'm heavily considering doing just that when I hear Kaden yelling.

I jerk away from Dempsey and he simply relaxes against the swing, smirking at me. I smooth my hair and wipe away the wetness on my face just as Kaden's head pops through the back door.

"Food's here!"

We're both still panting from our wicked appetizer of a kiss. What would a whole evening of kisses feel like with him?

Sinful. Delicious. Addictive.

He reaches over and grips my chin between his finger and thumb. Hooded eyes drop to my mouth before he flashes me a sexy grin. "We're going to do this again."

I mirror his smile. "We damn well better."

Yup, I'm going to hell.

Right now, I don't give a damn because that kiss was heaven.

CHAPTER FIFTEEN

Dempsey

W E KISSED.

I still can't get over it. Her lips on mine felt surreal. A fever dream come true. It didn't last long, but that kiss was everything to me.

It's been days since that moment on her back porch.

Each night, I've shamelessly stroked my cock to the memory. Her soft breaths of appreciation, how fucking cute she looked in her cozy outfit, the sweet taste of caramel on her tongue.

I'd expected to be pushed away, especially after how shell-shocked she was during dinner after, but she hasn't. We've been texting and I even brought her coffee each morning to surprise her. Tonight, I'll actually get to see her for Mom's birthday shindig.

Will I get to kiss her again?

The thought of having her in my arms once more has me willingly dressed in charcoal dress slacks and a black button-down. Since it's a fancy, catered event at my uncle's lodge, we're all expected to dress nice. Knowing Sloane will be there, I'm motivated to look good for a totally different reason.

I've been aching to text her more than the friendly correspondence we've been having. I want to tell her the kiss was pure fucking magic for me. I'm smart enough, though, to know Sloane is skittish like an alley cat. If I come on too strong, she'll pull out the claws of her stupid morality and that'll be the end of it.

Tonight will be especially tricky. With Mom here, I have a feeling Sloane won't be so cozy with me. We both have our roles to play. In time, however, I'm going to wear that woman down. The chemistry between us is fire and I'll be damned if I let it fizzle out.

"Waiting for Cinderella to show up at the ball?" Spencer teases as he sidles up next to me.

I shoot him a smirk. "Maybe I'm looking for Prince Charming."

He laughs, but I know I have his mind twisting and turning. It's not like he's ever seen me go after a woman or a guy before. In our family, you never know. I mean, he's in a relationship where he shares his stepsister with his dad. My other brother knocked up his student and then married her. And my reclusive brother? He found himself a man—his therapist of all people—to fall in love with. Hell, even my dad went and got weird way before all this when he stole my brother's girlfriend and made her his wife.

Our family doesn't exactly follow the typical route when love is involved.

Aubrey, Spencer's stepsister, sashays over to us, a deviant grin on her face. She's pregnant and will give birth before we know it. That'll make three babies in the past year to have joined the Park family.

As Spencer and Aubrey flirt, my thoughts turn dark. What if I'm just getting way ahead of myself with Sloane? I've fantasized about her for so long. I'm completely, madly in love with her. But she's barely acknowledged me as a man until very recently. We've shared one kiss. Where I'm at a level ten with my adoration for her, she's at a one or two at best.

I'm going to have to make quick work on getting her on the same page as me.

"Dempsey," Gemma calls out, waving me over to the massive buffet table that's covered in appetizers. "Look at this ice sculpture."

The excitement in her voice reminds me of when we were little kids. I can't help but be affected by it, making my way over to the sculpture with a grin on my face.

"Cool shit," I say as I inspect the piece. "Wait? Is that a dick? Mom's sculpture has a dick on it."

We both crack up laughing. She's trying and failing through her giggles to explain it's a replica of the statue of David.

My phone starts ringing in my pocket. I step away from my sister, quickly answering it in case it's Sloane wanting to meet somewhere.

"Hello?"

"Mr. Park?"

Okay, so it's not Sloane.

"Eh, Dempsey." I pull my phone away from my ear and see a number I don't recognize. "What's up?"

"This is Todd Wright at PMU. I'm the dean of the art department."

"Oh, hey, man."

"I've gone over all the submissions for the art expo and yours surpassed everyone's. Not just in skill and beauty, but you really captured a moment—an emotion of such utter longing."

My gut twists. "Cool."

Todd chuckles. "Yeah, cool. An understatement, though. I'd really like to showcase the piece. That would entail having your own roped exhibit area where you can include some other pieces if you have them. We'd also want to put your art on the banners and programs."

"Really? Wow. I don't know what to say."

"Say yes, please." He laughs again. "A lot of the digital artwork we have submitted is more illustrations than anything. Yours is realism and rivals actual photography. I know we'll have plenty of art students who will have questions, too. Not to mention, some of Seattle's artists will be at the event. You could easily be offered a place in one of their shops to sell your work."

Holy shit.

It's really happening.

"Yes," I say in a rush. "I mean, thank you, sir. It's an honor."

"Make sure you invite your family, too," Todd encourages. "I'm sure they'll be so pleased."

"Of course," I lie.

There's no way in hell I'm inviting my family to see my art. I'll tell them about my success after the fact. The last thing I need is to catch grief over something I'm really proud of.

"We're looking forward to having you in our art program, Dempsey. It's not often we have such talent come through our university's doors, but when it does, we don't sleep on it. PMU will be lucky to have you and hopefully, this will be the start of a fruitful career for you."

Sold, Todd.

After we end the call, I have this overwhelming urge to share the news with someone. The only person I feel like celebrating with, though, is Sloane. I scan the crowd of forty or fifty of Mom and Dad's closest friends and our family, searching for the familiar pretty face. When I finally land on it, I breathe a sigh of relief.

She's here.

In her signature navy-blue dress and looking uncomfortable as fuck around all these people. I smile tugs at my lips. Sometimes Sloane is so awkward, but it's adorable as hell. She's talking to my parents, giving them her best fake smile.

Her smiles are real for me.

I'm about to wave at her to get her attention when a man steps beside her. He's wearing a navy-blue button-down shirt that matches her dress almost exactly. As soon as I look at his face, I know who it is.

Her date from the pool hall.

The air is knocked out of my lungs as I stare at them in confusion. She didn't tell me she was seeing him again. Hurt needles its way into my heart, poking and poking and poking until I have to rub at the center of my chest to ease the ache there.

He's charismatic and rich and well put together.

With their matching outfits, they look like a couple.

Fuck. That.

He doesn't make her smile the way I do. I'm not sure many people have seen a true Sloane smile.

But then her face lights up, a stunning grin curving her lips up. Her blue eyes sparkle with excitement and happiness.

Well, hell. Maybe he can make her smile.

It takes a second for my brain to catch up to where her smile is directed. It's not at my parents or the goober beside her. It's for me. She's staring at me.

I make a subtle gesture toward the exit. Her small nod is all I need to feel like everything is right in my world again.

Quickly, before one of my family members can intercept me, I slip through the crowd and out the side door. The air is warm tonight and smells like pine. I step around the corner and wait for the woman of my dreams to make an appearance.

Moments later, her blond head peeks around the corner, still wearing that beautiful smile I love so damn much.

"Hey," I rumble. "I see you escaped from your date."

She smirks as she slowly approaches. The moonlight makes her hair shimmer almost like strands of silver. I want to draw her like this too—grinning, free and ethereal, like a sexy forest nymph.

"Not my date," she says, stopping just shy of our chests touching. "He pounced on me the second I got here."

Slowly, I reach for her hips, not eager to scare her off by jumping her bones as soon as she's in my space. She bites on her bottom lip, looking up at me through her lashes as my hands curl around her waist.

"I missed you," I murmur, dipping my head low so I can inhale her sweet scent.

"You saw me yesterday when you brought me coffee."

"True, but it was too long ago." I draw her closer to me until her breasts brush against my chest. "I have you now, though, and that's all that matters."

A shiver ripples through her. Tentatively, she reaches up to place her hands on the sides of my neck. Having her soft fingers against my skin is dizzying.

"You're the most beautiful woman here tonight," I murmur, running my nose along hers.

She lets out a soft laugh. "You're smooth with your words, Dempsey Park."

They're not just words, though. They're the truth. She's

not just the most beautiful woman here tonight. She's the most beautiful woman *every*where *every* night.

"I have been dying to kiss you ever since the other day at your house." My voice is a raspy growl filled with desperation. "Please tell me you're here so I can kiss you again."

Rather than answering, she stands on her toes, tilting her head up as she finds my lips. Our mouths meet gently at first and then, like the other day, it's as if a rubber band snaps us into action. A whimper escapes her as she opens her mouth, allowing me deeper access to her.

Tonight, she tastes like mint and *mine*.

My greedy palms slip down to her round ass and I squeeze her through her dress. I want to know what sort of panties she wears. Are they simple and plain or skimpy and sexy? Either way, I know they'll be the hottest thing I've ever seen.

One day, I will take them off so I can see the rest of her. One day soon.

I grip her ass and lift her. She goes with the flow, wrapping her legs around my waist. Our kiss grows more ravenous, each of us damn near trying to devour the other. She lets out a small yelp when I push her back against the wall of the building. Then it's my groan that erupts out of the wet, breathy sounds of our kissing the second my hard cock presses against her pussy.

"See what you do to me?" I rasp out, slowly grinding my hips so she can feel it. "Every damn time I see you."

She laughs, soft and fucking cute as hell. "That's a rather big problem."

I nip at her lip. "A problem only you can solve, babe."

Our lips and teeth and tongues continue to interrupt our

conversation. The need I have for her is so intense and unlike anything I've ever felt in my whole life.

She's mine.

She was always mine.

I just wasn't allowed to have her until now.

Totally worth the wait.

"This thing between us," I murmur, biting at her bottom lip. "It's not going to stop. You're not some itch to be scratched for me. You're everything to me."

She pulls back to stare into my eyes, searching with her probing stare for the truth in my statement. When she doesn't find a single lie, she graces me with another breathtaking smile.

"Dempsey?"

The sound of Dad's voice is ice water on my erection. Sloane claws her way out of my grip, forcing me to set her back down to her feet. We've barely separated when Dad comes around the side of the building.

Fuck. Fuck. Fuck.

Dad stops when he sees the two of us out here by ourselves, looking guilty as fuck, and frowns hard. I step forward, drawing his attention to me. "What's up?"

"We'll be cutting the cake soon. Time to get inside."

I stride ahead of him, forcing him to keep up with me. If I can get him back inside and away from Sloane, maybe he'll forget he ever found us alone.

That's a big maybe.

I just hope his surprise visit didn't scare away any and all hope of this budding relationship with Sloane.

I hope to fuck not.

CHAPTER SIXTEEN

Sloane

WHERE IS MY SISTER?

Focusing on Rhiannon and our family drama chases away the near-disaster that happened last weekend. I'd stupidly followed Dempsey, needing a repeat of our kiss and to escape Oliver. Like the first time, we fell together so easily, the attraction incredibly intense and undeniable.

It felt so good kissing him.

And then he picked me up like I weighed nothing.

Had Nathan not interrupted, would we have had sex right there against the wall?

Guilt and horror make my stomach churn. Though Nathan didn't see what we were doing, he's not stupid. The accusatory expression on his face won't stop haunting me.

That's our baby boy, you homewrecker.

I rub at my temple, hoping to ease the headache that's forming. It's been a week of overthinking that night and worrying Jamie will show up to tell me what a horrible person I am.

She hasn't shown up to hand me my ass yet.

So maybe we did get away with our stolen, passionate moment. It doesn't make me feel any less terrible about it, though. I clearly was feeling lonely and Dempsey showed up at the right time in my life, saying all the right things to make me feel cared for.

I chew on my bottom lip, barely focused on what Aisha is saying in the passenger seat. Early this morning—and like every morning since Jamie's party—I was eager to rush out of the station to go on patrol. I'm sure Tanaka thinks he scared me into leaving his shady dealings alone.

Unbeknownst to him, I've been doing my own investigating late at night when I can't sleep and I'm doing my best to blow Dempsey off via text. Not only have I been finding interesting information about the Ghirards, but I've also uncovered more about the motorcycle club Trevor has found himself mixed up with.

Without getting lost in Dempsey's handsome grins, I can actually stay focused and do my job.

"Where do we want to go to lunch today?" Aisha asks. "I'm thinking Thai."

Thai's not my favorite, but anything to keep me out of the station works for me. Now that I have a game console for Kaden at the house, I feel comfortable leaving him while I work rather than pawning him off on Tara.

"Sounds good to me," I say, my mind drifting back to my sister.

As Aisha continues to babble, this time about her kids, I wonder where the hell Rhiannon is. Each night, on my way home, I've stopped by her apartment to try to talk to her. Neither she nor Lenny is ever there, or at least they don't answer when I come knocking. Trevor isn't either. It's a mystery that may require me to speak to my mother. She may not answer my texts, but she'd have to speak to me if I showed up unannounced.

"You want me to surprise you?" Aisha asks, pointing to the Thai restaurant as we approach. "I'm assuming we'll eat on the run, right?"

"Yeah, surprise me."

As soon as she's out of the vehicle, I lean my head back and close my eyes. Dempsey's handsome, swollen, just-kissed lips come to the forefront of my mind.

This is absolute torture.

My phone buzzes and the usual guilty feeling threads through me. I peek at my phone to see another text from Dempsey.

Dempsey: Dad spooked you. I get that. Don't shut me out, though, babe.

Babe.

My eyes water and a ball of emotion clogs my throat. Of course the first time I actually feel attraction and connection to a man, it's the wrong one for me. Is that how Rhiannon felt when she got with Lenny? Mom with Dad? Are we all doomed in the Thurman family to fall for guys who'll destroy our lives?

Dempsey isn't anything like Lenny or Dad, but us having a relationship still hurts people. Specifically my best friend. I can still remember the prickly way she was toward me when she thought we were simply texting. As friends. If she knew we'd been kissing, she'd be disgusted with me.

Plus, I'm old and jaded.

Dempsey is young. He's going to college. There're thousands of girls in this town who would literally drop to their knees at his feet to worship him. He's a Park after all. They're basically gods around here. Gods and mere mortals like myself don't have any business playing together.

I want to let him know it's not him. It's me. There's absolutely nothing wrong with Dempsey. He's gorgeous, talented, funny, and incredibly sweet. He's a total catch.

For someone else.

With a heavy, resigned sigh, I text him back.

Me: Been busy. Talk soon.

It's another blowoff message, but hopefully, he realizes I need time. Maybe indefinitely.

Dempsey: Tara likes caramel macchiatos too. She says I'm going to have to show up a lot earlier if I want to make sure you get your coffee before you head out on patrol. Maybe I should show up at your house.

A smile tugs at my lips. He's persistent, I'll give him that. But I'm not supposed to think his persistence is cute.

Me: Thanks for the attempt. I really do appreciate it. Demps, I need time right now. Please.

The dots move and stop a few times before he replies.

Dempsey: I'll always wait for you.

This time, tears do form and I hastily swipe them away. I'm Sloane Thurman—emotionless, robot cop. I don't cry over texts. I know I've been on my period all week, but damn. These feelings are too much.

When my phone rings, my heart patters wildly. Except when I look down, I don't see Dempsey's name on the screen. I see his mother's.

Is this how it goes down?

She'll confront me over the phone after having a week to cool off her anger? This could be good news. Maybe not all is lost. There's no doubt in my mind Nathan tattled to her. He's always despised me because I'm a reminder of where Jamie came from. The gutter. His princess has a pet rat and he can't stand it.

"Hello?" I croak out, the emotions from earlier still lingering.

"Sloane? What's wrong? Is Kaden okay?"

Her concern is jarring. I'd been expecting a frigid greeting. Not the same, usual care she's always shown me since we were pre-teens.

"I'm fine," I say quickly. "Thai food. Spicy."

"You hate Thai food," she says with a chuckle. "You mean to tell me Aisha gets her way sometimes? Where was that generous heart when we were kids?"

Okay…so this is weird.

She's being nice.

Maybe Nathan didn't say anything to her.

Relief floods through me and I exhale sharply.

"She's convincing," I say lightly. "What's up?"

"I won't keep you long. I wanted to talk to you about something."

Great. Here we go.

"It's about Dempsey."

Bile creeps up my throat. I force myself to swallow down the nausea. "What about him?"

Don't sound guilty. Don't sound guilty.

"Tonight is his art expo. Did you know he's the featured artist?"

What?

"Uh, no." Honest answer. "That's good, right?"

"Good? It's wonderful. I'm a little heartbroken he didn't

invite us, though. I think he's still upset about the car thing and us making him go to college. If it were up to that kid, he'd goof off all day playing pool and razzing Spencer."

That kid.

Her baby boy.

Ugh.

"How do you know about it if he didn't invite you?"

"The dean of the art department called. Said there weren't any RSVPs for his family, aside from Gemma or friends. Todd was emphatic that this is an extremely big deal at PMU. It's an honor and will propel his career as an artist. Of course I told him we'd be there. I'm a little miffed Gemma didn't say anything either."

"Wow, that's impressive." Pride swells in my chest. I have the urge to text him to demand to know why he didn't tell me, but then that'd be opening the box back up. The same box I've been trying to keep closed all week.

"It's a fancy event. If you need to borrow a dress, come over early and you can wear whatever you want."

Wait.

Me?

"Huh? I wasn't invited."

She laughs. "Neither were we. You got him that iPad, seeing potential in him when no one else was taking the time to. I assumed you wanted to see him doing so well."

"I, uh, do. Of course I do. I just…"

"I have clothes," she reminds me.

"No," I blurt out. "I have my own stuff. I'll be presentable. Don't worry."

She sighs softly and then forces cheer into her tone.

"Absolutely. We'll pick you up then. I'll text you later when I know the time for sure."

I hang up the phone as Aisha exits the restaurant with to-go bags in hand. I'm really going to see him tonight? My heart aches at the prospect.

Seeing and touching are two totally different things.

Tonight, I'll keep my hands to myself.

Looking is okay, though. That's all I'll ever be able to do.

I'm a plainly dressed rat beside Jamie. Even pushing into her late thirties, she's gorgeous. Her sleek black dress fits all her curves and her hair is pulled up in a stylish way. Meanwhile, I'm wearing my ol' trusty blue dress and barely managed to run a straightener through my hair before they arrived to pick me up.

It's a reminder of how different I am than the Parks.

I'll always be different.

Jamie grins at me over her shoulder. She lives for these events. She and Nathan are always going to parties and galas. I suppose being the most influential couple in town, it's sort of expected of you. Jamie loves going, though. It's not a chore for her. I think it's a chance for her to be able to show this town that she crawled out of that gutter we came from and made something of herself.

Sometimes, it's a little nauseating for those of us still trying to claw our way out.

One day soon, I'm going to invest in another couple of dresses. I've worn this same stupid dress more times this summer than I have the entire decade I've owned it. It's past time for a wardrobe upgrade.

Cars fill the PMU parking lots and people dressed in black-tie attire litter the sidewalks. I follow behind the couple of the night, hoping to slip in and out unnoticed. This is Dempsey's night and I don't want to overshadow it with our…*thing*.

It's a thing that just won't go away no matter how hard I try to make it.

Before we reach the entrance, a man strides over to us with purpose. The cop in me has me readying myself for an attack. As soon as I lock eyes with the man, I stifle a groan.

Chief Tanaka.

"Officer Thurman," Tanaka greets, eyes narrowing as he glances at Nathan. "What brings you to such an event this evening?"

I straighten my spine. "I should ask you the same thing."

Our silent stare-off continues. Nathan interrupts, offering his hand.

"Nathan Park. And you are?"

"Hiroshi Tanaka. Chief of police."

Nathan grins at him and Tanaka turns on his charm. They begin a conversation where Nathan says how pleased he is to finally meet the new chief and how Tanaka has heard great things about Nathan's family from the mayor. The two men easily chat, no animosity whatsoever.

If Nathan and Tanaka get along, it only makes me even more suspicious of Tanaka.

"My son is being featured tonight," Nathan says with real pride. "He's an incredibly talented artist."

As he walks off, both men lowering their voices, I can't help but wish Nathan would share some of his pride with

Dempsey. I know Dempsey feels as if they see him as a screwup.

"He really is proud of him," Jamie says, looping her arm with mine. "We both are. Dempsey's always been a moody child. Maybe one day he'll realize we only want the best for him."

A moody child?

Maybe he wouldn't be so moody if they didn't think about him that way.

Bitterness at Jamie slithers its way in, but I squash it. She's his mother and I'm…just the local cop he likes to make out with. Obviously, she knows him better than me. Feeling protective over him around his own mother feels like a major overstep.

No one is more protective than a mother.

As we enter the building, we follow people heading down the hallway to the auditorium. Waitstaff bustles around with trays of bubbly champagne and appetizers that look too pretty to eat. Jamie snags us each a champagne flute before we make our way into the auditorium.

Everywhere art is displayed with lights highlighting each piece. People are crowding around a display in the center of the room, pointing and admiring the art. I see Dempsey first and lose my breath.

He's a good-looking man, but in a tuxedo, he's positively dashing.

His dark hair is slicked back and he seems to be at total ease as he converses with people. I detach my arm from Jamie's, taking several steps forward, needing to see him up close. Electric blue eyes find mine, searing into me and making me stumble to a stop.

I wait for the smile and the excited gleam in his stare.

All I get is panic.

Horror.

What?

I'm so stunned by his reaction, I visibly tremble. A man standing nearby gasps. Another woman points at me.

Do they all know?

How could they know I'm losing my damn mind over this man?

"It's her," someone says. "Wow."

I jerk my head to follow where he's pointing. The enormous print behind Dempsey is…*me.*

Me?

Unable to make sense of what I'm seeing, I push past several suited men until I can see the entire exhibit clearly. The highlighted piece is me in my navy-blue dress—the same godforsaken dress I'm wearing now. The expression on my face is sad. Lonely. Vulnerable.

Oh my God.

Each and every other display scattered around is also me.

Me. Me. Me. Me.

This is a nightmare, right?

Unfortunately, not.

CHAPTER SEVENTEEN

Dempsey

SLOANE IS HERE.

Holy fuck.

This was not supposed to happen!

Everyone is staring at her as though she stepped right out of the realistic art print and into their presence. Living art. Some new-age artistic show.

They gasp and croon, all clearly impressed by the spectacle.

Un-fucking-believable.

I didn't invite my parents or Sloane for this very reason. Somehow, they found out and showed up anyway. The three people who weren't supposed to see are gawking at the art I so lovingly worked hard on.

Sloane's gaze lands back on me. Her cheeks are flaming crimson and her eyes are watery. I feel like a total asshole. She's embarrassed and it's all my fault.

Before I can call out to her, Sloane turns on her heel and rushes out of the auditorium, pushing past people with surprising strength.

I need to go after her.

Right?

Mom's eyes find me next. Her mouth is curved into a disappointed frown and anger flashes in her gaze. She's pissed at me. As she should be. I've made a mockery of her best friend and our family. Rather than showcasing my talent, I've revealed my obsession with Sloane for the entire goddamn town to see.

Mom shakes her head at me and turns to follow Sloane's path. I'm sure Dad is around here somewhere, the disappointment etched on his face too.

What have I done?

"Mr. Park," a woman with sleek black hair purrs as she extends her hand. "I'm Mona Angel and I'm quite impressed with your style. I think your work would fit well in my Seattle gallery. I would love to discuss commissioning you."

This is what I wanted.

Seattle. Art galleries. Recognition for my work. Paid commissions.

So why does it feel hollow and unfulfilling?

Because you'd rather be chasing after the woman you're quickly losing.

Rather than ruining the only other good thing in my life, I force myself to stay despite wanting to run after Sloane. Nothing will be achieved by me going after her. Maybe a shameful argument in the parking lot that involves Sloane and my parents. I won't do that to her.

Mona pulls me aside, chatting about the opportunity she's presenting me. It sounds too good to be true. On one hand, I'm thrilled and proud to be acknowledged. On the other, I'm disgusted at myself that it's because of my love for Sloane.

After I make it through this evening, I'll go to her.

I'll make it right.

At the very least, I'll make her understand how sorry I am.

Knowing she's upset and hurting is almost too much to bear.

"You want me to go with you?" Gemma asks from the passenger seat. "I can try to help smooth things over."

I shut the Tahoe off and shake my head. "I need to do this alone. Are you okay to wait? I'm not sure how long this could take."

"I'm good. I'll make some content for my socials. It's quiet and I look good." She flashes me a wide grin. "You've got this, Dempsey. She'll understand you didn't mean to hurt her."

Earlier, I never did see Dad's reaction. My parents and Sloane were gone by the time I finished socializing with everyone. Gemma found me later and told me she witnessed the whole thing. At first, I didn't want Gemma to know about my crush on Sloane, but having someone to talk to about it helps.

Plus, twins take secrets to the grave.

I climb out of the Tahoe, softly closing the door behind me. Then I prowl through Sloane's dark yard to the back of her house where her window is. I'm not about to disturb Kaden. For all I know, she pretended everything was fine around him. I've embarrassed her in front of the entire town. I'm not about to extend that humiliation to her nephew too.

All the lights are off at her house even though it's not that late. Her curtains are drawn, not allowing me to peek inside. Gently, I rap on the window.

Nothing.

A heavy sigh rattles out of me. I'd avoid me too if I were

her. I tap at the window again with my knuckle, hitting a bit harder to make the sound carry.

Crickets.

I'm about to pound on the window but try to lift it instead. To my surprise, it's not locked and easily lifts. I climb through it, pushing past the curtains, hoping I don't get myself accidentally shot. When I fully make it through, she's standing a few feet from it, arms crossed over her chest, frowning. She's still wearing the notorious blue dress. The moonlight highlights her sad face, making her seem decades younger, and it fucking kills me.

I did this.

Fuck.

She bites on her bottom lip, eyebrows scrunching as I prowl toward her. I expect her to shove at me or back away. Instead, she holds her ground, lifting her chin to meet my stare. Like she's made of porcelain, I cradle her cheeks and stare into her glistening eyes.

"I'm so fucking sorry, babe."

Her eyes close when my lips brush against hers. She says nothing, so I continue.

"You were never supposed to see." My voice trembles and comes out raspy. "I never meant to hurt you."

"Is that how you see me?" she chokes out, lip wobbling. "So lonely?"

"Not anymore," I murmur, kissing her supple lips again. "Not with me."

A ragged sigh rattles out of her. "It was so raw…"

"And beautiful. Everything about you is so goddamn beautiful, Sloane. You—You're art to me. Something worth putting on display and sharing with the world."

"It just…" She swallows hard. "Took me by complete and utter surprise."

"I know," I grunt. "I should have told you or warned you. It's all my fault and I fucking hate myself for it."

She shakes her head, fingers whispering up my chest. "Do not ever hate yourself, Dempsey. You're so talented. You're a good, worthy man."

My heart stutters to a stop at her kind words.

"What I saw tonight," she continues, "took me by surprise, and obviously upset your parents, but the vulnerability I saw in your art was breathtaking."

"You thought so?"

I don't even want to think about the lectures I'll receive when I finally make it home. Sloane was the first and most important place for me to be. Everything else can wait.

"I did."

"I wanted to come after you," I explain. "But I also didn't want to make it worse. Old me would have. When I'm around you, though, I want to think things through and do what's right for everyone involved."

She graces me with a sweet smile. "You're a good man."

I'd been expecting her to yell at me or refuse to speak to me, but this is better. She's letting me in again. Forgiving me for my stupidity. Praising me. I love this woman. I always will.

I dip down and kiss her deeply. A small moan of pleasure hums out of her, giving me all the permission I need. Gently, I start maneuvering her toward her bed, my mouth owning hers with each swipe of my tongue. With my arm looped around her, I lower her to the bed, settling my strong body on top of her lithe one.

She's finally letting me in.

It feels like the sweetest reward after a night from hell.

Our kiss grows hungrier, but then her hands are pressing on my chest. Reluctantly, despite the throbbing in my cock and the growl escaping me, I pull back to stare at her pretty face.

"We can't."

I blink at her, her words confusing me. We totally can. We just were. She's into me and I fucking love her. Why can't we?

"Babe…"

Her head shakes as tears well in her eyes. "Please, Dempsey. Don't. I…"

I stroke my thumb over her cheek, searching her face. "What is it? Talk to me."

"I can barely say no," she whispers, shame coating her words.

"Then don't."

A long moment passes where we stare holes into each other. Her lashes flutter when I press a kiss to her nose. She sighs happily when my lips find their way back to hers. It starts sweet again but within minutes, we're both panting. Her heels dig into my ass as my stone-hard dick grinds against her center.

"Dempsey."

The pleading tone in her voice between kisses has me pulling away once more.

"We're meant to be," I murmur, rubbing my nose along hers. "I know you see it. Feel it."

She whimpers when I thrust my hips. "I do. I just, I can't."

Her eyes are full of shame and I know exactly why. She can't be with me because of my mother. I wish our bond were stronger than theirs. If only she'd give it a chance to be.

"This isn't just getting laid for me," I admit, voice broken and vulnerable. "It's about you. It's always been about you. I want you more than anything in this world, Sloane. Anything."

Tears leak from the corners of her eyes and she sniffles. "Then be strong for me. I can't. I'm too weak."

Everything in her expression begs to be held, cared for, loved. I ache to do all those things. But the words she's giving me starkly contrast that.

She needs space.

I close my eyes, knowing what I have to do. With a quick peck to her lips, I then roll off her and sit up. Running my fingers through my gelled hair, I attempt to squash the hurt lancing at my heart.

She sits up and slides her palm over my back, resting her head on my shoulder. "Thank you."

Twisting, I meet her face for one more chaste kiss and then rise to my feet. As long as we're touching, it's too difficult to do what's right. I vowed that I'd do anything for her and I meant it. If it means keeping her from doing something she'll regret tomorrow, then I'll do it.

That's what real love is.

Sacrificing what you want for the one who owns your soul.

"Promise me one thing," I say when I reach the window. "Anything."

My heart twists. "Don't shut me out after this. At the very least, just seeing you and talking to you is what I need. It'll have to be enough."

Silence fills the room and I start to panic. She finally agrees with a small sound of affirmation.

She won't shut me out.

She can't or I won't survive it.

I take one last look at the woman who has me tied in a

million knots. She's teary-eyed, completely wrecked, and so fucking sad. I've never seen a more beautiful sight in all my life.

"I'll wait for you. Until you're ready."

A small smile tugs at her lips. "You may wait a long time."

"For you, babe, I'd wait forever."

With those words, I slip out through her window and into the night. The window closes behind me and the locks engage. Slowly, I amble my way across the yard to where Gemma's face glows from her phone. I'm not exactly ready to face my sister or her barrage of questions, but there's nowhere else to go.

I climb into the Tahoe and buckle in, my entire body feeling shattered and ready to crumble.

"It didn't go well," Gemma whispers. "Oh, Dempsey. I'm sorry."

Her hand brushes over my arm. The comforting touch of my twin has me relaxing, allowing all the pain to settle deep inside my bones. I press my fingers to my eyes and slump my shoulders. The fingertips grow wet as my body trembles.

Gemma scratches her long nails over the back of my tuxedo jacket, murmuring soft words. It reminds me of when we were toddlers and I'd have a nightmare. We didn't need our parents. We just needed each other. I was never scared or upset as long as I had Gemma by my side.

When I've let out enough emotion for one night, I sit up straight, stare out the windshield, and make the drive back home.

This isn't goodbye.

It's just a pause.

Only a horrible, painful fucking pause.

I will get through this.

The prize waiting for me on the other side is worth it.

CHAPTER EIGHTEEN

Sloane

Jamie: How are you feeling today? Anything I can do?

I STARE AT MY PHONE IN DISBELIEF. LAST NIGHT, AFTER the art event at PMU, Jamie apologized profusely on behalf of her son while I tried desperately not to cry.

It felt as though everyone was privy to the secrecy of our forbidden romance. As if a spotlight were shone right in my face, revealing to everyone that I'm a mess over my best friend's son.

I'd expected ugly words from Jamie and Nathan.

Not apologies.

Not their shame and disbelief at what *Dempsey* had done to *me*.

I'd been too dumbfounded and brittle to correct them. Plus, I wasn't exactly looking forward to bringing their wrath down on me.

Rather than admitting to the fact that this thing between me and Dempsey wasn't one-sided, I allowed them to think it anyway.

I'm a coward.

**Jamie: He's out of control and I don't know what to do. This was clearly a cry for attention from me and

Nathan. You somehow got caught in the middle. I'm so sorry that happened to you.

I make no moves to respond. I'm caught in the middle because I put myself there. A bigger woman would tell her friend this and take the heat off the guy she likes.

And yet, I do nothing.

Dempsey definitely deserves better than the likes of me.

My chest aches as I think about him coming to my house last night. He'd been so eaten up with guilt for embarrassing me. I wanted, more than anything, to crawl under the covers with him so he could hold me until everything was all better.

I pushed him away.

He allowed me to.

Everyone is always talking about how wild and reckless Dempsey can be, but they don't see the real man he is. His heart is huge and he boldly goes after what he wants. It's admirable. Last night, he wanted me. Hell, I wanted him. Despite everything falling apart, I wanted him to undress me and make love to me so I could feel whole for one moment.

I'd asked him to leave because I didn't have the strength to tell him no. And he did. He didn't keep pushing for sex, sensing my hesitation, and pouncing on it. That's not irresponsibility like everyone claims is his number one character flaw. He's a deeply caring man I can't seem to stop thinking about.

After he left, I bawled my eyes out, hugging my pillow to me and wishing it were him. I missed him the second he slipped out the window. Still, the next day, I ache for him.

I shoot Jamie a quick text.

Me: I'm fine. Promise.

Nothing is fine, though.
Everything is far from fine.
My phone buzzes again. I expect more of the same from Jamie, but it's an unknown number.

Me: Hi, Sloane. It's Rhiannon's neighbor, Marianna. You asked me to text you if I saw her. Both her and Lenny just got home. They're fighting. I can hear them arguing through the walls. I don't want to get in the middle but just wanted to let you know.

Thank God.
Finally, a lead on my sister's disappearing act.
I fire off my thanks and then rush through getting dressed. I'd love to put on my uniform and burst into their house with enough authority to scare both of them into trying to be better people for my niece and nephews, but that would be a gross overstep as a cop.
No, this is personal.
After I'm dressed in jeans, a simple black T-shirt, and a pair of worn-out tennis shoes, I grab my purse and keys. I find Kaden sitting at the bar, scowling.
"Morning," I say, forcing false cheer into my voice.
"It's noon."
Okay, great. So he's in a mood, too. I'm not in the right headspace, though, to deal with a surly teenager.
"Wasn't feeling well," I lie. "What's wrong with you?"
He sits back on the barstool, glaring at me with narrowed eyes. "You're no better than Mom."
His harsh words strike me and I gape at him. "Kaden…"

"No," he bites out. "You say she neglects me, but you never have time for me either."

Ouch.

That's harsh.

I've had a few bad days since I took him into my home, but nothing remotely close to neglecting him.

"You're being unfair," I tell him, using my steady cop voice. "What do you want to do?"

He huffs, throwing his arms in the air, reminding me so much of his sassy mother. "Anything! I'm bored to tears. At least at the apartment, I had my friends."

Yeah, the bad type of friends.

An idea forms in my head.

"What if I took you over to Dempsey and Gemma's? You've been dying to hang out at their house again." I turn my back to him to start a cup of coffee I can take with me on the road. "What do you say?"

"Really?"

I swivel around to see a tentative smile forming on his lips. "Yeah, brat. Really. I mean, I'll have to drop you off for an hour or so because I have to run a boring errand. But we can even go eat somewhere greasy later since you're clearly dying to clog your arteries again."

His grin widens and he slips off the barstool. I'm taken by surprise when he nearly tackles me with a hug. After a second and the shock wears off, I wrap my arms around him and hug him back. Then he races off to get ready.

Everything is most definitely a mess, but I'll do my best not to let it spill over onto Kaden. I'm all he has right now and he's counting on me.

As we pull into Dempsey's driveway, unease claws at my chest. I didn't exactly ask if this was okay, but I don't anticipate anyone telling me no.

Kaden hops out of the car and bolts toward the front door. I'm barely climbing out when I see Dempsey talking to him on the porch. Kaden waves animatedly, and then Dempsey gestures in the house. As soon as Kaden disappears, Dempsey's intense stare lands on me.

He strides over to me, his usually smiling face stoic. It punctures my heart and makes it bleed with sorrow. Why does everything have to be so hard?

"Errands?" His eyebrow arches.

I let out a heavy sigh and keep my voice low so it doesn't carry. "A lead on Rhiannon. Neighbor says she and Lenny just got home. I'm going over there to talk to her."

His eyes widen. "That's good news. I'm coming with you."

Before I can formulate words to tell him no, he's already climbing into the passenger seat. With a frustrated groan, I get back into the driver's seat and shut the door.

"Dempsey," I start, but he waves me off.

"Don't." He reaches over and takes my hand in his. "Just let me go. You're worried. You need someone in your court. Let me be that man for you."

I stare down at our joined hands. His thumb rubs over my flesh, making goose bumps scatter up my arm. I'd be lying if I said this doesn't feel right and good.

"All right," I croak out. "Uh, thank you."

He brings my hand to his lips and kisses the back of it. "Everything's going to be okay, babe."

His words bring calm washing over me. I give him a quick nod and then reluctantly release his hand so I can back out of the driveway. It's then I get a whiff of tobacco.

"Have you been smoking?"

He barks out a laugh. "Want me to open a window?"

"You have. Dempsey, you're—" Too young? Smarter than that?

I glance over at him. He stiffens, waiting for me to finish that statement.

"Why?" I ask with a resigned sigh. "I've never seen you do it before or even smelled it on you."

He reaches over and takes my hand once more. "Up until last night, every day I've had with you has been fucking amazing. I'm not stressed around you. This morning, I spent a lot of time on the back porch, smoking and thinking."

"Thinking about what?"

God, I'm such a glutton for punishment.

His hand squeezes mine. "Us. Our future."

Why does my heart flutter at those words? So much for putting distance between us. When it comes to Dempsey Park, I'm hooked on him, allowing him to pull me wherever he goes.

"Oh." Oh? I sure as hell don't deny his words.

We sit in comfortable silence as I drive across town to my sister's apartment complex. As we grow nearer and nearer, worry threads its way through my veins. Whatever is going on with Rhiannon isn't good. My intuition is screaming that at me. Facing it today is going to suck.

I glance over at Dempsey again. He's watching me with a fierce expression on his face. The intensity of it nearly knocks me over.

"I'm sorry about last night," I tell him, voice cracking. "I said all the wrong things when you came over. It's just… This is hard. I don't know what to do."

"You don't have to do anything."

"Your mom…" I trail off and blink several times to clear the tears. "She thinks you're obsessed with me and I'm faultless."

"All truth."

I scoff at his words. "Not at all. I'm at fault too. You have me so wound up over you."

He pulls his hand out of mine and fumbles in his jeans pocket. When he retrieves a pack of cigarettes, I gape at him. He then rolls the window down and tosses it out.

"Dempsey!"

His deep chuckle warms my soul. "I needed to hear those words. Now that I've heard them, I don't need those anymore."

"You littered."

"You gonna arrest me, Officer Do-Good?"

My core clenches at the taunt. "Don't do it again."

He makes a silly show of crossing his heart. "Promise."

"I'm being serious. And you shouldn't have to take the heat from your parents. Last night was supposed to be wonderful for you."

"I got to kiss you," he reasons. "Pretty goddamn wonderful if you ask me."

I'm not done discussing this, but we've arrived at the apartment complex. After I park, we climb out and I lead the way into her building.

"You don't have to come with me," I tell him as we turn down my sister's hallway. "I can do this alone."

"Not a chance, babe. You never have to be alone again as long as I have anything to do with it."

I'm about to confront my sister and Dempsey still somehow

manages to make my heart skip a beat. I don't deserve his dedication.

When we reach her door, I pound on it hard, using my police knock that scares the shit out of people. Seconds later, the door cracks open, revealing an eye.

A blackened eye.

"Rhiannon."

"Who is it?" Lenny demands within the apartment.

Fear gleams in Rhiannon's one eye. She starts to close the door, buy I'm too quick, shoving my foot against it.

"Open it," I tell her, voice low and commanding.

She closes her eyes and steps back. I open the door and take in the apartment. A lamp is turned over and a broken beer bottle lies scattered all over the coffee table and floor beneath it.

"Who the fuck?" Lenny snaps as he rises from the sofa. "Oh, it's your cunt cop sister. Did you call her, Rhi? So help me—"

"You'll what?" I snap, striding toward him. "Hit her again?"

"She had that coming, pig."

"Sloane," Rhiannon pleads. "Just go. You'll only make it worse."

Lenny snorts out a cruel laugh. "Yeah, piggie, pig, pig. You'll make it worse."

It's then I notice the leather cut Lenny's wearing. It bears a patch that has the Park Mountain Shadows MC logo on it. Unbelievable.

Rhiannon whimpers again. She's terrified of this man and thinks it'll get worse for her. Not if I can help it. I glance over at my sister and really see her for the first time in a long time. She's too skinny, sadness swims in her blue eyes, and her usual fiery spirit has been snuffed out.

Fucking Lenny.

"Pack a bag, sis, we're leaving."

She blinks at me in surprise and then acts like she might actually listen. Dempsey, from behind me, is being eerily quiet, which I'm thankful for.

"You're not taking her anywhere," Lenny snarls, snatching up my sister by her elbow. "Now get the fuck out."

Unable to watch him abuse her any longer, I forget all police training and pounce on him, shoving him hard enough, he releases her to focus on me. *That's right, asshole, I'm the threat here, not her.*

"Pack," I bark at her. "Now, Rhiannon."

She scurries off toward the bedroom. I expect Lenny to chase after her, but he sticks to glowering down at me. I can smell alcohol on his breath and his pupils are dilated. He's fucked up. I wish I could just arrest his ass right here and now.

"She won't get far," Lenny says, spittle landing on my face. "She never does."

I jab a finger inches from his nose. "You're a fucking loser weighing my sister down and drowning her. She hasn't seen her kids in God only knows how long because of you. Time to let her go for good."

Lenny sneers at me. "Or what?"

"Or I'll make it my life's mission to get you sent to prison," I threaten. "An asshole like you doesn't belong anywhere but behind bars."

With shocking quickness, he snags a handful of my hair on the side of my head and jerks me to him. I don't even have a chance to defend myself before something—no, someone—barrels between us.

Crack!

Dempsey's fist slams into Lenny's jaw. He immediately releases his hold on my hair, falling flat on his ass on the dingy carpet. When Lenny starts to get back up, Dempsey kicks him hard in the center of his chest and sends Lenny sprawling out onto his back.

Rhiannon appears in the doorway of her bedroom, a backpack slung over her shoulder. Her eyes land on Lenny and she gasps.

"Let's go," I tell her, pointing to the front door. "Now."

She nods and then rushes past us. Lenny glares up at us with such hatred it makes my skin crawl.

"Leave them the fuck alone," Dempsey warns, voice harsh and threatening, "or I'll fucking make you."

As much as I'm grateful for Dempsey intervening, tendrils of fear work their way through my system. I can handle Lenny retaliating against me, but I certainly don't need Dempsey drawing away the target onto his own family.

Lenny stays where he's at as we slip back out of the apartment. Rhiannon speed walks ahead, clearly eager to get away from that prick. Dempsey lifts his hand and runs his fingers through my hair, massaging my scalp that still stings.

"I promise," he murmurs. "Everything is going to be okay, babe."

Right now, more than ever, I really want to believe that.

I take his hand in mine and pretend for a moment that it will.

CHAPTER NINETEEN

Dempsey

MY HAND HURTS.

Really fucking hurts.

It's been a while since I punched someone that hard—I certainly went easy on Trevor—but that Lenny asshole had my full wrath coming. Who the hell did he think he was putting his hands on *my* woman?

Sloane is extra tense as she drives. Every so often, she'll watch her sister in the rearview mirror a little too long or glance down at the way I rub at my bruised knuckles. The whole visit was a shitshow, but at least she has her sister away from that man.

Did he hurt Kaden?

Fury quells up inside me. I want to force Sloane to turn the car around so I can give that dude a proper ass beating.

"Where are we going?" Rhiannon asks from the back seat, voice shrill and alarmed.

"I was going to take you to my place—" Sloane starts but her sister interrupts her.

"Take me to Mom's. I need to see my momma."

Sloane grinds her teeth together as she pulls into a parking lot, does a U-turn, and then drives in the other direction. Other than the sound of Sloane's blinker clicking, no one says much. Sloane exhales a long sigh when we pull into an old, run-down neighborhood on the side of town Mom never lets us go to.

Walter Oaks.

"Jamie lived there," Sloane says, pointing to a dilapidated house with missing shingles. "We used to sit in front of that fire hydrant over there and make crowns from dandelions."

I know Mom didn't come from money, but I didn't realize how well off we were until now. The lawns are overgrown, with broken down vehicles peeking up from the grass. Screens hang from windows and one house has a storm door just propped up against the side nowhere near the actual door. Several houses have dogs chained out front, with shredded trash littering the area. One dog goes nuts as we pass, tugging fiercely against his chain in an effort to get to us.

This whole neighborhood is…sad.

I sometimes forget how good we have it. Hell, most of the time, in fact. My parents might be suffocating, but they've certainly spoiled us.

"Yes, I know. It's a shitty neighborhood," Sloane says tartly. "We won't be here long. You'll live."

Ouch.

Didn't realize I was so transparent.

We pull into the driveway of a yellow house. Well, it was once yellow but now has a film of dirt covering most of it. It could certainly go for a good pressure washing. Sloane hops out quickly. Rhiannon practically races for the door. I follow the two women, unsure of what to say or do in this situation. I know Sloane's relationship with her family is strained, hence her snippiness toward me. Despite it being uncomfortable, though, I'm still here as promised.

She doesn't have to be alone anymore.

She's got me.

Rhiannon barges into the house. Sloane casts an apologetic look over her shoulder at me before following her inside. I pull up the rear and am met with a wall of stale cigarette smoke. I'm a guy who lights up from time to time, but the stench of it overwhelms even me. I vow, in this moment, never to do it again. It's probably hell on the people who don't smoke.

The home is small—maybe twelve hundred square feet and that'd be pushing it—and it's full of people. Another woman who resembles Rhiannon and Sloane sits on a worn-out blue sofa with two children sitting with her. An older woman, but definitely related, stands by the opening of the kitchen, a lit cigarette dangling between her wrinkled lips. There are three more kids scattered about.

It's strange to imagine Sloane living here and growing up here. There's still so much I don't know about her. I'm going to eventually find out everything there is to know.

"Look what the cat dragged in," the woman from the kitchen says with hostility. "Sassy Sloane."

Sloane purses her lips before clipping out, "Nice to see you too, Mom. Ever heard of returning a text?"

The woman puffs on her cigarette and then waves dismissively at her. "Rhiannon was fine, obviously. I don't know why you suddenly felt the need to involve yourself in our family's affairs."

If her mother's words hurt Sloane, she doesn't let on.

"Fine? That piece of shit she shacks up with has been pummeling her," Sloane barks out. "And what about Kaden? You had nothing to say about me taking him in?"

Rhiannon perks up, looking a lot less pitiful at the mention of her son. "You have Kaden? How is he?"

"Fine, no thanks to you," Sloane grumbles.

Rhiannon's shoulders hunch and she drops down onto the sofa near her other sister. They reach for each other, holding hands. My heart aches that Sloane is the outsider in her own family. I, of all people, know how that feels.

"I think we've all had more than we can handle of your self-righteous bullshit," her mother says as she stubs out her cigarette in an ashtray on the bar. "It's time for you to go now."

Sloane's flinch is slight, but I catch it. It's not my place to put in my two cents, but I do think we should go. Rhiannon is safe with her mother and family. Now I need to see to Sloane's mental well-being.

"Don't go back to him," Sloane says to Rhiannon. "And text me when you're ready to see your son. He misses you."

Rhiannon starts to cry and the other sister soothes her. I slip back outside with Sloane on my heels. When we reach her car, I gently take the keys from her hands and give her a push toward the passenger side. Shockingly, she goes without argument.

"This is how the other side lives."

I arch a brow at her as I turn the vehicle on. "I didn't say anything."

She shoves the seat belt buckle into place with a snap. "You didn't have to. I can read the disdain written on your face."

"It's not disdain."

"Right," she huffs, glaring out the side window. "What then? Pity? Second-hand embarrassment?"

She's prickly and upset. I'm an easy target. Is that what

she needs? To vent out all her frustrations? I know one thing's for sure. She's in no mood to deal with Kaden. Rather than driving us to my house, I take the route to hers. As soon as we pull into her driveway, she climbs out and slams the door so hard the whole vehicle shakes.

"Sloane," I call out, trotting after her. "Talk to me."

She waits by the door, arms crossed and scowling, for me to unlock it. As soon as I do, she shoves inside and starts letting it all out.

"I bet you're rethinking your 'future' now, huh? Got a taste of the other side and it's not so pretty, is it?" She gestures at herself. "Some of us come from nothing. We will always be nothing."

Now she's starting to piss me off. I toss her keys onto a table and grab the front of her T-shirt, hauling her to me.

"Take it back."

Her nostrils flare. "Take what back?"

"The part where you're indicating you're somehow less than me. I fucking hate that. Take it back."

She claws at my hand clutching her shirt. "No! It's the truth, Dempsey! I'm me and you're a damn Park! In what world did we ever think this could work?"

I crowd her, forcing her back until her ass hits the closed front door. Her eyes widen as she stares up at me. They continue to flicker with anger, but heat is also there.

"I don't give a fuck where you came from, babe, only that you're here. Got that? I only care that you're here. With me. Where you fucking belong."

Her lips part and she blinks, frozen in my penetrating stare. Unable to keep from touching her like I want to, I crash my mouth to hers. The kiss snaps her out of her daze and she fucking bites my lip. I growl, pushing my hips against her, letting her feel how hard that defiant act makes my cock.

As though her anger has finally conceded to lust, she stops trying to push me away and instead tugs at the button of my jeans. I realize she's finally ready for me and that silent, small act is her permission. Testing my theory, I yank at her button and then draw her zipper down on her jeans. She cries out when I slip my hand beneath her jeans and panties, going straight for her pussy.

"Dempsey," she whimpers the second my fingers reach her clit. "Oh, God."

I continue to kiss the hell out of her, nipping and sucking at her lips and tongue. She claws at my shirt and manages to pull it up my body and over my head. It hangs around the arm that's working her clit.

"Are you hot for me?" I rumble, ghosting my teeth over her jawline. "I'm not fucking you until you're nice and wet, babe. Got it?"

She whines and quivers. With each circle of my fingertip over her clit, she grows a little wilder. I abandon her clit to rub at her slick opening, coating my finger in her arousal before going back to attack her pleasure point with slippery fervor.

"Dempsey!"

Sloane detonates with an explosive orgasm that has her clawing the hell out of my shoulders. Then she desperately tries to get my pants undone. She gets them shoved down my hips and her small hand finds its way into my boxers. Once she grips my throbbing cock, I let out a feral sound of pleasure.

I yank at her T-shirt, damn near ripping it off her body. As much as I want to tear her bra off too, I don't have the time. If I want to match her frantic energy, I need to get us naked enough to have sex and nothing more. The rest can wait until later when we can take our time.

She toes off her tennis shoes while I push her panties and jeans down her thighs. After some shimmying, she wriggles out of them and kicks them away. I help her by pulling my boxers down my own legs, readying myself to be with her.

"Hold on, babe. This is going to be so goddamn fast."

Her hands snake around my neck as I grab her ass and lift her. She hooks her legs around my waist while I grab onto my cock. Then I line the tip against her slick entrance.

Our eyes meet as I slowly sink into her tight body. It's tighter than my hand ever could be and a thousand times more wet. Her heat sucks me in and it's the single best feeling in all my life.

She claws at my hair, drawing me to her mouth for a ravenous kiss. I kiss her deeply, erratically pumping my hips. Fucking Sloane—always a dream until now—is surreal and phenomenal.

There's so much of her I want to taste and touch, but all I can do right now is fuck. A couple more thrusts and I feel my nuts tighten. I'm going to come.

And I'm inside her bare.

Fuck.

With the restraint of a saint, I pull out of her body seconds before my release and slide my slick cock against the lips of her pussy. My cock erupts, sending thick ropes of cum between us, coating both our stomachs. I'm dizzy with pleasure and nearly lose my hold on her.

"You're perfect. Holy fuck, you're so goddamn perfect."

She whimpers as I slowly release her so she can stand on

her own two feet. Her body trembles wildly, so I steady her hips to keep her from falling.

The tension returns to her body and she stiffens.

With a smack to my chest, she shrieks, "You didn't use a condom!"

I sigh because she clearly is still freaking out about earlier and taking it out on me. "I pulled out, babe. It's okay."

She shoves at me, pushing me back far enough she can escape my hold. "Thank God I'm on the pill!"

Her words sting. Not that I'm mad she doesn't want to get knocked up the first time we have sex, but because she's already pushing me away again. I drag my boxers and jeans back up as I chase her naked ass through the house. Her bedroom door slams in my face, the lock engaging almost immediately.

I scrub a palm down over my face, getting a hint of the smell of her arousal. God, she smells fucking amazing. One day I'll take my time getting to know her pussy very, very well.

Today, though, I need to get her to calm the fuck down.

"Come on, Sloane. Talk to me. You're being unfair."

This brings on the tears. She starts crying, which makes me feel like a total dick. I want to hold her and promise everything will work itself out. Instead, I'm stuck on the other side of the door, listening to the torturous sound of her pain.

"Babe," I mutter, rapping my knuckle on the door. "Let me in."

Nothing but more sobs.

"Do you want me to leave you alone for a bit? Do you need time to process this? Us?"

The crying gets louder.

"I'll go and get Kaden. Just…try to relax. Take a hot shower. When I come back, we'll talk about all this."

Still no response other than her breakdown on the other side of the door. Guilt seeps into my every pore. Maybe I hurt her. Maybe I went too fast. Maybe she regrets being with me.

"Babe," I choke out. "I should have gone slower. I…I fucked you when I should have made love to you. You deserve better than that."

"That's not… Y-You didn't use a condom," she rasps out between hiccups and tears. "What w-we did was reckless. I don't even know w-who you've been with or if you've been tested lately."

I lean my forehead against the door and squeeze my eyes shut. "You're safe. You'll always be safe with me." I try the locked doorknob to no avail. "I was tested during my last routine checkup, but even still, you wouldn't have to worry. I'm a virgin." I bark out a laugh. "Was. I was a virgin."

This makes her cry even more.

With a heavy sigh, I leave to pick up all her scattered clothes, using her T-shirt to swipe off the leftover cum on my stomach. The last thing Kaden needs to see is his aunt's clothes all over the foyer. I then toss all her clothes in the laundry room before snagging my shirt up from the floor. After stalling long enough and realizing she's not going to come after me or let me in, I leave to go get the kid.

This thing with Sloane is complicated and messy.

And worth every second, even the miserable ones.

CHAPTER TWENTY

Sloane

WHAT'S WRONG WITH ME?

I treated him like he was a monster, even though for a short while when we were having sex, it was one of the best moments I've ever experienced.

Being with him felt right and good.

I've surely ruined it now.

I took a quick shower like he suggested and dressed at record speed. I'd heard voices when he and Kaden returned, but I was too chicken to speak to him. He tried to talk to me again through the door, but after me not answering, he finally left.

How did he get home?

Did Gemma follow him with their car?

I clutch my phone, desperately wanting to text him to make sure he made it home okay, but I can't make myself do it.

He's better off thinking I'm a heartless, cold bitch.

Dempsey needs a warm, vibrant, loving woman.

Not me.

Anyone but me.

To be fair, had I not dealt with the drama of Rhiannon and my family, things may have gone down differently between me and Dempsey. Our first time could have gone slowly and cherished as it should have been.

I treated him like a filthy whore.

I got the sex I desperately wanted and needed then sent him out the door without so much as a thank you or a kiss.

God, that was so wrong.

Why is life so hard?

The chemistry between us was so intense. Fire burned inside me like never before. I was happy when he was inside me and kissing me. I'll probably never get a chance to feel anything like it ever again because I've undoubtedly ruined this thing between us.

Have I, though?

Dempsey has proven time and time again he's there for me, even when I lose it. He just keeps showing back up with such patience. My heart aches for him. He really is perfect. How no one besides me has ever seen this is beyond me.

He deserves the world.

I could give it to him.

I could fix it.

Shame creeps over me, but I straighten my spine. Yes, it'll be awkward to admit my shortcomings and to apologize for freaking the hell out, but he'll make it better with his sweet touches and kind words. I know this without a shadow of a doubt.

Not all is lost.

My life may be a shit show of epic proportions, but Dempsey is one of the best things about it. Maybe I don't have to fight so much when it comes to him and just let it happen.

Images of us together in bed, kissing and cuddling, make my chest tighten. I want that. I want to be with him in whatever capacity that may be.

I'm about to text him and ask him if he wants to come

back over to talk when my phone buzzes. A smile tugs at my lips as I eagerly read his message.

Except, it's not him texting.

It's an unknown number calling.

"Hello?" I croak out, frowning.

The line is quiet and then I hear a sniffle. "Aunt Sloane?"

"Trevor?"

My nephew has been a thorn in my backside for weeks, but hearing him break down on the other end of the phone shreds my heart into tiny pieces.

"Hey, hon, calm down. What's wrong? Are you hurt?"

If those club assholes touched one hair on his head, I'll bring the entire wrath of the PMPD down on their heads.

"C-Can you come g-get me?"

"Of course. Where are you?"

"The ap-apartment. S-something's h-happened."

"I'm on my way. Keep your phone on you."

We disconnect the call as I race to throw on my shoes and grab my Glock. It's dark outside now, which means I've hidden away all damn day in my room. When I finally emerge from my cave, Kaden is glued to the screen, playing a video game with an open pizza box beside him.

Dempsey made sure he was fed.

God, I don't deserve that man.

"Hey," I say as I hurry through the living room. "I have to go check on Trevor. He just called."

He tears his gaze from the screen to gape at me. "He did?"

"Yeah. Can you hold down the fort until I get back?"

"Yeah. You don't have to worry about me, Aunt Sloane."

I drop down to give him a kiss on his head and he playfully pushes me away. I'm going to fix all of this. My family.

Dempsey. My love life. It's time to harness that fiery, stubborn girl who climbed her way out of her hard life and into something better. I can do this.

I'm tempted to call Dempsey on the way to the apartment complex, but since he's already had an altercation with Lenny and Trevor both, I don't want to make things worse. I'll be protected because I have a weapon. Hopefully, it won't come to that. If Lenny put his hands on Trevor, I'll call it in and get that prick arrested.

The trip goes by in a blur and all too soon I'm at the building, storming inside. When I reach the apartment door, I try the knob. Locked. Softly, I rap on the door.

"Trevor?"

Footsteps thud toward the door and the lock disengages. Trevor slowly cracks open the door, his entire body slumping with relief when he sees me.

"Aunt Sloane!"

He throws himself at me, hugging me so tight I nearly lose my breath. "Thank God you're here."

I squeeze him back, cringing at how frail he feels. Whatever he's been mixed up in is bad for his health. The last time I'd seen him, he'd been stocky from playing basketball with the neighborhood kids. Now he's a waif.

"Tell me what happened," I say, gently pulling away from him. "It's okay."

He shrinks away from me and slowly walks into the apartment. I close the door behind me, surveying the space. It's still a mess from earlier, but Lenny's missing.

"Did Lenny do something to you?" I demand, unable to keep my anger in check.

He shudders and shakes his head. "No, uhh…you better go look for yourself."

Trevor points toward the bedroom Rhiannon and Lenny share but makes no moves to go that way. I withdraw my weapon and turn off the safety, unable to shake the sinister feeling crawling up my spine. This time, with Lenny, I won't be caught unaware. I'll shoot his ass in the kneecap if I have to.

I prowl toward the bedroom. On the other side of the bed, legs stick out on the floor. Bile creeps up my throat as I approach. As soon as I see the body, my heart sinks. Not because of whom it is, but because of how he died. Lenny, eyes wide open and tongue lolling out, has had his throat slit and now lies in a huge puddle of dark, sticky blood.

Despite my hatred for this man, I snap into police officer mode and carefully approach to check for a pulse. His skin is cold, firm, and rubbery to the touch. No pulse. Time of death must've been hours ago—sometime between when we left and now.

Who all came here in that time?

Just Trevor?

Sickness roils in my gut as I rise to my feet. He stands in the doorway, a horrified expression marring his once-handsome face that's now littered with scabs.

"What happened?" I ask, voice even and calm.

He stares at Lenny's feet. "I came home to get some stuff and…and I found him like that."

Trevor's hands don't have blood on them and he appears to be terrified of entering the room. I believe him, but I'm not sure if that's the aunt in me or the cop.

"It's okay," I assure him. "I just need to call this in. You can explain everything to the police—"

"The police?" he hisses, stepping back with his palms raised. "You are the police, Aunt Sloane. That's why I called you."

As much as I want to take the lead on this, I can't. I'm too close to this case and Tanaka would can my ass. If I want Trevor to have any hope of getting out of this unscathed, everything needs to be by the book.

"I'll be here the whole time," I say gently. "We'll explain it together and get to the bottom of what happened."

He shakes his head in vehemence. "N-No. They'll arrest me. I'm an adult now. I don't want to go to prison."

"But you didn't kill him, though, right?"

"What? No!"

"Then you don't have anything to worry about, hon."

His eyebrows scrunch together as he mulls this over, then without warning, he turns on his heel and bolts. It takes me a second to snap into action. By that time, he's already out the front door and racing down the hall. I chase after him, calling his name over and over. He's much quicker, though, and tears out the door into the night.

I can't abandon the crime scene to chase after my nephew. Dammit.

Trotting to a stop, I fish out my phone and make the call. This whole day is the biggest shit show of my entire life and that's saying something because my life has been hell since the day I was born.

After I place the call, I make my way back inside the apartment, not closing the door all the way. The detectives are going to want this place dusted for prints and the less I contaminate the scene, the better.

It feels like an eternity later, but officers begin arriving and taking over. When the detectives—two colleagues I speak to every single day—show up, the realness of this situation begins to set in, especially when I'm immediately relieved of my Glock that's bagged and tagged into evidence.

They're not joking like they do in the break room. No, I'm being drilled with questions from two hard-assed cops. I tell them everything from the issues Lenny and Rhiannon had, to Trevor getting mixed up with a bad drug-using crowd, to Kaden staying with me because of it, to the altercation from this morning, to the point we're at now. By the time I finish, another man shows up, crisp and out of place in an expensive suit.

"Officer Thurman," Tanaka says, voice icy cold. "Detectives, I'll take over from here with Thurman."

My two colleagues give him a firm nod and then move on to do their jobs. Tanaka's eyes narrow, resembling a hawk before it swoops down to snatch up a field mouse.

Am I done?

The look in his gaze says I am.

What if this was all some setup to get me into trouble? Tanaka knows I'm onto his corruption. This could be a way to silence me, right? Have my sister's lowlife boyfriend murdered and put me right in the middle of it. I'm forced to retell the entire thing to the man I've been secretly investigating.

"Am I in trouble?" I ask, voice shaking when I finish.

"Not if you continue to cooperate," Tanaka says smoothly. "You were just worried about your nephew, right?"

My stomach sinks. "He didn't do it if that's what you're thinking."

Tanaka's black eyebrow arches up, reminding me of an

evil villain. "He ran from the scene of a homicide, Thurman. It's not a good look."

They'll haul him in, though, and interrogate him like I tried to. Trevor is innocent. They'll come to that conclusion too. In the meantime, a real killer is out there.

What if Rhiannon had been here? Or Lucy or Kaden?

"I'm going to follow you back to the station," Tanaka says, gesturing for the door. "We'll continue this talk while the detectives work the scene."

Great.

Being brought in for questioning at my own workplace has to be a new low for me. It's humiliating and infuriating. But if I want to move past this, I have to go through the thick of it first. I concede with a nod and head out the door. There's one thought that replays in my mind.

Thank God Dempsey wasn't here with me.

The last thing I need is to pull him deeper into my shit.

CHAPTER TWENTY-ONE

Dempsey

COME ON, SLOANE. WHERE ARE YOU?

I pace her front porch as I wait for her to come back home. I'm still reeling from her text from earlier.

Sloane: Someone killed Lenny. Trevor found his body and called me. He ran off after, so it looks really bad for him. I'm on my way to the station now with Tanaka to finish giving my statement. Can you keep an eye on Kaden until I get back?

Of course, after receiving that text, I'd blasted her with questions, none of which were answered. I slipped out of the house and came right over, not bothering to follow Dad's stupid rule about taking Gemma with me.

I wasn't sure if Sloane wanted me to tell Kaden, so I stayed tightlipped and told him I'd come over to hang out for a bit. We played video games while I checked my phone every three minutes. Eventually, I made spaghetti and we watched a movie. He fell asleep on the sofa, but I've been unable to sit still, my mind racing with worry.

Sloane was already having a terrible day after the run-in with Lenny when she took her sister away, but for it to end like this? My chest aches. I just need her in my arms so I can hold my girl back together. Something tells me she's going to need it.

Will she let me?

I think so.

Yes, she sort of freaked out after we had sex and clearly needed some space, but I didn't think she'd let it go on forever. Knowing I was the person she reached out to with the information of Lenny's death and needing help with Kaden proves that I'm still her man.

Headlights bounce as a vehicle comes up the road. I stop pacing to strain my eyes, searching for any sign that it's her car.

"Thank fuck," I mutter when she pulls into the driveway.

She shuts off the car, climbs out, and then softly closes the door. Her entire body trembles. I've never seen her look so lost or broken.

Snapping into action, I stalk across the lawn over to her. When she sees me, she surprisingly flings herself into my arms. Grabbing her ass, I lift her up and she wraps her legs around me. Her grip on me is fierce, like she's afraid I'll vanish into thin air.

I'm not going anywhere.

"I'm here, babe. I've got you."

She makes a choked, pained sound that kills me. I hate that she's hurting.

"Kaden's asleep on the sofa," I murmur. "Come on. Let's get you inside."

Her breath is warm and ragged against the side of my neck where her face is. With Sloane still clinging to me like a koala bear, I quietly let us back inside and then take her to her bedroom. This time, I'm allowed inside. I close the door and then carry her to the bathroom.

Once I ease her to her feet, I take a moment to inspect her face. Dark circles rim her eyes and her skin is pale. Tears swim in her pretty blue eyes, threatening to spill over. I press a soft kiss to her nose and then let go of her long enough to turn the shower on. When I return, I help her out of her clothes until she's fully naked in front of me.

God, she's a fucking vision.

I'd love nothing more than to fall to my knees right now and worship her, but she doesn't need that. She needs someone to hold her together and be the strong one. I can do that for her. I can and will do anything for her.

"Do you want to shower alone?" I ask, voice raspy and soft.

She gives me a sharp shake of her head.

I pull my shirt off and bite back a smile when her nostrils flare. We'd been in such a hurry earlier today that neither of us was able to appreciate each other's bodies. Knowing she's just as mesmerized by mine as I am by hers is such a relief.

The bathroom fills with steam as I strip out of the rest of my clothes. Her eyes widen when they land on my cock.

"You're pierced," she utters, shock in her words. "How? When?"

I snigger as I grab her hand. "You don't want to know, Officer Do-Good. Probably wasn't legal."

"Who would pierce a teen—"

Her words fade away as I kiss her supple lips. "Don't worry about it, babe. It's done."

I pull us under the hot spray of her shower. Water sluices over our bodies as I hug her to me. Our naked skin on skin feels incredible. She pulls slightly back to look up at me with hooded eyes. Need flickers in her gaze, but I ignore it for now in favor of bathing her.

"Put your hair under the water," I instruct. "Let me take care of you."

She obeys and gets her hair wet. Once it's soaked through, I dump a glob of shampoo that smells like her onto the top of her head. A soft groan escapes her when I start massaging it into her hair and scalp.

My dick certainly can't ignore that sound.

I gently tug on the strands of her hair, indicating for her to tilt her head back so I can rinse out the suds. Her eyes close and a contented sigh rushes past her lips. Smiling, I continue to bathe her, taking special care to add conditioner to her hair and then to soap her down from head to toe.

I'm about to quickly wash myself, but she takes over, running a bar of soap over my chest. Our eyes meet as she soaps my body. I grunt when she avoids my dick that's aching for her touch.

"You're a good man," she murmurs, eyes watering again. "I don't deserve to have this—*you*."

I scoff. "Zip it."

A smile curls her lips up. I quickly rinse us both, shut off the water, and grab us towels. After drying our bodies off and running a brush through her hair, we abandon our towels and climb into her bed naked. She sighs happily when I lie flat on my back and pull her against my side.

"Tell me what happened. All of it."

I sit quietly as she explains the call from Trevor, his behavior when she arrived, seeing Lenny's murdered body, and then the relentless grilling from her superior. By the time she finishes, she's trembling.

"I'm so scared for Trevor," she whispers. "He's mixed up with bad people and now the cops are looking for him. I just want to fix it all, but I don't know how."

"I know you do," I say, running my fingers up and down her arm. "You're doing the best you can."

She tilts her head up, her hot breath tickling over my face. I twist so I can meet her lips with mine. At first, she kisses me softly but then, like earlier, she claws at me, tugging on my shoulders. I roll over until I'm on top of her, caging her in between my elbows.

"I need you." Her legs tighten around my hips. "Please."

"I didn't bring a condom. I was planning to just take care of you."

"Making love to me *is* taking care of me."

"Babe…"

She tilts her hips as she attempts to rub her pussy along my shaft. "I screwed up earlier. I said a bunch of crap I didn't mean. We can go without the condom. Please, Dempsey."

How the hell can I deny her when she asks so sweetly?

I kiss her mouth and then trail kisses down her chest, stopping briefly to show each of her pert nipples my attention. They're nothing like my imagination. My drawings don't come close to the real thing. I nip and suck at each nipple until she's clawing at my hair.

"Dempsey…"

I chuckle against her flesh and continue my trek south. My tongue teases her bellybutton and then I'm right where I want to be. With my thumbs, I pull apart her pussy lips and seek her clit, eager to give her pleasure when she's had the world's shittiest day. As I suck her clit into my mouth, she lets out a garbled sound.

"Shh," I murmur against her pussy. "You'll wake your nephew."

She arches her back, stifling the sounds attempting to make their way out of her as I feast on her perfect pussy. I can't get enough of her sweet, unique taste. I want it all over my fucking face, running down my chin and seeping into my pores.

I've never gone down on anyone before. When I'd told her I was a virgin, it was the damn truth. It's hard to get laid by some rando when you're in love with someone else. I never wanted to just get my dick wet. I wanted Sloane. Always Sloane.

She tugs at my hair when I nip at her clit. I ease a finger into her body, marveling over the tight, slick channel. Accidentally, I run my fingertip over her G-spot and she shudders wildly with pleasure.

"You like that, babe?" I murmur against her pussy as I stroke that same spot again. "Like when my finger is inside you, fucking you?"

"Y-Yes," she hisses. "Feels g-good."

I continue sucking on her clit while fingerfucking her. It doesn't take long until she's coming apart with a strained moan. One day, when we're completely alone, I'll make her scream for me. Her body convulses with her orgasm, long after I remove my finger. Gripping my cock, I press against her soaked hole and inch slowly inside.

Fuck. I've always known my dick was on the large side, but being inside her body that barely accommodates my size forces me to go slow so as not to hurt her. After a few thrusts of my hips, I'm fully seated in the body of the most beautiful woman in the world.

Our lips meet for a tender kiss. I don't fuck her like a madman like earlier, but instead take my sweet time with her. I memorize every soft whimper and groan that comes from her luscious lips. She scrapes at my shoulders with her blunt nails and rips at my hair. I love how desperate she is when we make love.

Stars glitter on the edges of my vision. Her breaths are coming out fast and ragged. To help bring her to orgasm again so we can come together, I reach between us to work her clit between my fingers.

"I'm going to come soon," I rasp out. "I want you to come too, babe. Don't worry. I'll pull out."

"N-No. Don't. I want to feel you inside of me when we come."

I nip at her bottom lip. "That sounds like fucking heaven."

We kiss like two starved people feasting on one another. Within seconds, she cries out in ecstasy. Her pussy clenches around my cock, completely sending me over the edge of sanity. I growl against her lips as my cum jets inside her hot body. When I'm completely spent, I don't pull out, instead resting my elbows on either side of her head again so I can see her gorgeous face.

"You're it for me, babe," I murmur. "It's always been you for me. It always will be."

Her features turn stony for a flash and I expect instant regret from her like last time. Maybe even her bringing up my mom and the whole moral issue of our relationship once more.

I get none of that.

"I'm lucky to have you," she says, smiling at me. "I don't know how it happened, but I'm glad it did."

Running my nose along hers, I whisper, "I love you, Sloane. I know you're not there yet like I am, but I can't go another minute without telling you. I love you so goddamn much it makes my chest fucking hurt."

She runs her fingers through my hair, studying me like I'm something wonderful to her. I don't ever need to hear those words in return as long as she continues to look at me like I'm fucking special.

"I have never had a connection with a man like this," she admits, cheeks blooming crimson. "I, uh…"

I kiss her nose. "What, babe? Never had sex this good?"

A laugh barks out of her. "Actually, I…" She squeezes her eyes shut. "God, this is really embarrassing."

"It's just me. Spill."

With a heavy sigh, she pops open her eyes and meets my stare. "I've never done that before."

"Which part? No one's ever gone down on you?"

Those selfish assholes should feel ashamed for neglecting this beauty.

"No," she huffs. "None of it. I was, uh, a virgin too."

I gape at her, her words shocking me. She's Mom's age and she's never had sex before? "Really?"

"I never got close enough to anyone to want to be intimate."

I grin at her. "So you're saying I'm special?"

"Yeah, Demps, you really are."

CHAPTER TWENTY-TWO

Sloane

ACON?

Why do I smell bacon?

I slowly wake, realizing it's morning and I'm alone in bed. The ache between my legs is a reminder of how I spent most of my night.

With Dempsey.

We came together off and on throughout the night, each time more intense than the time before. I've never orgasmed so many times in such a short period in all my life. Probably because it's always been up to me and I can't be bothered to make it happen more than once.

Dempsey has made it his mission to get me off as often as he can.

I stretch my arm across the bed to the empty spot where he slept. The sheets are cold, which means he's been out of bed for quite a while. From the smell of it, he's been cooking. For some reason, this makes me grin like an idiot.

Is this why people are in such a hurry to find a significant other?

I guess if I'd known this feeling was a possibility for me, I'd have been searching a long time ago.

Like before Dempsey was born?

My stomach twists at that intrusive thought. When I can

separate Dempsey the man from Dempsey my best friend's son, everything is great. I see him as an equal, a fantastic sexual partner, and a confidant. But when I am reminded of exactly who he is, it makes me feel like some sicko who's been preying on her friend's son.

I tried denying the attraction between us and that didn't work. That means my only option now is to keep it between us. It's such a bitch move, but I'm too greedy to let him go. I want Dempsey. So much. If this is the only way I can have him—in secret—so be it.

After a quick shower, which Dempsey sadly doesn't join, I finally make my way into the kitchen. Kaden is awake, playing a video game, while shoving bacon absently into his mouth.

"Plate's in the microwave," Kaden says around chewing. "Dempsey said don't cook it without reading the note first."

Note?

I don't have an opportunity to be sad about Dempsey having already gone as curiosity gets the better of me. I open the microwave to see a plate of scrambled eggs, bacon, and pancakes waiting for me. A tented piece of paper addressed to "Babe" sits on top.

My heart melts.

He's so sweet and thoughtful.

I pull the note out and then turn on the microwave. Once the food starts reheating, I read his message in surprisingly neat handwriting.

Morning, sleepyhead!

I got a call from Dad chewing my ass out for breaking his car rule. I figured I'd head home and do some damage control. You didn't have shit for groceries, so I ran to the store first and whipped you guys up something to eat. Do you ever feed that kid anything besides takeout? Don't worry, babe, you've got me now. I'm more than a spoiled shit. I actually learned how to cook. Anyway, I'll call you later. Just wanted to make you feel special this morning. Get used to the feeling because I plan to do it every damn day if you'll let me.

Love you,
Dempsey

My heart hammers in my chest. I kind of panicked when he told me he loved me last night, but I'm not going to lie. It feels good to hear it. He's right about our level of feelings, though. Where he's been in love with me for a long time, I'm slowly getting there. It may happen sooner than I'm expecting because everything about him makes me smile.

I'm happy with Dempsey.

Truly happy.

It's the first time in my life I could say that and mean it. I thought I was happy when I'd gotten accepted into the police academy or when I took my first ride in my squad car as an official police officer. Looking back, it was just pride or satisfaction.

Not this light, giggly feeling that's gotten a hold of me.

This is happiness.

The microwave beeps, bursting my bubble, and reality slowly trickles in without Dempsey to distract me.

Trevor is on the run. Lenny is dead.

I'm going to have to tell Rhiannon today.

I'll need to tell Kaden too, but I will do it all at once. I'm not about to tell this story twice in a row if I don't have to.

"Hey, kiddo," I call out to Kaden after I wolf down the best damn breakfast I've had in a long time. "You want to go see your mom?"

The game pauses and he makes his way into the kitchen.

"I need to talk to her. I can go alone or—"

"Let me grab my shoes!"

A flutter of happiness presents itself again. Reuniting Kaden with my mother is a good thing. Now that she's away from Lenny—for good—I think things might get better for both of them.

◎

"Kay-Kay!"

"Mom!"

Kaden nearly tackles Rhiannon in Mom's cramped living room, overcome with joy at seeing his mother. Rhiannon sobs and laughs as though the moment is equal parts happy as it is sad. She's not a bad person but just got wrapped up with one. Those kids love their mom. Maybe now she can be the parent they've desperately needed.

"Thank you for bringing him to see me," Rhiannon says as the two of them sit on the sofa. She gives me a soft smile. "Don't worry. Mom just went in for the lunch shift. She's just being Mom and didn't mean what she said yesterday."

As much as I appreciate the words, I don't believe them.

Me and Mom have always had friction. That's not going away anytime soon.

"I, uh, actually have to tell you something. Both of you."

Before I can speak, the front door opens. Lucy, smelling like hashbrown grease, staggers in, eyes drooping from having to do the early shift. When she sees her mom and brother together, she joins them on the sofa, grinning happily.

All they need is Trevor now.

That one is going to be a lot trickier.

"What is it?" Rhiannon finally asks after Lucy rambles about all the things that went wrong this morning at work. "You said you had to tell us something."

I force myself to sit in the aged recliner Mom uses and drag my gaze over Rhiannon and her kids. There's no easy way to say this.

"Lenny's dead."

The three of them stare at me as though I never said a word. Finally, Rhiannon's brows pinch.

"What do you mean Lenny's dead, Sloane? I don't understand. We just saw him yesterday."

I run my fingers through my damp ponytail and let out a tired sigh. "Last night, someone cut his throat. It was a homicide."

"That's why you had to go to work last night?" Kaden asks, confusion on his face. "Because there was a murder?"

Lucy gapes at me. "You're joking, right?"

Rhiannon continues to blink, still trying to make sense of my words. "You worked the scene? You saw him? Is this real?"

"Yes," I mutter. "I, uh, was the first one on the scene. It was definitely a homicide. You may get a visit from the detectives who are working the case."

A strangled sob rips from Rhiannon's throat. Fat tears well in her eyes and then spill over. Both kids, though not crying themselves, cling to their mother to show their support.

Fact of the matter is, even though Lenny was an abusive prick, she still loved the guy.

Rhiannon shakes her head and then shoots me a pleading stare. "Who would do that to him?"

I don't dare breathe a word that Trevor was the one who called me. Letting them think I was at work and came across the homicide is better for now. The last thing the three of them need is to worry about Trevor being implicated for the murder. That's on me to worry about for now.

"We're not sure," I say quickly, "but the detectives are working diligently on it. I was going to call today to see if there were any leads. I'll keep you informed."

Rhiannon continues to softly cry. When she gets her bottom lip to stop wobbling, she says, "I'm…Sloane, I'm pregnant. Lenny was going to be a dad. Now…" Another sob. "Now this child will never know their father."

The other children don't have a relationship with theirs either and that's not necessarily a bad thing.

"I'm sorry," I murmur. "I really am."

"I'm going to have a little brother or sister?" Kaden asks, gently patting his mom's belly that's not showing. "No way."

This has Rhiannon drying up her tears and giving her son a smile.

"Well, we really should get going," I say, rising to my feet. "I just wanted to deliver the news in person."

"Can I spend the night here with Mom?" Kaden asks, eyes lighting up with hope.

"No," I blurt out at the same time Rhiannon says, "Of course, honey."

My sister frowns at me and her features harden. She's

not exactly in a position to suddenly care about her son, but she is his mother.

"That's fine," I rush out, waving in the air as though it's nothing. "Call me if you need anything."

The statement is for Kaden, but Rhiannon nods. Looks like I'm going home alone. Maybe Dempsey will come back over later when I'm no longer trying to be quiet. The thought sends a thrill down my spine.

After saying goodbye, I slip out of the house and head back out onto the road. Instead of going home, though, I take the route to the station. I'm not exactly keen on being back there after the rigorous questioning I received from Tanaka last night, but I do want answers.

Since it's the weekend, there's an entirely different crew of officers than I'm used to seeing. A guy I've never met mans the front desk. I guess they do give Tara a break every once in a while.

To my surprise, Bishop and Montgomery are both at work. As I approach, Bishop takes a call and walks off, leaving me with Montgomery.

"Hey," I say, voice clipped. "Any leads?"

Montgomery frowns. "On what?"

I blink, waiting for the punchline of a stupid joke. "The homicide from last night. Don't play cute. I'm not in the mood today."

His jaw muscle ticks. "I'm not being cute. I thought you were expressly told not to touch this case."

"I'm not touching it," I grumble. "I'm asking about it. That's not a crime, Montgomery."

"No, but it goes against a direct order." He crosses his

arms over his chest and leans back in his desk chair. "Back off, Thurman."

I know he's right, but it doesn't mean I have to like it. With a frustrated sigh, I storm over to my desk and decide I'll do my own digging. I'm barely scratching the surface when Tanaka breezes past me, motioning for his office along the way.

"Now," Tanaka barks over his shoulder.

I glower at Montgomery for tattling and he simply shrugs. As I pass Bishop, he mouths, "sorry," to me. Whatever. If I could survive last night's interrogation, I can survive another bitch out from Tanaka. As soon as I close the office door behind me, Tanaka lays into me.

"You have to distance yourself from this case," Tanaka hisses. "Why is that so damn hard to understand?"

I take in the fury flickering in Tanaka's dark eyes and the grinding of his molars. The cool, unflappable chief of police is actually pissed.

Because I care about this case?

Or because he's hiding something and I'm dipping my toes somewhere they don't belong?

"Let the detectives do their job," he says icily. "I don't know how many other ways I can say that for you to get it through your thick skull."

My nostrils flare with anger, but I reel in a scathing remark that might get me canned. "Montgomery is an idiot. If we actually want to catch this killer, we need all hands on deck, Chief."

"I disagree with one of those statements." He narrows his eyes at me. "And we don't need all hands on deck. Especially not yours. The deceased is your sister's boyfriend, for fuck's sake, and your nephew is a suspect!"

I shake my head in vehemence. "I told you. He didn't have blood on him. He was scared."

"You're his aunt. Of course you're going to see what you want to see. Like I said, you're too close to this case. Goddammit, don't make me put you on leave over this."

Shrinking back from his words, I study his eyes for the truth. He's hanging on by a thread. If he puts me on leave over a disciplinary action, I may as well kiss my career goodbye. Gritting my teeth, I force back all the arguments I'm desperate to unleash.

"Got it, sir."

Tanaka nods and huffs out a sharp breath. "Good. Thought so. Now go enjoy the rest of your weekend. We'll handle it from here. I promise."

His promises mean nothing to me.

"Thanks," I grind out. "I hope you catch the *real* killer soon."

While Montgomery chases his tail in circles, I'll get to the bottom of this on my own time. If I have to submit anonymous tips, I will. Maybe I can even get Dempsey to help me.

One way or another, I will figure out who did this and clear my nephew's name.

Hopefully, I'll manage not to lose my job in the process.

CHAPTER TWENTY-THREE

Dempsey

Sloane: Can you come over again tonight? I miss you already.

GRIN AT MY PHONE. SEEING THOSE WORDS FROM SLOANE makes this relationship of ours all the more real. It's not one-sided or unrequited.

She's one-hundred percent in it with me.

Me: I have to make it through our family dinner tonight but then I can escape.

Sloane: Where did you tell them you were last night?

I hate that I lied to my parents. I'd wanted to tell them where and with whom I shared a bed last night, but I played it off and said I was at a friend's house.

I'm such a pussy.

Not that I'm afraid of getting in trouble or anything. It was more that I wanted to stay in my little bubble of undisturbed happiness for a while longer. When they find out who I'm sleeping with, they're going to make it a huge dramatic thing.

I'd rather put all my energy into pleasing Sloane, not fighting with my parents.

Me: A friend's. How are you feeling? Sore?

Sloane: Very. Not sure I can handle any more tonight. I'm down for kissing and cuddling.

Me: Can I kiss and cuddle your pussy?

She sends me a bunch of shocked emojis that make me snort with laughter.

"You never smile at me like that," Tate says as he crosses the road between our houses. "Should I be jealous?"

Jude gives him the side-eye and hugs him tighter to his side. It amuses me that my brother is so damn possessive over his man. No one wants to steal Tate away, but he protects him as though everyone he encounters does.

"Very," I say with a smirk.

I rise from the porch chair, shove my phone into my pocket, and fist-bump Tate when he approaches. Jude reluctantly releases him and saunters into the house. Tate lifts a brow at me, waiting for some sort of explanation.

Like always, I keep my lips zipped.

"Fine, don't tell me," he grumbles playfully. "I'm happy you're happy, though. It's a good look on you."

My chest expands at his words. I *am* happy. Sloane has that effect on me.

We head inside where the usual Sunday family dinner chaos ensues. Gemma, Mom, and Aubrey are all crowded around Willa and her newborn baby boy, Bane. Callum stands behind them, tense and ready to intervene if anyone makes the little squirt so much as whimper. It's funny seeing him as a dad. Even more so than seeing Spencer as a dad. Where Spencer has fun with little Rex, Callum seems terrified and treats Bane as if he's made of glass.

Dad, locked in a conversation with Hugo, watches me

with narrowed eyes as I follow behind Tate. He didn't buy my bullshit answer this morning, but I didn't stick around for him to probe. I escaped to a shower where I replayed every hot as fuck moment between me and Sloane.

Something tells me I won't be able to avoid him for long.

Dinner is loud but not a good enough distraction from my thoughts. I keep daydreaming about Sloane, unable to keep up with the conversations around me. When my phone buzzes again, I discreetly pull it out to read under the table.

Sloane: Oh my God. Did you do this?

She sends me a picture of her in the mirror, her blond hair pulled aside to reveal a big-ass hickey. Whoops.

Me: Sure as hell better have been me…

I send her a devilish smiling emoji. She returns it with a few middle finger emojis.

"Dempsey."

Mom's sharp tone cuts through the noise and everyone falls quiet. She's not one to yell or get pissed about anything, especially not at family dinner.

I lift my gaze to find her staring at me with narrowed eyes and pursed lips.

"What?" I snap, her sudden focus on me that's drawn everyone else's focus too irritating me.

Her nostrils flare at my rudeness. "Something's going on with you. You're being secretive. Are you doing drugs?"

Spencer barks out a laugh but smothers it when Aubrey smacks his shoulder.

"Mom," I say, unable to keep from laughing too. "No. I'm not doing drugs. Chill."

She drops her fork to her plate with a loud clatter. "I will not *chill*, Dempsey. Whatever is going on with you is turning you into someone I don't recognize. Tell me what you're hiding."

A spear of anger pierces my chest. "Maybe I'm finally becoming who I really am."

"A reckless jerk?" Mom asks, voice shaking as her eyes brim with tears. "That's what it seems like. First, you buy a motorcycle, then you embarrass us and Sloane in front of the whole town, and now you're staying out all night. I think it's drugs. Is it drugs?"

Tate clears his throat. "Jamie," he says gently, "perhaps the three of us could pop into Nathan's office to discuss this."

She ignores him, hastily swiping her tear that races down her cheek. "Tell me. Are you still harassing my best friend? She's too old for you, you know."

Ahhh.

So my parents aren't as blind as I thought them to be. Especially not Mom.

"She's not too old for me," I grind out, unable to keep the lid on this any longer. "She's perfect for me."

Gemma gasps and shakes her head as if to warn me to stop talking. I'm done keeping secrets. If they want to accuse me of shit, they may as well get it right what I've done wrong.

"Sloane has known you since you were a baby," Mom hisses. "She's changed your diapers. Why in the hell would she ever be romantically interested in you? You're a child, Dempsey!"

Fuck this.

I jump to my feet, sending my chair scraping across the wood floors. Glowering at my mother, I growl, "I am not a fucking child, Mom, and you know it."

"Dempsey," Dad warns, voice deep and authoritative. "Sit down."

"No," I snap. "I'm tired of being told to sit down, shut up, and obey, obey, fucking obey. From day one, me and Gemma have been your two perfect children the two of you have loved parading around town. I'm sick of it. I don't want to be a god-damn trophy like the rest of your kids. I want to enjoy my life and love whoever the hell I want to love."

"She'll never love you back," Mom yells, tears freely falling now. "She won't. She'd never do that to me."

"It's not all about you," I grit out. "And we're well on our way, *Mother*. You want to know what's really going on with me? Where I really was last night?" I smirk at her. "In your best friend's bed."

As soon as the words tumble past my lips, I know I've gone too far. Mom shrieks, covering her mouth with a dainty hand, and shakes her head. Dad glares at me as though he wishes I were a kid he could bend over his knee and spank the snot out of.

"I love her," I say softly. "She loves me too."

I can feel everyone's eyes on me. It's annoying as fuck to be the center of attention and for my big secret to be served as dessert, but at least I only have to say all this shit once.

"I'm going to her house and I'm staying the night. Maybe we can talk again when you're done treating me like a fuck-ing kid."

Dad stands and crosses his arms over his chest. "You won't be taking the Tahoe."

And yet, they still treat me like a fucking kid.

Ignoring him and Tate's whispered calls to me, I storm out of the dining room and up the stairs. Angrily, I stuff a bunch of clothes and shit into a bag, grab my iPad and some toiletries, and then am back downstairs within minutes. Mom is hiding out in the kitchen, sobbing. The rest of the family is whispering. Dad stands beside the garage door, holding the Tahoe keys hostage.

"Dempsey," Dad rumbles. "We're not done discussing this."

I stop in front of him and sneer. "Yeah, Dad, we are. Everyone always assumes the worst of me anyway, so what's the big deal, huh? I'm the worst. Yay me. I'm just an afterthought anyway. Gemma's your real prize. Forget I even exist. Should be pretty easy for you."

Shoving past him into the garage, I hit the button to open the overhead door. I dig out the motorcycle key and stalk over to the bike. Dad calls after me, but I drown him out with the roar of the motorcycle engine when it flares to life.

I hate this stupid bike and what was at stake for me before I won it. Right now, though, it's my saving grace. I back out of the garage and then turn it around before zipping off down the road. The farther I get away from my house and family, the more I can breathe. I suck the cool evening air into my lungs and exhale all the shittiness I feel.

Within fifteen minutes, I'm pulling into Sloane's driveway. I turn off the engine, put the kickstand out, and climb off the bike just as she opens the front door. Needing her in my arms more than anything right now, I race over to her and yank her to me. As soon as she hugs me tight, everything wrong in my world is righted.

"God, I missed you, babe."

"Missed you too."

I kiss the top of her head. "Can we stay like this forever?"

"Mmm. Tempting, yes."

And we do stay like this forever. Or maybe it's just five minutes. Regardless, it does wonders for my aching heart.

"I think I just fucked up everything with my family. For me. For you. Jesus, I'm sorry. I just got so pissed."

Sloane tenses at my words and then gently pulls back so she can look up at me with her big blue eyes. "What happened?"

"Us," I say sadly. "We happened. My family thinks there's something wrong with me for getting you involved."

She frowns and shakes her head. "There is nothing wrong with you, Dempsey Park. Nothing."

"I didn't corrupt you?"

"Well, maybe a little bit," she teases. "You didn't do this all on your own. We're in this together, no matter the consequences."

I straighten at her fierce admission. Friends. Lovers. Partners. Sloane Thurman is a helluva lot more than just my mom's best friend. She's everything to me.

"Everything around us is falling apart," she whispers, sliding her palms up my chest to cradle my face. "Us, though? We're falling into place."

Dropping my head down, I rest my forehead to hers. "Falling in love."

"Yeah," she admits with a sexy grin. "That too."

The time for words is over. Now I just need to taste her sweetness and bury myself in her scent. I capture her mouth with mine and greedily kiss her.

Being with her is like living in a dream of my own design. Reality is fuzzy around the edges and easy to ignore as long as I have her to distract me. Fuck reality. I'm living the dream.

Maybe we can kiss like this all night.

Maybe we can kiss like this forever.

CHAPTER TWENTY-FOUR

Sloane

"Where's Kaden?" Dempsey asks once we break from our kiss and head inside. "Usually, his ass is planted right there." He gestures for the floor in front of the TV before turning a questioning look my way.

I sigh heavily. "A lot happened today while you were gone."

His expression darkens. "Is he okay? Are you okay?"

"Yes," I say, forcing a smile. "We're fine. I just had to break the news to Rhiannon about Lenny. Kaden went with me."

He takes my hand, eyes darting back and forth. "How did that go? Your mom give you any more shit?"

"No, she wasn't there. Rhiannon was devastated because she somehow still loved the monster. I also learned she's pregnant."

"Damn." He tucks an errant strand of hair behind my ear. "How did she take knowing Trevor was the one to find him?"

I bite on my lip, tearing my gaze from his. "I didn't tell her. It would only upset her more. Anyway, Kaden opted to stay the night there."

Dempsey pulls me in for another one of his warm, comforting hugs. When he has me all wrapped up in everything that's him, it's easy to block out the world and stay in a suspended moment of bliss.

"That's not the worst of it," I grumble. "I went by the station to see if they had any leads and they treated me like a criminal who was involved. Tanaka handed me my ass and told me to stay away from this case."

He strokes his hand up and down my back. It soothes me more than I would have thought.

"I'm sorry," he murmurs against my hair. "You've had to deal with a lot lately. I wish I could do something to help."

"Actually," I say, pulling away. "Maybe there is."

His brows furl together as he studies me. Genuine concern and desire to help gleam in his magnetic stare. "Anything, babe."

"Tanaka doesn't want me to investigate as a cop, but maybe I could as a civilian—as a concerned aunt. If we find something helpful, we can submit it as an anonymous tip."

"You want to go look for him?"

"Maybe we can kill two birds with one stone. We can check out where those arrogant asshole bikers hang out while also hunting down Trevor."

Dempsey smirks. "A stakeout?"

"An unofficial one."

"We'll take the bike, Officer Do-Good. Can't be rolling up to the enemy's lair in a cop car."

He drops his backpack onto the sofa and then gestures at me. "As much as I love when your hair is down, you'll want to put it up for our ride."

After putting my hair in a tight bun and changing into darker clothing so I don't stand out so much, I climb onto the bike behind Dempsey. He fires up the engine, which is deafening, and then peels out. I shriek in shock, tightening my hold around his middle. His laughter can be heard over the engine and his whole body shakes with amusement. I playfully pinch his nipple to let him know what I think about him making fun of me.

Through my research, no thanks to Montgomery or Bishop, I learned the Park Mountain Shadows MC hangs at a bar called Pipe's on the edge of town and also seem to have a presence in one of the older neighborhoods not far from Rhiannon's apartment complex. I motion for Dempsey where to turn to take us by Pipe's first. He slowly drives by while I scope out the place. There are a few old trucks and a couple of beat down minivans, but no bikers.

He guns it when we pass the bar and then I guide him to our new destination. There's a lookout point at one of the smaller mountains near the neighborhood. I direct him to it and when we arrive, he shuts off the bike, bathing us in silence.

"Romantic," Dempsey teases as we climb off the bike. "If you wanted to take me on a date, you didn't have to dress it up as a stakeout."

A smile tugs at my lips. I give him a quick peck before walking over to the edge of the lookout. While I can't see details, I can hear music in the distance and the rumble of motorcycles. Near one of the bigger houses that backs up to a field, there's a giant bonfire going.

"You think that's their club?" Dempsey asks. "Too bad we didn't bring binoculars."

I put that on the mental list for next time. Right now we're not looking to engage but more or less getting a lay of the land. There's a gigantic barn about a hundred yards from the home close to the edge of the woods. I wonder if we could enter from those woods and take cover behind the barn to get a closer look.

Glancing over at my partner, guilt suddenly punches me in the gut. Dempsey, though a strong, capable man, is not a cop. Bringing him on this little mission is dangerous and reckless.

But Trevor is at risk and I'm not thinking as clearly as I should be. Plus, I feel so much calmer with Dempsey around. I won't let anything happen to him.

Dempsey walks over to the rocky ledge and sits down. He pats the ground beside him. "Come sit. You're wound up really fucking tight, babe."

I relax and give him a clipped nod before joining him. Once I'm settled, he wraps an arm around me, tugging me to his side.

"That's better."

I smile. "Much."

We sit for a while, neither of us speaking. There's an easiness about being with Dempsey that I've really come to love. He's right. I'm wound up a lot of the time, but he unwinds me. I relax and can just be myself around him.

"Does your mom hate me?" I ask, cringing at how everything went down between Dempsey and his family this evening. "Is she going to kill me?"

"Nah," he says with a chuckle. "She's pissed at me and thinks I'm out here wrecking lives for fun, but she'll get over it."

"You seem so sure."

"We're Parks. Despite all the bullshit we've gone through, our family always sticks together and prevails. Deep down, I know this. They do too. Doesn't mean we don't blow up on each other from time to time."

I'm not a Park, though.

It would be easy for Jamie to write me out of her life for good.

The thought of never speaking to her again is an ache deep in my soul. But the alternative? Not speaking to Dempsey is worse. That feels like a blade tearing through my heart, a visceral pain I don't care to experience.

Maybe one day she'll forgive me for getting involved with her son.

At least, I hope so.

We stay on our perch, watching the people down below go in and out of the house, gather by the fire for a while, and the occasional person on a bike showing up or leaving. Not much to go on other than to observe that this is definitely their home base.

Where are you, Trevor?

Are you mixed up with these losers?

We stay for hours, watching and quietly chatting about both serious things and silly things. He was joking, but it really does feel like a date. A bike ride with my man and then spending time with him someplace with a great view while having engaging conversations.

All the other men I've dated until now fall so completely flat in comparison to Dempsey. He's life and color and fun—something I was clearly missing desperately until he came along.

"Come on," he murmurs, squeezing my thigh. "It's late and you have work tomorrow. We can do this again another day."

I know he's right, but it doesn't help squash the guilt at not having found Trevor. He's out there, traumatized by Lenny's death and doing drugs. If only I could just find him, tear him away from the bad people he's found himself with, and help my nephew get back to the sweet boy he once was.

Tomorrow.

There's always tomorrow.

Dempsey holds true to his word. When we got back home, we fell into bed naked, but he didn't push for more sex. He simply held me to his strong, solid body and stroked my hair. I keep waking up, despite being so comfortable, wondering if maybe just maybe my body could handle another round.

His soft, measured breaths tell me he's asleep, which is the only reason I'm keeping my hands to myself. I'd love to wake him up with my hand around his cock, but sleep really does need to take precedence if I have any hope of functioning at work in the morning.

I'm just drifting off when I hear the sound of motorcycles in the distance. It gets louder, signaling the approach of several on my road.

It's them.

It's the Park Mountain Shadows MC.

They knew we were lurking and have come to pay us a visit.

I shake Dempsey awake and then slide out of bed to find clothes. We hear shouts outside, though I can't make out what they're saying. I throw on clothes as fast as I can before grabbing my shotgun from my closet safe since my Glock is still in evidence.

"Stay back. Let me handle them," I tell Dempsey over my shoulder as I creep out the bedroom door.

"Fuck that," Dempsey growls. "You're not going out there alone."

I stop to glower at him but the deafening sound of an explosion cuts me short. The entire house rumbles as glass shatters somewhere near the front of the house. Dempsey hooks an arm around my middle, dragging me back into the bedroom.

What just happened?

We then hear the squeals of tires and then the motorcycles leaving. As soon as it feels safe, we both run to the front door. I open it, shotgun drawn, and survey the scene before me. The bike Dempsey had been driving is on fire and in pieces. That explains the explosion.

"Was this retaliation for me winning that bike?" Dempsey asks, voice shaky with anger.

"That or they saw us tonight." I scrub my hand over my face. "Crap. I have to call this in."

Dempsey gives me a nod and then walks over to talk to the old lady who lives next door, who's watching us from her front porch. I rush back inside to grab my phone and make the call I don't want to make.

By the time the fire department and the first responding officers arrive, I'm bursting at the seams. I want to get in my car and chase after those bastards who did this.

The next half hour I spend, long after the fire has been put out, explaining to the officers who I think did this. They take their notes but don't seem impressed by the fact I think it's a motorcycle gang responsible. I'm about to give up completely and do whatever I can to get them to go away when a shiny red Porsche pulls up along with the twinkling of the sunrise.

Great.

Tanaka climbs out of his overpriced toy and stalks my way. It's not even six in the morning and the man is wearing a crisp suit with not a black hair out of place. Must be nice to always be so put together. He probably sleeps in his stupid suits.

"Thurman," Tanaka greets, voice icy. "What happened here?"

One of the other officers fills in our chief, their tone almost mocking as they parrot what I'd said about the motorcycle club. The statement doesn't bore Tanaka but instead enrages him. A vein throbs on his forehead as he glowers at me.

"It's true," I grit out, needing to defend myself from his anger. "I heard them with my own ears. I'm not crazy."

Tanaka clenches his teeth, nostrils flaring. "And what did you do to provoke such an attack?"

Seriously, asshole?

Dempsey, sensing my tension, comes to stand right behind me, the heat of his body giving me much-needed strength.

"They're criminals," I say, seething. "Why don't you go ask them instead of giving me the third degree?"

Tanaka glances at Dempsey and recognition flickers in his eyes. Then he turns his attention back to me, his features returning to their normal, cool, stone-like facade.

"You're making a lot of bad decisions lately, Thurman. Decisions that could ultimately impact your career. I suggest you take the day off and get yourself in order." He waves a dismissive hand at me. "See you Tuesday."

As Tanaka drives away, my heart dive bombs to the ground at my feet. I can't let the new, corrupt chief destroy my career just because he has a vendetta against me for doing my damn job.

I can't let him take this job from me.

I won't.

CHAPTER TWENTY-FIVE

Dempsey

ER CHIEF IS SUCH A DICK. I WANTED NOTHING MORE than to put him in his place, but luckily, Sloane can hold her own. Even though he treated her like dirt, she kept her chin up.

Now that it's just the two of us again, she's grown somber and withdrawn. So much has happened to her lately. I wish I could relieve the burden in some way. She settles on the sofa, losing herself to her phone screen. I'd love nothing more than to sit and pull her into my arms, but she needs to eat.

I busy myself in the kitchen, making waffles, fried eggs, and sausage links. By the time I'm finished and dusting powdered sugar on the waffles, she appears in the kitchen, eyes wide and curious at the spread I've made.

"Careful, Demps," she says with a sweet smile. "You keep this up and I'm going to get used to it. You'll have to cook me breakfast every day."

Chuckling, I hand her a plate. "Don't threaten me with a good time."

We decide to eat at her bar, side by side, neither of us speaking much as we inhale the food. When we finish, she helps me clean up and put away the leftovers. I love how we work around each other with what feels like practiced perfection.

"Come on," I say when finished. "We're going to grab some coffee and then head to the hardware store."

She beams but then her smile falls at the last part. "Wait? What?"

"I want to board up those broken windows for you. Don't worry. I'll make it quick."

Based on the grimace on her face, I can tell the hardware store is not her favorite place, but coffee was the perfect lure to get her to go with me.

As we run our errands, we actually have a nice time despite the shitty morning. I learn a lot about Sloane as we drive.

She loves going to the movie theater but never has anyone to go with.

At least I know where I'm taking her on our first actual date.

She also dislikes doing laundry but enjoys playing in the flowerbeds. Cooking is the bane of her existence, but my girl loves to eat.

I also reveal things about myself like how I've always felt overshadowed by my sister. That I hate being referred to as a kid instead of the man I am. How I love hanging by the pool but haven't done so much this summer. I even admit to how much I've always wanted a dog but Dad never let us get one.

By the time we've ordered plywood and nails to be delivered and made a coffee run, I feel as though we just had a speed date. Holding her hand as we drive, while chatting, feels right and the highlight of my day.

The hardware store said they'd deliver our supplies within the hour, so we head back to her house to start cleaning up on all the broken glass. My phone buzzes in my pocket and has been all night and morning. I'm sure after last night's blowup at dinner, I have my entire family trying to reach out to me. When Sloane runs inside the house for a bathroom break, I bite the bullet and read my messages from last night.

Dad: Come home so we can talk. Your mother is upset.

Gemma: Are you okay?

Tate: Call me!

Callum: I think they call this Karma. Good job, little bro.

Spencer: Dinner and a show! Rex is a fan!

The rest came in this morning.

Tate: Let me at least know you're alive.

Jude: Tate's worried about you. Check in or I'll hunt you down.

Hugo: Do you want to have lunch with me and Aubrey?

Gemma: Mom's been crying. A lot. I'm worried about you.

Willa: Callum showed me his text. Ignore him. He's an ass.

Callum: Dad's freaking out. His baby boy ran away. I bet he wants to call the cops…but, plot twist, you're banging one. He can't easily fix this and doesn't know what to do. Quite amusing if you ask me.

Aubrey: Lunch??? Miss your face.

Dad: Can we please talk, Son?

Then there's a text from Spencer where he's holding up Rex's middle finger and grinning evilly behind his son. That actually makes me laugh.

"Are they blowing up your phone?" Sloane asks when she returns.

"You have no idea."

I hand her the phone so she can read through them all. She also laughs at the picture of Rex. After handing me my phone back, she leans against me, resting her head on my chest.

"Who knew loving someone could be so difficult," I say absently, kissing the top of her head. "I thought love was supposed to be easy."

She pulls back slightly to smile at me. "It's easy for us. Everyone else is just having a hard time with it."

I can't fight the grin that tugs at my lips. Her little slip about her feelings for me gives me hope we'll make it the long haul.

"Mom is going to have to get over it. I'm not letting you go just to spare her feelings."

Sloane squeezes me. "Me neither."

All the challenges we're facing seem manageable as long as I have this woman in my arms, reciprocating the way I feel. As long as we have each other, we can face them fearlessly together.

Eventually, the hardware store drops off the pre-cut plywood. Sloane hammers while I hold up the wood for each blown-out window. Earlier, while I made breakfast, she went online and made an appointment for a window replacement company to put in new windows this week. Aside from the charred bike in the driveway, we've finally managed to get past all the drama from this morning.

"I'll find someone to haul the bike away," I tell her as we make it back inside. "It's trashed and I never had a clean title on it, so it's not like I can get any money for it."

"I hate that your bike was a casualty in my war against those stupid biker assholes."

"Our war," I remind her. "We're in this together."

I'm graced with another beautiful smile that does wonders for soothing my aching heart. I don't like being at odds with my family, but I don't see any other way around it. I'm not about to let them dictate who I love. Not happening.

"BLTs for lunch?"

"Do I even have stuff for BLTs?" she tosses back, eyebrow arched.

"I bought real food for your fridge considering all you had were condiments and takeout boxes." I playfully smack her on the ass. "Told you I was going to take care of you."

Her cheeks redden and the grin she flashes me is brilliant. "I'm starting to believe you."

"Good girl."

"Show me," Sloane says, poking me in the chest. "You brought it, so show me. As your muse, I demand it."

Anxiety crawls up my spine, but I try not to let it affect me. If she wants to see all my drawings, then I'll show her. I just hope she likes them. With a heavy sigh of resignation, I leave her side on the couch to dig my iPad out of my backpack. Once I sit back down, she scoots closer, resting her head on my shoulder.

I open the Procreate app and then hand it to her. Slowly, one by one, she opens each piece to look at the illustrations.

"Wow," she murmurs. "Your work is so…real. I didn't have time to truly appreciate it the night of the event. You're so incredibly talented."

Her words are a surge to my ego. It's nice to hear when you're good at something and not just the family fuckup.

When she finds one that shows her nipple, she gasps. "Dempsey."

"I know, I know. I just…you know I can't stop thinking about you. This was before I knew what you looked like naked. My imagination."

She laughs. "You make me seem perfect."

"You are perfect, babe. I don't see a single flaw when I look at you."

"Your eyes are lying to you."

"Maybe my eyes are the ones that see the truth."

She closes the iPad and places it down on the sofa beside her. Then she sits up and straddles my lap.

"How about now? What do you see?"

I slide my palms to her ass, drawing her close to me. "You. All I see is you."

"With no makeup and dark bags under my eyes from lack of sleep."

"Nah, just you, babe. Beautiful fucking you."

She pounces on me, crushing me in a hungry kiss. I squeeze her ass, urging her to grind on my dick that's now hard as stone.

"Still sore?" I rasp out. "Too sore to fuck?"

"Y-Yes. Ugh. I hate that I am."

"Take off your shirt and let me see your pretty tits then."

She wriggles out of her shirt, tosses it away, and then quickly discards her bra. Her bottom lip is trapped between her teeth as she waits for more instructions.

"Put it in my mouth," I rumble. "I want to taste your nipple."

Her breath catches, but she sits up to bring her breasts closer to my face. She threads her fingers into my hair and guides me down to her chest. I flick out my tongue and circle her peaked nipple, marveling over the sweet moan that comes out of her.

"So perfect," I growl, nipping at the tender pink skin. "Mine."

She pulls back and then offers me her other tit. "Yours."

This time, I suck as much of her breast into my mouth as I possibly can. She groans with pleasure. I love how fucking responsive she is to my touch.

"The second your pussy feels better, I'm going to wreck it again."

She giggles—so young and carefree. Such a foreign sound from my beautiful girl, but I absolutely can't get enough of it.

"I have an idea," she says as she pulls away again. "Unbuckle your pants."

I lift an eyebrow at her, curious as to what she has planned. She slides off my lap and down onto the floor between my spread thighs.

"I can still make you feel good," she purrs, eyes hooded and cheeks a pretty shade of red. "I think. I mean, I'm not sure if you'll like it or—"

I cut her off with a sharp shake of my head. Then I shove my jeans and boxers down. My cock slaps against my lower belly over my T-shirt. Sloane licks her lips and then pushes my clothes farther down so she can access me better.

"Tell me if I do something wrong," she says, a frown marring her features. "Okay?"

"You could yell at it or spit on it or call it names and it'd still be right as long as it gets your attention."

"Spoken like a true man." She smirks at me before wrapping her small hand around my thick cock. "At least I can inspect this piercing up close now."

The view of her on her knees, tits out, and my dick in her hand has got to be the hottest thing I have ever witnessed in my entire life. I could probably come just from staring at her like this in this position. I don't have to, though, because she leans forward, tentatively licking the crown, swiping away the dot of pre-cum there.

"Fuck," I choke out. "Jesus, fuck."

"I haven't done anything yet."

"You're doing everything to me, babe. You're fucking unraveling me and you're not even trying."

Challenge gleams in her eyes. My eyes roll back when her lips wrap around my cock and then she starts bobbing up and down my length. I can't help but grip her blond tresses, eager to keep her exactly where she is.

I reopen my eyes, watching her take my length in as far as she can before gagging. Her eyes water as she slowly draws herself back up. The hot slickness of her mouth is heaven.

"You're so damn good at this," I praise. "If drawing your gorgeous tits gets me a blowjob, I'll draw you a thousand times."

She slips off my cock, saliva running from her bottom lip

down to my crown. "I like seeing you lose control. Your eyes right now… You look like a wild animal."

I curse when she swallows me down again. This is fucking bliss. No wonder the other guys I went to school with were always raving about blowjobs.

"You keep sucking dick like a champ and I'm going to drown you in cum. Better let me come all over your tits so I don't make you choke."

She increases her efforts and easily sends me right over the edge of pleasure. Like a good girl, she pulls off as I start to come and points my cock at her tits. Rope after rope of thick cum shoots out of me, decorating her breasts.

I love seeing my girl so messy.

"Rub it in," I rasp out, drunk on this wonderful feeling. "Smear it all over, babe. I promise I'll clean you up in a bit."

She releases my dripping cock to run her fingers through the mess on her chest. I groan when she pinches her nipples and then sets to sucking each finger clean.

"Officer Do-Good, that was very, very naughty."

Her wicked grin has my softening cock perking back up.

My God, this woman is going to kill me.

I'll never get enough of her.

CHAPTER TWENTY-SIX

Sloane

WORK IS WEIRD.

I knew it would be, which is why I mentally prepared for it. And by mentally prepared, I lost myself in Dempsey all day yesterday and last night. Leaving him naked in my bed was really difficult.

It's crazy to me that he sleeps naked. Honestly, I never considered it until him. Now, I've been sleeping naked as well, resting beautifully in our sexy love cocoon.

Shaking away thoughts of Dempsey's muscular, clothe-less body, I attempt to focus on the day ahead. Bishop keeps shooting me curious looks while Montgomery gives me the stink eye. As for Tanaka, he watches me like a hawk from his office.

This is so awkward.

For once, I'm eager to get out on patrol with Aisha. She's focused on a file, but I know her. If I'm ready to go, she'll drop everything to get the hell out of here.

I check my phone to make sure I haven't missed any messages from my sisters. Nothing. I'd kind of expected some sort of nasty message from Jamie, but she's yet to contact either me or Dempsey. I hate that there's this wedge between us and his family. Furthermore, I hate that my best friend is handling this so poorly.

I mean, I get it. On the surface, it might seem gross to her since it's her kid and there's a significant age gap. However, I'd like to think she'd at least hear Dempsey and me out. If she could see how happy we are together, maybe she could find a way to be happy too.

It definitely hurts to feel abandoned by my best friend. Especially since I was there for her during one of the most difficult moments in her life. When she cheated on Callum to be with his father. I was also there before the Parks came along, protecting her the best I could from her abusive family. I've come to realize that I can be the right sort of friend for Jamie, but she's not the right friend for me.

Dempsey is who I can confide in and tell my darkest secrets. There's trust there between us where I know that no matter what happens, he'll stand by my side. It's comforting to have that level of support. If I have to trade Jamie for Dempsey, unfortunately for our lifelong friendship, that's what I'll do.

He's worth it.

"You ready?" I ask Aisha. "I'm not liking the vibe around here."

Bishop snorts at my comment. Montgomery ignores me altogether. Ethan Montgomery and Hiroshi Tanaka can both kiss my ass. I'm a good cop and I refuse to let them make me feel less than. This job has never been easy. I knew that from day one and I'd be wise not to forget it.

Aisha waits until we pass the cherry-red show-off Porsche before she leans in. "Girl, tell me the scoop. It's ice-cold in there. What did I miss?"

We spend the next twenty minutes patrolling while I word-vomit my life. I don't hold anything back either. I tell her about Dempsey, Jamie, my family, the motorcycle club…everything. When I finally finish with the attitudes of this morning and Jamie's silence, she whistles.

"Wow. That's…a lot."

"Right?" I sigh heavily as we pass by Nadine's Diner. I can't help but look through the windows as we drive by, searching for any sign of my family. Lucy, standing by a booth, sees the squad car and waves. I smile and wave back. "At least she doesn't hate me."

"Your family doesn't hate you," Aisha assures me. "They're just being ridiculous like all families. Trust me. My family is dramatic as fuck." She shifts in her seat to look at me. "You really think Tanaka is a bed egg, huh?"

"Either that or just a big douchebag."

"I mean, he can be both, right?"

We both snigger.

"You're right about that."

I take us past Rhiannon's apartment complex, unable to stay away despite what Tanaka says. Because Aisha is a good friend, she keeps her eyes peeled, both of us looking for Trevor. Unfortunately, we don't see him or any of his loser biker friends.

We get called out to a minor fender bender and are just finishing up a half hour later when we get another call.

Domestic disturbance.

The address is familiar.

"That's the biker hangout," I hiss as soon as we tell dispatch we're on our way. "What if it's Trevor? What if they've hurt him?"

"We'll get him," she assures me.

I know Tanaka told me to leave them alone, but this

is my job and I was actually called to it this time. I'm not going to risk the safety of the persons involved because my corrupt chief doesn't want me snooping.

The drive over to the location is unnerving. With each passing mile, I feel more and more agitated. If Trevor's there, I'll do whatever I have to in order to get him out. Hopefully, Aisha will have my back.

I park the squad car a couple of houses down and we both exit, tense and ready for anything. As we come up to the big house, I notice an older woman and a man around her age arguing. She keeps swinging at him even after he shoves her hard to the ground. The woman is relentless, hell-bent on hitting the guy.

"Ma'am," I call out. "Sir. What's going on here?"

The man throws his beefy arms in the air in irritation. "She's a psycho bitch. That's what."

"I ain't a bitch," the psycho yells, making to charge at the man again.

Aisha is quicker, wrapping her arms around the woman and physically dragging her away to a safe distance. I step between the man and woman, facing the guy.

"Tell me what happened," I say in a firm tone. "I'd rather be eating lunch right now than playing referee. Let's see if we can get this resolved so we can all go about our business."

The man huffs and darts his eyes to the house. It's an insignificant thing, but alarm bells ring in my head. I quickly glance over my shoulder, find nothing of interest, and return my stare back to the sketchy redneck. There's something familiar about him.

Wait.

I think he might've been at the pool hall that night.

The psycho lady starts to laugh and the guy in front of me smiles too. I reach for my gun, realizing something is amiss, but am too late. The guy in front of me shoves me hard, like he did with the woman earlier, to the ground.

"You bit me, you bitch!" Aisha yells.

Panic seizes me. This isn't a domestic disturbance call. This is a trap. They somehow knew I'd be on patrol today and drew me in. Blowing up a bike in my front yard wasn't enough?

I roll on the ground onto my hands and knees to take off, putting distance between me and the redneck. I'm not fast enough. His boot slams into my ribs, sending me rolling.

"She's mine," a guy calls out as he exits the house.

His flaming red hair is also familiar. This guy was the second-in-command at the pool game.

"Fuck the pig, Bozo!" the redneck hollers. "She's got a nice ass at least!"

Bozo pulls a Desert Eagle from the back of his jeans, pointing it right at my face. I surge toward him, catching him off-guard and knocking him on his back. He squeezes off a deafening shot, that whizzes past my hair before he loses hold of the weapon.

Another shot happens somewhere near me and I hope to God it's Aisha taking control of the situation.

"You fucked with the wrong guys, cunt," Bozo snarls, easily flipping us, pinning my body under his massive one. "Prez says you need to be dealt with since you're causing all sorts of fucking problems in our lives."

He rams a fist into my face. I black out briefly before

quickly coming to. If I don't figure this out, he's going to kill me. I need to get me and my partner out of here.

More shots can be heard, echoing around me. Bozo barks with laughter as his hand encircles my throat. With a slight squeeze, he nearly crushes my windpipe.

Oh my God.

I'm going to die.

Not willing to go down without a fight, I claw at him, grabbing hold of his beard and yanking. He howls in pain, lessening his grip, and I'm able to grab my service weapon. Miraculously, I manage to flick off the safety and get the gun between us.

Bang! Bang! Bang!

I squeeze it several times. Bozo's body jerks each time and his eyes widen in shock. Then he slumps off me. Two rounds got him in the belly but one, which is probably the fatal one, got him in the chest.

Aisha.

Grass explodes beside me as someone shoots my way. I shriek and scramble toward a rusted BBQ pit for cover. It pangs as bullets pierce the corroded metal, sending shards into my hair. I don't stay there for long and run while crouched toward a row of bushes.

"Officer down!" Aisha croaks out from somewhere nearby. "Thurman, where the fuck are you?"

I race past the psycho whose bullet-riddled body lies sprawled out in the grass and take cover behind a motorcycle.

"I'm here, Patel, where are you?"

Swiping my hair out of my eyes so I can see better, I

survey the property, looking for threats and my partner. I don't see the shooter anywhere. Maybe Aisha got him.

A familiar, pained moan carries over to me. She's close and clearly injured. Fuck. There's a small garden wall separating the biker property from their neighbors. It's made of cinderblocks, which would be a great place to take cover.

Please, God, let her be there and alive.

Sirens wail in the distance and it's a sweet, beautiful sound. If I can just get the two of us to safety until backup arrives, we'll take down these assholes.

"I'm coming," I mutter, knowing Aisha can't hear me but needing to coax myself into running the distance from my hiding spot to the garden wall.

With a deep breath, I ignore the throbbing pain on my face and in my skull from Bozo's punch and take off toward the waist-high wall. I'm nearly there when I hear the shooter again.

Bang!

Fire explodes in my back and I stumble, landing face first in the grass. The pain radiating through me is overwhelming. It'd be easy to curl into a ball and pray for it all to go away.

That would mean sure death.

I can't die when I've finally found happiness in life.

Pushing through, I crawl the rest of the way with what little strength I have left. When I launch myself to the other side of the wall, I'm met with a gun to my face.

Here's where I die.

"Thurman," Aisha hisses. "I nearly shot your eye out!"

Groaning, I fall to the ground beside her. "You're injured. We have to get the hell out of here."

Aisha twists around and fires her weapon a couple of times over the wall before dropping back down beside me. "Easier said than done." She groans in pain again. "Fuck. Is that my blood or your blood? Oh shit. You're bleeding a lot, Thurman. Fuck! Sloane, fuck!"

Her voice grows smaller and smaller and smaller.

All the light vanishes in a blink.

CHAPTER TWENTY-SEVEN

Dempsey

"**D**EMPSEY! OPEN UP!"

I walk out of the laundry room and make my way to the front door, where my sister keeps pounding. Should have known I couldn't ignore my family forever, especially not her.

"What?" I grumble as I open the door. "It's called space. Give it to me." Her tearstained face has me tensing up and panic slamming into me. "What's wrong? Gemma, are you okay? Mom? Dad?"

She swipes at her tears, throwing herself at me for a hug. "You haven't heard? It's been all over the news. I tried calling you like a million times."

Gripping her shoulders, I pull her back so I can look at her. "Heard what? You're fucking scaring me right now."

A sob escapes her. "T-Two officers were involved in a shootout."

My blood turns to ice in my veins.

"Two female officers, Dempsey. Have you heard from Sloane? I have this sick feeling it was her."

There aren't a lot of female officers in the Park Mountain PD. Sloane told me they're the only two women who go on patrol. The rest are men.

It's her.

It's fucking her.

"No," I hiss, panic clawing at my throat and making it hard for me to breathe. "This can't be fucking happening." I know it's a fruitless effort, but I race to my phone to call Sloane. No answer. "No!"

"What do we do?" Gemma asks, bottom lip trembling.

"Hospital," I grunt. "Let's go."

I snag the keys from her and bolt out the front door with my sister on my heels. We break every speed limit and traffic law on the way there. I park our massive boat in a fire lane, not bothering to take the keys out of the ignition. Since Gemma isn't right behind me anymore, I imagine she's dealing with the car for me.

"Two officers," I bark out to the receptionist. "Where were they taken?"

"Sir," the woman with a name tag that reads "Candace" says, "slow down. Who is it you're looking for?"

"Sloane Thurman. I need to know if this officer was brought in."

The woman's features scrunch. "I, uh, let me see."

She taps away on the computer and then gives me a grim look.

"What?" I demand.

"Perhaps you should have a seat in the waiting room."

"What? No. I want to know where Sloane is!"

She leans forward and whispers, "I can confirm she was brought in and is being prepped for surgery. I'm sorry, but that's all I can offer right now."

I stumble back, the breath leaving my lungs. Prepping for surgery. She was shot. My fucking girlfriend was shot. I tug at my hair, attempting to keep the terror from consuming me. Gemma arrives, eyes darting back and forth in question.

"She's been shot, Gem. She's in surgery."

My sister bursts into tears. "Call Mom and Dad."

It's been what feels like hours. Gemma and my parents sit together nearby, but I've taken up residence in a chair near the receptionist's desk. I've been asking her for updates every five minutes. I know I'm driving her crazy, but she's at least trying to help. I notice Dad speaking to the police chief, Tanaka, and have the urge to pummel that fucker's face.

Since I don't know anything or who's responsible, I'm forced to sit still, waiting for any news whatsoever.

"Sir," Candace, the receptionist, says to me. "They say she's out of surgery now and in recovery. You should be able to see her soon."

Thank fuck.

My eyes well with tears as relief floods through me. I blink my eyes furiously to keep from full-on sobbing. Despite Candace's assurances, I won't calm down until I have Sloane's hand in mine. Until I can witness with my own two eyes that she's alive and well.

More time ticks slowly by.

"Are you her son?" Candace asks, the phone pressed to her ear but eyes on me. "Family?"

"Her son? What the fu—No! I'm her boyfriend."

Candace frowns. "But not family?"

Are you fucking kidding me right now?

I rise to my feet and glower at the once-helpful woman. "No. Is that a problem?"

"Sir, only family is allowed back at this time—"

"BUT I FUCKING LOVE HER!" I roar, rage and despair clawing at my very soul. "I NEED TO SEE HER!"

When I slam both fists onto the counter, the woman shrinks back.

"Sir, please don't make me call security. I know you're upset—"

I cut her off with a string of curse words that silences her completely. A firm hand squeezes my shoulder.

"Miss," Dad says, voice calm but brimming with authority. "Who's Sloane's doctor?"

The woman looks like she might cry, which makes me feel like a total dick. I shouldn't have yelled at her, but I'm fucking terrified. I just want to see my girl.

"Uh, Dr. Crow."

"Ian Crow? Ah. He's a friend of mine. Tell him Nathan Park is here. He'll speak to me."

Candace nods and places the call, whispering softly. Then she passes the phone to my dad. Dad talks lowly, chuckles, and then thanks him before handing the phone back. Candace nods and then hangs up.

"You and I are cleared to go back there," Dad says to me. "Dr. Crow said they've almost got her situated in room number 1238. He said to give them ten minutes and then we can head up."

Ten minutes may feel like a lifetime, but it's something. I grab hold of Dad and hug him to me. He squeezes me tight and murmurs that everything's going to be okay.

I sure as hell hope so.

The beeping within the hospital room has me stalling at the open door. Dad gently nudges me to keep going. I suck in a breath, preparing for the worst. As soon as I walk in and see Sloane attached to various machines, my heart cracks in two.

Her face is bruised—painted blacks and purples and blues. It looks painful as fuck. I rush over to her to take hold of her hand. She's sleeping and doesn't stir. I can hear Dad's soft voice as he talks to someone just outside the door.

"Babe," I choke out. "Hey, babe. It's me. It's Dempsey. You gave me quite the fucking scare."

A tear races down my cheek. She's alive. This could have been a lot worse.

I bring her hand to my lips and kiss the back of it. She's so beautiful, even damaged and wrecked beyond recognition. I still see her. Every perfect part of her.

"You'll get out of here soon and I'm going to be the best nurse who ever lived," I assure her, forcing a laugh. "Fuck. You better get out of here soon."

I'm unsure where she was shot. Her arms and upper body appear to be unharmed aside from the big-ass bruise on her face.

"Ian thinks no more than a couple of days and she'll be out of here," Dad says, approaching me from behind. "The bullet clipped her spleen, but they were able to salvage it. She's really lucky it went straight through and didn't ricochet inside her rib cage."

Bile burns at my throat. "She was shot in the stomach?"

"Back. Someone shot her in the back, Son."

What kind of lowlife shoots a woman when she has her back turned? A fucking spineless coward.

"Who?" I demand. "Who did this?"

Dad sighs and makes his way over to one of the chairs in the room. He motions for me to sit down beside him. I lean forward and gently kiss an uninjured portion of Sloane's face before joining him.

"Well?"

"Hiroshi says—"

"Who?"

"Chief of police."

"Go on."

"He said that the two officers were ambushed. Biker gang."

I snap my head. "Those motherfuckers."

"Hiroshi said you and Sloane had a run-in with them?"

"Run-in? Dad, they blew up my fucking bike."

His eyes widen. "And you're just now telling me this?"

"I didn't exactly leave on good terms."

"Like I give a shit about that, Dempsey. If you have problems, you come to me. I will solve them. You know I'd do anything for you kids."

It's relieving to hear this. Deep down, I know it, but it's easy to forget when they're always on my ass.

"The first run-in was when I won the bike in the first place," I admit with a huff. "That was an actual run-in that turned nasty."

He listens with rapt attention as I replay that night. When I mention Gemma's involvement, his features turn murderous.

"I won that shit fair and square."

"So this is all over a bike?"

"Hardly." I scrub my palm over my face. "Sloane's nephew, Trevor, is mixed up with them. She's been investigating and trying to find him. Her sister's boyfriend was wearing a leather cut with their club patch on it. I think those motherfuckers felt like she was meddling in their business and wanted to teach her a lesson." I pin Dad with a pleading look. "Can you do something about them? They need to rot in prison."

"I'll have Jude pick apart their entire organization and do what I can. In the meantime, you and Sloane need to stay away from them. The two of you should come back to the house to stay where it's safe."

At this, I scoff. "Right. So Mom can smother us in our sleep?"

Dad frowns, disappointment etching his features. "You know good and damn well your mother lives and breathes for you and Gemma. That would hurt her deeply if she thought you felt that way."

Do I think Mom will literally kill us? No.

Do I think she could make my life a living hell by constantly throwing our "betrayal" in our faces? Yes.

"You know," I mutter. "I wasn't trying to be outrageous or reckless or whatever it is you guys are thinking. I didn't seek out Sloane just to piss you off or hurt Mom. I love her, Dad. I fucking love her."

Dad's eyes soften as he regards me. "You didn't give us an opportunity to understand."

"Mom didn't give me an opportunity to get my point across." I blow out a harsh breath. "Sloane's it for me. I want to be with her. If that means having to choose, I'm going to choose her, Dad. I'll choose her over everything."

Dad nods in understanding. "I can respect that and I

can see how serious you are. Your mother, well, she'll need a little more time to come around to this idea. Just don't shut us out. Please."

Before I can say anything else, Sloane whimpers from the bed. I bolt out of my chair and over to her. Her blue eyes peek out from her cracked eyelids.

"Dempsey?"

"I'm here, babe. I'll always be right here."

A ghost of a smile dances over her lips. I dip down and press a soft kiss to her mouth.

"Wait… Where's…?" She scrunches her eyes shut as if to clear away a fog. "Aisha."

The other cop.

Her partner.

I shoot Dad a panicked look because I have no idea. My only concern was Sloane. Dad approaches the bed and gently pats Sloane's foot through the blanket.

"Aisha is fine, Sloane. Dr. Crow said the bullet grazed her arm but didn't do any significant damage."

Sloane starts to cry, clearly overjoyed with hearing that her partner is going to be okay. Dad slides a chair over to me and allows us our privacy. I hold on to Sloane's hand, listening to her cry and hoping like hell I can mend my girl back to health soon.

"I love you, Sloane Thurman."

She nods and mouths back a similar sentiment.

We're going to get through this.

We'll get through anything as long as we're together.

CHAPTER TWENTY-EIGHT

Sloane

GETTING SHOT HURTS.

Like really, really hurts.

Now that I'm back home and don't have the good stuff being pumped into me whenever a flare of pain happens, I'm noticing the pain a lot more than I did for the first couple of days in the hospital.

Thankfully, I have Dempsey as my nurse. He's great about feeding me, making sure I'm comfortable, keeping me company, and cheering me up. Plus, he's easy on the eyes and rarely wears a shirt, which prevents me from getting bored.

Aisha: Girl. These kids think I'm on vacation. They've asked me to take them to the park a dozen times this morning. I never thought I'd say this, but I'm already eager to go back to work.

Smirking, I reply to my partner.

Me: Every time I get bored or anxious, I just look at Dempsey's abs.

Aisha: Pictures or you're lying…

"Aisha wants a picture of your abs," I tell Dempsey, who's in the kitchen.

He saunters into the living room and flexes, flashing me

a cheesy grin that makes my heart squeeze. I snap a picture and send it to her.

Aisha: Lucky bitch.

She sends back a picture of one of her toddlers, whose face is smeared with something sticky-looking. The kid is crying in the picture, both eyes and nose running like leaky faucets. Yeah, I don't envy her a bit.

Me: We won't be on administrative leave forever. We'll be back before we know it.

Aisha: To desk work. How long until they'll let us patrol again? My mother-in-law is hovering. Her living with us isn't so bad until I'm home all day with her. I wish she'd go hover over the kids so I could just breathe uninterrupted for five seconds.

Why do people ever want to have kids?

Me: You could always run away and come watch Dempsey's abs with me.

Aisha: Don't tempt me.

Dempsey has disappeared again. He spent all morning cleaning out my pantry and griping the whole time because everything was stale or expired or inedible. He's been making a massive grocery list. It's cute how much he cares about my food situation. Jamie, who was underfed in her younger years, clearly overcompensated for her childhood by making sure her children have access to good food. I, however, was used to eating free food from the diner Mom worked at. When I finally got out on my own, it was more of the same but different restaurants.

Aisha: Heard from Trevor?

The playfulness between us is gone. She knows how worried I am over my nephew, especially now if he's involved with those bikers. They set a trap for me, planning to take me out. I vaguely remember the Bozo guy yelling at me. What did he say?

"You fucked with the wrong guys, cunt. Prez says you need to be dealt with since you're causing all sorts of fucking problems in our lives."

What problems specifically was I causing them?

Everything I've done is because of my family. What exactly are they trying to hide anyway? You don't ambush and attempt to murder a cop just because they're snooping around or trying to protect their nephew. But if you're inadvertently getting too close to something they want far away from the cops, perhaps that could be it.

So what are those bastards hiding?

And for whom are they hiding it?

That's the real question. My gut tells me it's related to our police department. Tanaka has been making my radar go off since day one when he arrived in his flashy car. Does he have something illegal going on with those bikers? What could it be?

My mind races around and around in a never-ending circle. It doesn't help being on pain meds. I can't think as clearly as I'd like. If only I could put a finger on what's going on so I could put a stop to it once and for all.

"Babe," Dempsey says, appearing in the living room again, this time, disappointingly, with his shirt back on. "Don't be mad."

Don't be mad?

I can hear car doors slamming outside. Someone's here and he doesn't want me to be mad about it.

"Who?"

He cringes and says, "They came up to the hospital yesterday to see you, but I told them to just come over here today since you were being discharged."

"Who are *they*?" I demand, voice tight.

"Your family."

Before I can process his answer, said family just walks right in, Kaden leading the pack. Though I'm happy to see him, and Lucy too, seeing Mom in my house for the first time ever is a punch to the gut.

"I told your sisters that job was dangerous," Mom says in her gravelly smoker's voice in lieu of a greeting. "Been predicting you'd get shot since you told us you joined the academy."

Rhiannon, whose bruises are fading, rolls her eyes behind Mom's back. Kaden and Lucy both rush over to me, hammering me with a thousand questions.

"Did you shoot them back?" Kaden asks, eyes wide with curiosity. "I hope you killed all those assholes."

"Don't say assholes," me and Rhiannon both say at once.

"It's an ongoing investigation, right, Aunt Sloane? I bet you're not allowed to talk about it, huh?" Lucy squeezes my hand, brows furled together. "We're just glad you're okay. We all were really worried."

I don't see Nevaeh or her kids, so maybe not everyone was really worried. I'm honestly surprised Mom is here. Rhiannon probably guilted her into coming.

"I'm not at liberty to say," I tell Kaden. "Like Lucy said, it's an ongoing investigation."

"Lame," Kaden grumbles. "Dempsey, want to play Call of Duty?"

Lucy sits on the floor beside the couch where I'm laid up. Rhiannon sits on the coffee table nearby, while Mom inspects everything in my living room with a critical, judging eye.

"Fancy place you've got here," Mom says, crossing her arms over her ample chest. "Didn't know cops paid so well."

"Got a good deal on rent here. Jamie knows the landlord."

"Of course she does." Mom flutters her fingers in a dismissive way. "Jamie's something special now, huh?"

Dempsey, thank goodness, is in an intense conversation with Kaden about the game to even notice my mother bitching about my best friend.

"She's happy," I say through gritted teeth. "Have a seat, Mom. Stay a while."

To my surprise, she sits down in the recliner. Despite Mom being Mom, it's kind of nice that they came over. Our relationship may be shitty, but they must care, otherwise they wouldn't be here. For someone who's spent her lifetime feeling isolated from her own family and as though she doesn't belong, the feeling is refreshing.

"Some of your friends from the station came by," Rhiannon says, face scrunching. "Asked me questions about Lenny and Trevor." Her eyes water. "You didn't tell me he was there the night of Lenny's murder."

"Ongoing investigation, Mom," Lucy interjects on my behalf. "Have you guys ever seen a cop show before?"

I stroke my hand over Lucy's head in a quiet gesture of thanks.

"I didn't want you to worry," I say to my sister. "You'd already been through a lot. Plus, if the detectives came to see you, then you would have plausible deniability. I didn't want them investigating you too."

"Is he going to get into trouble?" Rhiannon asks. "I wish he'd answer his phone or come see us."

"No," I lie.

Maybe not be in trouble with the cops, but the bikers are a whole other story. Rhiannon definitely doesn't need to worry about that.

"The detectives said it was safe to move back into our apartment," Rhiannon tells me, worry gleaming in her eyes. "There's part of the carpet that's been cut out, but the land-lord is supposed to be replacing it soon."

My stomach roils. "But Lenny was murdered there."

"Probably by someone he had beef with," she counters. "I don't have beef with anyone. I just want to go back to work and be with my kids. I want a simple life."

"Nadine says you can come back whenever you're ready, sugar," Mom says to her, voice soft and gentle, a tone she has never used on me.

"I'll protect them," Kaden says from where he sits on the floor in the middle of his video game. "Detective Bishop taught me some self-defense moves a few times when I went with you to work."

"Will you at least check in?" I ask Rhiannon. "Or answer when I text you?"

She nods, a sad frown marring her face. "Lenny wouldn't let me reply to you or take your calls. He's not here anymore."

I hate that she's carrying his kid and dealing with the fact he's been murdered, but I'm not sorry that loser won't be in her life anymore. It was a blessing in disguise.

"Just don't shut me out," I say to her. "Please."

"I promise. I won't."

My family stays for another half hour and then they leave because Mom has to get back for her shift. I learned Nevaeh and her kids didn't show up not because they didn't want to, but because there wasn't enough room in Mom's car for everyone. Nevaeh was, however, worried about me according to Rhiannon. That reduced the sting.

After Dempsey sees them out, he takes Lucy's vacated spot on the floor beside the sofa. I run my fingers over his stubbly jaw, realizing this is the first time I've ever seen any sort of facial hair on him. Either he left his razor at his house or he's been too busy catering to me to shave.

"This is new," I murmur, smiling at him.

He smirks. "I almost used your razor but then decided that might get me kicked out."

I laugh but wince when a sharp pain lances through me. "You feed me and spoil me. Going to have to do a lot more than dull my razor before I even think about making you leave."

A bang on the door has us both jolting in surprise. Dempsey hops to his feet and trots over to it. He huffs and looks over his shoulder at me.

"Tanaka."

I grimace but give him a nod to let him in. As much as I don't want to see the man, I can't exactly avoid him forever. He's still my boss and I was shot while on duty. Aisha already warned me he stopped by her house yesterday to deliver some paperwork for her to sign.

The chief strides into my living room all business. His eyes are narrowed as he quickly glances over my entire body before landing on my face.

"How are you feeling?" he asks, voice crisp.

"About as good as one can feel after taking a bullet in the back."

He nods, lips pressing into a firm line. "Years ago, when I was a beat cop in Seattle, I got hit in the shoulder. Hurt like a sonofabitch. Even after lots of physical therapy, it still gives me fits all these years later. Here's to hoping you heal quickly and fully."

I offer him a polite smile, but it's difficult. I'm not exactly comfortable with this man standing in my living room.

Dempsey, bless him, remains right beside him, arms crossed over his chest and wearing a scowl. I love how protective he is. It's nice knowing I have someone to confide in who will always have my back.

"Officer Thurman, I'm just going to get right to it and cut to the chase," Tanaka says, dropping a file folder on the coffee table. "Internal Affairs will be investigating you."

I start to sit up but wince in pain, deciding not moving is a better option if I want to continue to breathe without crying. "What? Why? I'm on paid administrative leave. I was defending myself and another officer."

"Patel said the same thing. The shooting isn't why you're being investigated. It's why you were there in the first place."

"Because it's my job," I hiss, fisting my hands. "We were called there. It was an ambush!"

"Again, I know this because Patel said the same thing."

"You don't believe Aisha? Me?"

"Aisha, yes, as she's not given me any reason to question her. You, however, have been there every damn time I turn around. You're in every case, nosing around, working cases you're not assigned to, responding to situations that are a conflict of interest."

I gape at him, blinking in shock. "Since when is caring about doing the right thing a bad thing, Chief?"

Don't cry.

Don't freaking cry.

Stupid meds have my emotions clogging my throat.

Dempsey, seeing my reaction, clenches his teeth together. His expression is murderous as if he'd like to punch Tanaka in his perfect face.

"I took this job because our precinct was in dire need of cleanup. I'm still trying to determine if you're the source of the mess or an annoying distraction." Tanaka gestures at the folder. "I'll come back later for the signed documents. IA will be reaching out to talk to you. If you're hiding anything, Officer Thurman, they'll uncover it. You'll learn nothing gets past me."

With those words, Tanaka turns on his heel and brushes past Dempsey on his way out. Neither of us speaks until we hear his engine start outside.

"That guy is such a dick. I want to knock him off his high horse," Dempsey grumbles as he comes to sit back down on the floor beside me. He takes my hand, stroking my skin with his thumb. "You have nothing to hide. He's reaching. Your job is safe, babe. Don't worry."

I want to believe him.

I really do.

My job may not be safe now that IA is involved, but that doesn't mean I have to go down without a fight. If Tanaka wants to report me, so be it. I'm about to sing like a canary about all his wrongdoings and all my suspicions of him.

Tanaka is hiding something, not me. He's corrupt and I suspect he might have more information on Trevor that he's let on.

Two can play at this game.

I will win.

Losing my career over all this mess may be inevitable, but I'll be damned if I lose my nephew over it too.

CHAPTER TWENTY-NINE

Dempsey

"**D**AMMIT, WOMAN, SIT YOUR ASS DOWN," I GRUMBLE, rushing over to take a plate out of Sloane's hand. "I'll unload the dishwasher. You're supposed to be resting."

She was shot a week ago. A goddamn week ago. You'd think she was completely healed by how eager she is to do stuff around the house.

She blows out a huff of air. "I can't just sit around all day. Yes, it still hurts, but I'm going stir-crazy. The doctor doesn't want me lifting anything heavy, but I can handle unloading the dishwasher."

As much as I want to coddle her and make sure she's taken care of, I know she's right. Sloane's best bet at healing is to start doing more and more. I just fucking worry about her hurting herself.

"Fine," I grumble. "But don't do anything that requires you to stretch."

I'm rewarded with a triumphant grin at having gotten her way. I decide it's sexy and I'll let it slide.

"You should be working anyway," she tells me, eyes narrowed. "That piece won't illustrate itself."

She's right. I've been commissioned by the artist lady, Mona Angel, I met at the art gala for a couple of pieces. One for her and one for one of her high-end clients. They'll earn me five thousand a piece, which I thought was ridiculously high but am not going to complain. Then she went on to tell me if I do a good job and as word gets around, the commissions will go up in price, meaning they'll pay me even more than five thousand. Of course she's taking a small cut on anything she refers to me or later if I sell anything in her gallery, but it's still better than I could do on my own.

I dip down and give Sloane a peck on the side of her neck before leaving her to her task. Once in the living room, I settle on the sofa with my iPad and tackle the piece for the client first. He sent some videos of his wife who lost her battle with cancer last fall. There are pictures of them but not many in the last few years. He wants something that shows her as she was in those final months as she battled her illness, but still show her strength and their love for one another. Watching the two of them banter in the videos and then some where she breaks down in tears, overcome with grief at what the cancer was taking from her is heartbreaking. I hope I can bring the emotions to the art that he's hoping for.

A soft knock on the door interrupts my work. I set the iPad down and walk over to the door to see who it could be today. We've had countless visitors since Sloane was discharged from the hospital. I'll be glad when it slows down and goes back to just being us.

I peek through the side window and nearly choke on my own tongue when I discover who's on the other side.

Mom and Dad.

Why are they here?

Fuck.

With a sigh, I open the door. Mom's eyes drop to my

shirtless body and her face sours like she's been sucking on a lemon. I wave for them to come in and snag my shirt off the couch. By the time I've thrown it on, my parents are standing awkwardly in the living room.

I never really thought my parents were uppity, but seeing them in Sloane's cozy, normal living room, they certainly look out of place. Mom's designer handbag probably cost double what Sloane pays every month for rent.

"Hey," I say in greeting. "Have a seat."

They both sit side by side on the sofa. Sloane slowly walks into the room and stands close to me. The tension in the air is thick enough to damn near choke on.

"You need to sit down too, babe," I say, gently guiding Sloane over to the recliner. "You got your way and unloaded the dishwasher. Now rest."

She smirks at me but obeys. I help ease her into the chair and snag her blanket from the end of the couch. Once she's settled, I can relax. I find my mother watching me with confusion in her eyes.

That's right, Mom.

I'm a man who cares for his woman. Not some reckless child you think I am.

I bite my tongue, choosing not to say those very words. I don't want to cause any more tension. Sloane is broken up about the idea of Mom hating her. It hurts me too. They're best friends. Their friendship can't end over something like this. It's just not fucking fair.

Dad clears his throat. "So how are you feeling, Sloane?"

"Better than you'd think considering I took a bullet in the back. I'm anxious to get back to work."

My father nods as though he approves of her answer.

Mom purses her lips but doesn't speak. I suppose it's better than her yelling at me.

"Jude sent me information on those bikers," Dad says, voice tight. "Basic stuff like all their criminal records, police reports, family, etc. Nothing telling. More than likely, their illegal activities that they haven't been caught for have remained off the radar, especially if they're dealing with cash. If there was something to find worth anything to tell, he'd have found it."

Annoying as fuck, but not surprising. Silence fills the room and awkwardness settles over everyone. It's obvious they didn't both show up just to give me that useless update.

"Jamie," Sloane says softly, voice filled with pain. "I'm so—"

"Please," Mom chokes out. "Don't."

Sloane slumps, defeated by Mom's dismissal. Anger swells up inside me. I sit on the arm of the recliner and take Sloane's hand in mine, squeezing it to show my support.

"Mom," I grind out. "This has to stop. You're making this all about you and it has nothing to do with you."

She gasps, eyes widening. "Dempsey."

Dad frowns but doesn't interrupt. I take it as a sign to keep pushing.

"No," I say firmly. "You've punished us enough. You need to either get on board with us or get out. I won't have you making us feel like shit for loving each other."

"I…"

"You, you, you." I sigh heavily. "Think for five seconds, Mom, that this is real because it is. You're hurting two people you care deeply about because you don't approve of the relationship. It's selfish."

Sloane is tense, her hand turning clammy in mine. I stroke her with my thumb and bend down to kiss her hand.

"I know this is hard for you to believe," I tell my mother, "but I love Sloane. More than you could ever understand. I will do whatever I can to take care of her and make sure she feels adored like she absolutely should be. You of all people know what sort of shitty life she's had when it comes to family. You—all of us—were her found family. She found and chose you to be hers. Now you want to throw it all away because she fell for your son?"

Mom looks at Sloane, her bottom lip trembling.

"Dempsey is so good to me," Sloane says in a hoarse voice. "The best. I never knew a man could be so kind and loving. He's breathed life into my bleak world, Jame. He's a good man and doesn't get enough credit for it. I wish everyone could see what I see."

Her words make my chest tighten. "Aww, you love me, Officer Do-Good."

She huffs out an annoyed laugh. "Yeah, you gave me no other choice."

When I look back over at Mom, she's studying us with new eyes, darting back and forth between us. Then she bursts into tears. Dad hugs her to him, stroking her hair and consoling her. Finally, she composes herself and gives us a watery smile.

"I just want you to be happy. For you both to be happy." Mom swipes at her wet cheek. "If this is how it happens, then so be it. I'm sorry I've been such a witch about it. I love you both so much and can't stand for either of you to get hurt."

Something unfurls deep inside of me. Mom's words are

heartfelt and genuine. Maybe we can get through this shitty time sooner rather than later.

"Do you plan to come back home?" Dad asks, back to business. Always business with that guy. "What about school? Your career? I hope you're not losing yourself in all this."

"Dad," I say in exasperation, "I'm finally figuring out who I am. I'll start college in the fall like I said I would, but I'm going to actively pursue my art. I already have two paid gigs lined up."

Dad nods, a smile tugging at his lips. "I think that's a wonderful idea. Your talent is too incredible to be wasted. The world needs to see what you can do."

Pride surges through me. I *am* a good artist. My father agrees. Holy fuck. Shocking as hell, that's for sure.

"I'm also going to take my earnings and buy my own car," I tell him. "Something I can afford on my own. Something I'll drive on my terms and no one else's."

Dad grins. Actually grins. I haven't seen him look this happy in, well, ever. What the actual fuck?

"And I'll get my own place, too," I continue now that I'm on a roll. "I'm eighteen and a man. When Sloane is ready to have me forever, then I'll be there. Until then, I think I'll be happier not living at home."

"I'm ready," Sloane says. "Don't go."

I tear my gaze from Dad's weirdly twinkling eyes to look at my girl. "What?"

"I want you here, too, Demps. I finally found someone who loves me and who I love back. You think I'm going to let that go?"

Holy shit. Sloane's asking me to move in with her.

"You just like that you're getting home-cooked meals on

the regular," I tease. "And that I cleaned out all the stale cookies from your pantry."

"Hey, I know a good thing when I see it," she jokes back.

"You've been cooking?" Mom asks, surprise in her tone. "So you do pay attention."

I shrug my shoulders. "It's your other kid you need to teach. That is, if you can get her to stop videoing herself for longer than five seconds."

Dad chuckles. "She's 'influencing.'"

Sloane pokes at my thigh. "Be nice. She's good at it. My nephew worships her."

"It's weird, though, right, Dad? She developed a cult of followers who buy what she tells them to buy. It's like she's mastered mind control. Fucking creepy if you ask me."

Mom sighs in exasperation. "It's not creepy. She's a savvy, young businesswoman."

"I'm sure half her followers are jerking off in their parents' basements as she moisturizes her face live."

"Dempsey!" Sloane and Mom both bark out at once.

Dad's humor evaporates and he scowls. "They better not be."

Sorry, Gem, I owe you coffee for that one.

"I'm sure everyone has innocent intentions," I say to Dad, giving him my best angelic smile that used to get me out of trouble when I was a toddler.

He shakes his head, rolling his eyes. "Sure." With a huff, he rises to his feet and offers a hand to Mom. She joins him and they both look over at us as Dad says, "We'll see you soon."

"At Sunday dinner when Sloane is feeling well enough

to travel," Mom says in her stern mother voice. "I'm not taking no for an answer."

"I'll think about it," I tease.

Sloane pokes me again. "We'll be there. I'm fine."

I hop up and see my parents out the door. Despite a rocky start, their visit turned out okay. When I return to the living room, Sloane has stood up and waits with a sexy smile that makes my dick perk.

"I could use a shower now, boyfriend. You going to wash me?"

Up until now, I've helped her shower every time and kept it G-rated. Something tells me she has a little more in store this next time.

"Boyfriend?"

"You moved in. It's official."

We're official.

That I can get on board with.

CHAPTER THIRTY

MONTGOMERY'S EYEBROWS LIFT WHEN I WALK into the station in uniform. Tara greets me with a hug and then I get a fist bump from Aisha, who's been back a couple of weeks before me. Eight weeks was a long time to be out of work. Bishop gives me a nod and a small smile.

Now, if I can just avoid Tanaka.

Internal Affairs held their investigation, and I was cleared. I'd threatened Tanaka about investigating him as well, but in the end decided not to. I'll just be sneakier about uncovering what he's up to. Rest assured, though, I'll get to the bottom of it.

"Be prepared to be bored out of your skull," Aisha says from her desk. "Chief says I can go back on patrol soon, thank God. I don't know how much more of those dweebs' daily banter I can take."

Montgomery flips Aisha off and Bishop cracks up laughing. Idiots. I don't blame her. It's going to be a long few weeks of desk work until Tanaka deems me fit for duty. I plan on using this time wisely to obtain more information starting with any leads on Trevor.

I spoke with Rhiannon last night over the phone. They've been living back at the apartment for weeks and haven't seen any sign of him. I'm worried that he's vanished. Did something happen to him? Is he still alive or did he just skip town to avoid the heat? Whatever happened to my nephew, I will figure it out, no matter the result.

My desk is as I left it. Tidy and untouched. As much as it pains me to admit, I'm grateful to work the desk for a while. I'm healed physically, but I still am not at full strength. I get winded easily and tired after anything strenuous.

The morning goes surprisingly easy. Just about everyone at the station drops by my desk to give me shit about getting shot. I think it's all in good fun. I certainly don't let it bother me. When I have a lull between people coming over, I check my phone.

No texts from Dempsey.

He started classes at PMU this week. So far, he's not happy that he only has one art-related class. I don't blame him. School's not his favorite place to be and they're making him take gen-ed courses like English and History. But he's not complaining about it, which I'm hoping means he's focused and taking notes. I decide to refrain from texting him so as not to disturb him.

I'm so lost in my thoughts about Dempsey that I almost don't see Tanaka breeze by. It's nearly lunchtime and he's just now showing up to the station today. As expected, he doesn't stop to talk to me or acknowledge my presence. It's satisfying knowing he tried to get me out of here and failed since I didn't do anything wrong. I guess I'd be bitter if I were him too.

"Montgomery, my office," Tanaka barks over his shoulder. "Now."

I smirk at Montgomery and shrug. *How does it feel to be in the doghouse, asshole?*

As soon as he disappears, I realize Bishop is nowhere to be found. The two detectives on Lenny's case are away from their desks and Tanaka is distracted. This is one of those golden opportunities I'd hoped for with having desk duty.

Quickly, I slip out of my chair and make my way over to Montgomery's desk. Since he runs his mouth more than he works, his area is clean and no files are anywhere. Bishop's desk, however, is a goldmine. It's clear to see who does all the work between those two. I take a seat, ignoring Aisha's wide eyes as she watches me while on the phone. I'm sure she'll give me crap about this later, but I don't care. It's now or never.

Several folders on his desk are ones I'm unfamiliar with. I do, however, come across one called Tate Prince. I'd been the one to take Tate's statement when his vehicle had been vandalized and then again when he'd dealt with a stalker. The perp has been in jail for nearly a year now. Case closed. Why in the hell is it on Bishop's desk?

As much as I want to dig around to see what that's all about, I have something more important to worry about. Trevor. I end up finding the file I'm looking for buried under a few more, including the Ghirard file.

Maybe I'm not the only one who's had a problem with all these cases. It's annoying that Bishop can dig all he wants but Tanaka rides my ass for it. Does Tanaka know Bishop is looking at these files? If me and Bishop put our heads together, perhaps we can uncover what Tanaka is hiding after all.

Bishop's phone that's sitting on the desk lights up. Because I'm nosy, I take a peek. It's a text message.

Mayor: You can't change the price, Andre. Not how this works.

An oily feeling slicks over my skin. What price? How does Bishop even know the mayor? His phone lights up again with another text. Of course I read that one as well.

Mayor: Just make it go away like you promised. We can renegotiate later. This is too important to stall on.

"Can I help you?" a deep voice rumbles from behind me.

I slam Trevor's file closed and wheel around to face Bishop. He cocks his head to the side, studying me as though he can see inside my mind. The penetrating look causes me to shiver.

"Just looking for this." I wave the folder at him. "Since no one is looking for my nephew anymore or looking into who killed my sister's boyfriend, I thought I'd tackle this to see if I could find out anything new."

Bishop glances at Tanaka's office and then flashes me a goofy grin. "You're in luck. Me and Montgomery were about to follow up on a lead." He gestures at Tanaka's office. "He's going to be there a while, I imagine, and this is time-sensitive. Want to ride with me and ask your questions?"

A lead on Trevor?

My heart leaps at the prospect.

"Of course. What's the lead?"

He snags his phone and keys off his desk. "I'll fill you in on the way. Let's go."

Aisha, who's still on the phone, frowns when I walk by with Bishop. I mouth the word "lead" and drop the file on her desk. Before she can tell me this could get my ass fired, because it could, I follow after Bishop to his SUV.

"So," I ask once I'm buckled in and we're on the road, "what's the lead?"

"A guy called in. Said he thinks Trevor's been staying with some bad people. I told the guy we'd meet up so I could ask more questions."

A guy. Bad people. Vague much?

I drill him for more answers, but he cleverly diverts the conversation back to work and fills me in on what I've missed. I'm starting to get a really gross feeling about this. Alarm bells are ringing inside my head. As soon as we pull down the road where the bikers' place is, all the hairs on my arms stand on end.

This doesn't feel safe.

Thank God I have my service weapon on me.

That didn't help last time when you got shot, dumbass.

"Across the street," Bishop says, pointing to a dilapidated house. "He says he sees people coming in and out all the time, but there's this one kid who's young and doesn't seem like he belongs with them." He pulls up in front of the old house. "If you want to stay in the car, that's fine. You won't hurt my feelings. I know it might be triggering to be back here."

Fuck off, asshole.

As if I'll give up this opportunity to get information on Trevor. It's not like I can rely on Bishop or Montgomery to do their jobs. We'd have found him already if they actually worked every now and again.

I climb out of the vehicle and follow after Bishop as he goes to the front door. He bangs on the door and holds his badge out. The door cracks open and a greasy-looking guy peeks out.

"Detective Bishop," Bishop says, voice deep and commanding. "You called about a kid who looked out of place?"

The man nods and points past us to the barn on the property behind the bikers' house. "Yeah. He was comin' and goin' pretty frequently until a few weeks ago. Then he went in that barn and hasn't come out. Gotta bad feelin' about it."

Bile surges up my throat and it takes everything in me not to puke. If he went into the barn and never came back out, does that mean they killed him? Oh God.

I'm still staring at the barn when a skinny man is shoved out the side door. He stumbles and falls face first into the grass.

What if it's him?

I take off running, ignoring Bishop's barked order to wait for him to call for backup. All that matters is getting to Trevor. If it's not Trevor, there's a kid out there who needs help. My back immediately starts to ache from the exertion, but adrenaline keeps me from slowing. I run through the yard where a couple of months ago I was shot and into the field. The skinny man climbs to his feet and starts waving at me.

It's him.

As I draw in, I recognize his build and shaggy hair. He's much skinnier than when I last saw him and bruises mar every inch of exposed flesh. Anger explodes inside me. These motherfuckers hurt my nephew.

Trevor is shaking his head and rasping out words I can't seem to make out. I nearly tackle him when I reach him.

"Honey, Aunt Sloane is here. You're okay."

He lets out a pained sob and rasps out, "Run!"

Run?

I turn to look for Bishop, ready to yell for him to get back up here now, when a large shadow casts over me. The scent of whiskey and body odor permeates the air. Before I can whirl around to face the person coming up to me, something slams into the back of my head.

The crack echoes in my skull and I black out before my body hits the ground.

CHAPTER THIRTY-ONE

Sloane

Ow.

The first thing I notice as I start to regain consciousness is that my head is throbbing inside my skull. Something warm trickles down the back of my neck. Has to be blood. What the hell did I get hit with?

I blink away a wave of dizziness, attempting to make sense of my location. It's musty and smells of mildewed hay. I must be inside the barn. It's dark aside from a few slivers of daylight shining in through the cracks of the worn building. When I go to touch the back of my head, I realize I've been cuffed to a pipe with my own handcuffs.

Naturally, I've been divested of my weapon, keys, phone, and anything else that could've been useful in my predicament.

A surge of panic swells up inside me as my fragmented thoughts begin to piece together.

Trevor!

Where is he?

"Trevor?" I croak, scanning my eyes across every viewable surface in my line of vision.

Nothing but dust and hay.

"Trevor," I say louder, forcing my voice to project beyond my near vicinity. "Are you okay?"

Nothing.

I'm dizzy and slightly nauseous, probably sporting a nasty concussion, too. It'll be okay, though. Bishop saw what happened. He'll call for backup. This place'll be crawling with cops in no time.

Breathe in, breathe out.

I attempt to keep the storm of fury and terror from overwhelming me. Running my palm across the dusty floor, I search for anything I could use for a weapon. A rusty nail would be great. Unfortunately, all I have to use in defense is hay and my free fist.

Voices can be heard just outside, but I can't make out what they're saying. Then there's a squeak of a door that floods daylight into the barn. I squint against the harsh light that exacerbates my headache.

Who hit me?

What do they want?

A shadowed silhouette saunters my way. Is it the Prez guy? One of his goons? The figure stops a few feet in front of me and then squats.

"You should have left well enough alone, Thurman."

The voice. I know the voice.

My brain short-circuits as I try to make sense of it. I finally am able to focus on the man's face when he turns slightly. His profile is one I see every day at work.

Andre Bishop.

This doesn't make any sense.

"I actually liked you," he says with a cold chuckle. "Feisty as hell. Thought many, many times of what it'd be like to fuck someone like you. I bet you're an animal in the sheets."

"Fuck you," I hiss, swiping the air in front of me and missing him by a mile.

"Too late." He shrugs and sighs. "The time for those ideations is over. This is all business, I'm afraid."

Thoughts blink inside my head, little flashes here and there. This stupid concussion is making it impossible for me to think straight. I remember the files on his desk and the texts from the mayor. Then he easily lured me out of the station with the promise of news about my nephew dangling on his hook.

He knew where he was all along.

"You were nothing more than a nuisance until you started picking at the Ghirard case. I had that shit buttoned up so tight," he complains. "But you just couldn't let it go even after Tanaka rode your ass about it."

I knew it.

I knew there wasn't something right about it all along.

"You work for the mayor, doing dirty deals behind the scenes? Never pegged you for a corrupt cop."

He chuckles. "You call it corruption. I call it business. Everything was fine until you got into my business."

How can he be so smug and chill about this? It's like he's confident he'll get away with it. There's no telling what all he's been getting away with since he's been working for the PMPD.

"You made it pretty easy to deal with you, though," Bishop says, continuing his arrogant speech. "Your family is trash, and when I discovered your nephew and your sister's boyfriend were involved with some local bikers, I realized there was a way out of all this. A way to get your thorny ass out of my side."

My heart hurts that my family was brought into this because of me. Trevor's in real trouble right now, and apparently, I brought all this on myself.

"Me and Prez were able to strike a deal," he reveals. "Money and sex, Thurman. Those two things make the world go round."

"You can't do this forever," I bite out. "You'll get caught sooner or later. Maybe you'll get rid of me, but there'll always be someone out there looking to stop corruption and uncovering the truth."

"That's me, woman. I'm the detective with the impeccable record and a favorite among my peers. Even you liked me and you don't like anyone."

"Where's my nephew?"

"Oh, he's around. I promised a lead and I led you right to him. We have a plan for your delinquent nephew. He has your blood on his hands." He makes a gesture at the back of his head. "And he'll have the murder weapon on him. I'll have to shoot him in the head, of course, for killing my colleague and friend. If only I'd gotten to you sooner."

His sarcasm makes me grind my molars together. "You won't get away with this."

"Oh, but I have. Tanaka's stupid ass thinks it's you—that you're the problem in our department. He thinks you're covering for your nephew murdering Lenny. Prez cut Lenny's throat and later sent Trevor home. You both played beautifully into our hands."

I was wrong about Tanaka all along.

We were looking for the same person and were too focused on our dislike for each other.

What a waste. I feel like an idiot.

And now, because I didn't figure this out quickly enough, my nephew is going to die. We'll both die. I'll never see Dempsey again.

A lump forms in my throat. Crying won't help me. Grieving over a future with a man I love that I'll never go on to have isn't going to get me out of this situation.

"You were supposed to die weeks ago, but you were too slippery then," Bishop says, jerking me back to his villain speech. "You're not slipping away this time. I'm being paid a lot more to get my hands dirty to make you go away."

The mayor is dishing out the cash to have me murdered all because I was digging into the Ghirard case?

"You're going to kill me yourself, Bishop?" I bark out a harsh laugh. "They'll catch on. They're not stupid. Your DNA will be all over this place."

He rises to his feet and clucks his tongue. "Like I said, Thurman, me and Prez have worked out a deal. He gets to kill you, we frame Trevor, and everyone walks away happily ever after. Well, except for you. You'll be dead."

Without another word, he strides off. Someone else approaches and swings at me. I barely have a chance to react or move and take a fist to the jaw.

I see lights again and then nothing.

"Aunt Sloane."

"Go to sleep," I murmur. "Night night."

"Wake up," Trevor croaks out. "Please."

I jerk fully awake with a massive migraine. In one of the now-muted light slivers, I find my pale nephew shivering with snot running down his lip. Adrenaline courses through my veins, the need to protect Trevor pushing past the pain in my head.

"It's okay," I rasp. "We're going to get out of here."

How? I have no freaking idea. But we have to. We can't die like this.

Light enters the barn again, this time dimmer, like maybe just the moonlight. It makes me wonder how many hours I've been trapped in this barn and unconscious.

People will be looking for me.

Aisha knows I went with Bishop.

They'll piece it together. They're cops.

But will it be too late?

Considering they have Trevor in here with me, I'd say my time is running out. Quick. The scent of body odor and whiskey invades my nostrils, making me nauseous. Whoever is here is the person who knocked me out before.

"Lookie, it's the bitch pig who shot my fucking friend."

Prez.

"He deserved it," I spit out and brace for him to hit me. Nothing comes.

"Andre says I have full rein. I can do whatever the fuck I want to you." He kicks some hay toward me. "Blondie, there's a lot I want to do to you, but we'll start by making you squeal like the pig you are when my dick is rammed up your tight cop ass!"

"No!" Trevor cries out, launching himself at Prez. "I won't let you hurt her!"

Prez easily body slams Trevor to the barn floor. Something cracks—which sounds like a bone snapping—and my heart is crushed. Trevor wheezes, giving me renewed hope that he's still alive. Prez drags Trevor to where I can see him in a ray of moonlight and then begins strangling him. Trevor is too weak and no match for the burly guy on top of him.

"Stop," I cry out. "Please, Prez. Just do what you have to do to me. Get this over with. I can't watch this."

He rains punch after punch down onto Trevor's face and then finally abandons him to look my way. My nephew's blood spatter is on this monster's face.

The monster who's coming for me next.

With surprising quickness, he grabs my foot and yanks. The cuff cuts into my arm as I'm stretched as far as I can go. I try to fight this man off with my free hand, but he easily swats it away. He's yanks at the top of my pants, ripping the button off in one tug. Then he starts peeling my uniform slacks off my body.

He's going to rape me as promised.

God, I can't do this.

Think of Dempsey.

Dempsey, sweet Dempsey.

I'm flipped onto my stomach and my arm screams in pain at being twisted. Then a punch to my back has me in so much pain I vomit.

He punched me where I got shot.

That bastard.

Someone is sobbing hysterically and it takes me a second to realize it's me. I'm crying. No, I'm freaking the hell out. I may be a tough cop, but even this is too much to deal with.

I need help!

But help isn't coming.

My panties are torn painfully from my body and dirty fingers probe at my ass crack. I wish he'd just kill me instead. That would be more preferable to what's coming.

Shouts.

Lots of men shouting.

Bright white lights start dancing all over the barn in every direction. Chaos ensues with people yelling and crashing into things. Prez lets go of me, taking off in a bolt. I whimper and sob, painstakingly trying to twist my body back around. My ass meets the dirty hay floor and it's a relief. I'm trembling so hard my teeth keep clacking together, but all I can focus on is pulling my uniform pants up to provide some sort of protection. Heavy boots thud toward me, causing me to shriek, shying away from my attacker.

"It's okay," a smooth, deep voice says. "PMPD has arrived. Let me get you uncuffed."

A light from somewhere in the barn reveals my rescuer. Andre Bishop.

I open my mouth, ready to scream at him to get away from me, when he brutally grips my jaw, cutting me off.

"Say a single word and I'll finish what Prez started," he warns, voice low and dangerous. "And then I'll do the same to every goddamn person in your family."

Another man rushes over to us. I recognize the nauseating cologne immediately. Bishop's partner, Ethan Montgomery.

"Grab the kid," Bishop barks. "Right there. I think he's injured. I found Thurman. She's in bad shape too."

"Fuck," Montgomery growls. "I hope every single one of these assholes goes down for this."

"You and me both," Bishop agrees.

I'm too stunned, and frankly terrified, to speak. Bishop unlocks the handcuff, finally freeing me. I'm too weak to stand on my own and am forced to lean against him once he has me on my feet. More tears freely fall down my cheeks.

I'm not dead and neither is Trevor.

I need to get to safety before I can figure out a way to

bring Bishop down for all this. In the shape I'm in right now, though, I'm powerless and relying on his physical strength to get me out of this barn.

Once outside, the chill of the fall air makes me shiver. Bishop crushes me against him. Bile burns my esophagus, making me wonder if I'm going to puke again. I hope I do it all over him.

EMTs rush over to nephew, immediately taking over for Montgomery. More EMTs come to my aid. Bishop gives me a painful warning squeeze on my arm before releasing me to them.

I'm free.

I'm free from that psychopath.

Tanaka stalks past me, giving me a nod and an apologetic smile. I'm confused that I didn't just receive another reaming for getting involved with these bikers again. Instead, I see him stop Bishop. He says some words that have Bishop backing up, but then Montgomery and another officer are manhandling him into cuffs as Tanaka reads him his rights.

Am I imagining this?

Nope.

They put him into the back of a squad car and shut the door. Tanaka and the other officers are talking, but the EMT asking me questions and probing the back of my head distracts me.

"Ma'am, tell us where you're hurt."

"I, uh, got hit in the back of the head. Then punched in the face." I grimace. "And punched in the back where I was recently shot."

A wave of nausea has me gagging.

"Were you sexually assaulted?" the woman asks,

gesturing at my unbuttoned pants that aren't doing anything to hide what my panties would have if I still had them.

"N-No, well, y-yes. I, uh, he didn't get to penetrate me, b-but that was the plan."

She nods, a sad look on her face as she covers my lower half with a blanket. The next few moments are a blur as they check my vitals inside the back of the ambulance. Before we leave, someone enters the ambulance and sits down beside me.

"Thurman." Tanaka stares down at me, an unreadable expression on his birdlike features. "I'm sorry."

"For?" I rasp out. "Is Trevor okay?"

"He'll be fine. I popped in to check on him before coming to see you. They're already on the way to the hospital with him. One of the officers is calling your sister."

I relax, thankful that he's alive and family will be told.

"I feel stupid," Tanaka admits with a scowl. "I seriously thought you were the rat."

"Same to you, buddy." I grimace when another wave of pain explodes inside my head. "I mean, what police chief can afford to drive a Porsche?"

"One who married into wealth," he says, shaking his head. "We fucked up."

That we did.

"I came here from Seattle because of the corruption of the previous chief. From experience, I've learned there's not just one snake, but usually a couple. I've been watching everyone but then got distracted by your…pursuits."

"And I," I say with a sigh, "found out a little too late that Bishop was the real source of infection in our department."

Tanaka gently touches my arm, and surprisingly, I do find comfort in it. "We were both fooled. It won't happen again."

"There's someone else too," I tell him, cautiously side-eyeing the female EMT.

"I know." His eyes flicker knowingly. "Montgomery actually cracked things wide open. He's been watching Bishop's interactions for months now and even followed him to a couple of meetings. The other person in this equation is being apprehended now."

Relief floods through me, knowing the mayor's not getting away with his part.

"What about that sick piece of shit biker president?"

"On his way to jail with all his buddies." He squeezes my arm. "We could have avoided all this had you stayed at your desk like you were instructed to. Imagine my surprise when I came out and you were both gone."

Great timing, Sloane.

"How did you know where to find me?"

"Officer Patel said she got a bad vibe when she saw you leaving with Bishop. She was ready to rescue you, guns blazing. We weren't sure where the two of you went. Both of your phones were turned off. But when he turned around to come back, he switched his phone back on. Then, to our surprise, he came in with an outlandish story about how your nephew had taken you hostage."

"You had to go along as though you had no idea," I grumble. "I bet that sucked."

"Indeed. I had to send Patel home because she was seconds from blowing the lid off the entire operation."

A smile tugs at my lips as I think about Aisha ready to rip Bishop's head off for me. She really is a good friend.

"What now, Tanaka?"

"Now we let justice prevail. Those men are going away for a long, long time."

"Good." I smile at him even though my bruised face hurts. "Next time, let's try working together instead of against each other."

He smirks. "Fantastic idea, Thurman."

CHAPTER THIRTY-TWO

Dempsey

" **I** 'M SURE SHE'S FINE," GEMMA SAYS AS SHE WATCHES ME pace Sloane's living room. "Probably just working late. She's been gone a long time. I bet her boss gave her a boring task like organizing the file room."

Her babbling, though I don't believe a word of it, soothes me. Just like always. It's why I called her first—why I always call her first. Plus, she has our car until I get one of my own. I don't like being stranded.

"Or," she continues, "maybe she went to see her family. You said they're getting along better."

I rub my hand over my face, unable to shake the terrible feeling in my gut. She'd have called or responded to my texts if that were the case.

"Does it make me a psycho boyfriend if I drive around looking for her?"

Gemma sniggers. "Yeah, kind of. It's still weird knowing you two are a thing and Mom and Dad are okay with it."

"Something doesn't feel right, though."

Headlights flash through the front windows and my heart does a somersault. Thank fuck. I'm going to bend Sloane over my knee and spank her pretty ass for giving me heart palpitations. Dating a cop—one who's been shot in the line of duty—is hard on the nerves.

"I guess you don't need me anymore," Gemma says as she stands, tossing her long brown hair over one shoulder. "See you in the morning."

I give her a fist bump as she leaves. Until I find a car, she's been picking me up for school since our university schedules are pretty much the same. She's gone for ten seconds or so before she's walking back in, a frown on her face. Kaden bursts into the living room behind her.

"Aunt Sloane's at the hospital," he says, tears in his eyes. "Trevor too. The cop dude came by our apartment to tell Mom. I told her you'd want to know, but she didn't have your number."

Holding up a hand, I rasp out. "Wait. What do you mean she's at the hospital? Did something happen to Trevor?"

"The cop told Mom they'd gotten hurt. He didn't give us much more than that just that we'd probably want to get to the hospital to be with them."

"Fuck," I snarl, shooting a panicked look at Gemma. "We have to go. Now."

She nods and the three of us rush out of the house. Kaden jumps back into the car with his mom, and me and Gemma take off in the Tahoe. I'd expected her to hand me the keys, but she didn't. I'm thankful, too, because I'm shaking so damn bad with panic that I'd have a hard time keeping the vehicle on the road.

Sloane's at the hospital.

She's hurt.

I fucking knew it. I had a feeling and I chalked it up to my obsession with her. All along, she wasn't avoiding me or rudely failing to communicate with me. There was a problem.

Please be okay.

What if she's been shot again? This time worse? What if she was in a traffic accident? Too little information and too many what-ifs keep ping-ponging inside my head.

Minutes later, we arrive at the hospital. I'm having triggering memories of the last time I was here when I was denied access to seeing her. Luckily, I do have her family with me, so that might help my case to see her.

The chief meets us—the guy Sloane has had so many issues with—and it takes everything in me not to deck the fucker. Was he involved in this? Is he responsible?

"What happened?" I demand, storming over to the guy. "Where's Sloane?"

Tanaka holds up a placating hand. His usual asshole sneer is gone. "She's okay. We got to her in time."

We got to her in time.

What the actual fuck?

"What about my son?" Rhiannon asks, voice trembling. "Is he okay?"

"He's going to be okay too." Tanaka frowns at us. "I'm not going to sugarcoat it. They went through an ordeal, but they've both made it to the other side. They'll need family support to get them through the mental anguish they've experienced."

I feel sick to my stomach.

"Spit it out, man," I choke out. "You're freaking me the fuck out."

"One of the detectives lured Sloane to the biker compound with the promise of a lead on Trevor. When she arrived, she was ambushed."

Ambushed.

My knees buckle, but my sister hooks her arm in mine to keep me steady.

"Both Trevor and Sloane were assaulted," Tanaka grits out, eyes flashing with fury on their behalf. "The degree and specifics will be up to them to share."

"So let me get this straight," I growl. "You were harassing my girl because you thought she was doing something shady and all along it was someone else?"

Tanaka's head bows and his black eyebrows pinch together. "Unfortunately, yes."

"Where is that fucker who tricked you all? I'm going to fucking hurt him."

Gemma tightens her hold on my arm. "Dempsey, don't."

"You can't," Tanaka says with a shake of his head. "He's been arrested along with every person involved." He meets my furious glare. "I understand you're angry. I'm angry too. I feel like I was fooled. But, in the end, we got the bad guys, and Sloane and Trevor are going to be okay. It's the best outcome we could have asked for."

"I want to see my son," Rhiannon says. "Please."

Tanaka turns on his heel, gesturing for us to follow him. We walk past the receptionist—a different one than the one I'd flipped out on last time—and toward the ER. Once there, he guides us to where Trevor and Sloane are in beds in the same area, their curtain pulled back so they can see each other.

I stumble to a stop when I see her bruised face and wrapped head. She also has a bandage on her wrist. Her hair is sweaty, bloody, and covered with bits of hay. What the hell happened to my girl?

When she sees me, her tough, stoic expression crumbles. I'm by her side before the first tear drips from her jaw. Gently, I take her hand in mine and lean forward to press a whisper of a kiss on her battered face.

"This job of yours sucks," I whisper, voice thick with emotion. "Like, it really, really fucking sucks."

She barks out a teary laugh. "Would you believe up until we started seeing each other, it was actually kind of boring?"

"What are you saying?" I grumble, "Am I your bad luck charm?"

"There's not a bad thing about you, Dempsey."

After several minutes, once Sloane has calmed down, I tear my gaze from hers to check in on Trevor. His face is a lot worse looking than his aunt's. Rhiannon has crawled into the bed with her son, holding him like he's three and not a grown-ass man like myself. Kaden, Lucy, and Gemma all hover nearby, their worried glances bouncing between Sloane and Trevor.

"What happened?" I ask, turning back to study Sloane. "Tell me everything."

She sniffles, not meeting my stare. "I stupidly went chasing after something that felt way too easy and too good to be true. I knew, in my gut, that it was a bad idea, but I went anyway."

I bring her hand to my lips and kiss it. "That's just you, babe. It's not a bad thing. You're a cop. You chase down leads. You're also an aunt who cares about her family. Anyone in your place would've done the same."

Her smile is sweet. "Thank you."

"So tell me when it went downhill."

"Bishop, that lying sack of shit, brought me into another trap they'd sprung for me. This time, they caught me right where they wanted me." Her chin quivers. "I saw Trevor and he was emaciated. I was so relieved but also terrified at seeing him in such a state that I blindly ran for him. Someone hit me from behind and I woke up handcuffed to a pipe."

Only the fact the perps have been arrested quells the rage that burns hot in my chest. She and Trevor are safe from those bastards.

"Then," I urge, voice murderous. "Go on."

"Bishop admitted he was doing all the sketchy things I was suspicious of. It was never Tanaka. I feel like an idiot now."

"Hey," I say softly. "If it's any consolation, he said he felt like an idiot too."

A smile tugs at her lips. "We were both idiots, but I think we might be on the same page from here on out."

I tuck a dirty strand of her hair behind her ear. I'm eager to get her back home where I can spend all the time in the world washing away the horrors she endured today.

"After telling me he was going to frame my murder on Trevor and then kill him too, I was knocked out again. I'm not sure how long I was out for, but when I woke up the next time, Trevor was there with me. Prez showed up and started talking trash. Trevor tried to defend me and ended up taking a horrible beating for it. I was able to get Prez's attention back on me…"

Her eyes glaze over and terror gleams in her blue eyes. I'm not sure I want her to continue, but I can't pick and choose what I hear.

"Did he rape you?" My voice is so soft, it's barely audible.

She swallows hard and shakes her head. "He, uh, was going to. Had my pants down and everything." A full-bodied tremble quakes through her. "Then the cops showed up. Bishop was back pretending to be one of the good guys. But when we got outside, Tanaka was ready and arrested him along with all his biker cronies."

Sloane may have not been raped, but she was sexually and physically assaulted, terrorized, and held captive. I'm calling Tate tomorrow to set up an appointment with him. I may give him a lot of shit, but he's a great therapist and Sloane's going to need a professional after this. I'll give her love and support. However, she still needs counseling after this. Anyone would after such a traumatic event.

"It's over, babe," I murmur, squeezing her hand in mine. "You're safe. Trevor is back with his mom. You did it. Time to rest."

As though my words were exactly what she needed to hear and the last of the adrenaline has left her body, her eyes flutter closed and she passes out.

When I look back over at Trevor, Rhiannon is no longer in the bed with him but sitting in a chair beside him. Her other two kids and my sister are gone.

"Where'd they go?"

"Gemma said she'd take them back home. Now that they know their brother is safe, they don't need to sit up here." She looks over at her son, who is also now sleeping. "My sweet boy got on the wrong path. This is all my fault."

"You didn't force him to join a biker gang, Rhiannon."

"I know," she says with a huff, "but because of my relationship with Lenny, he was exposed to that life."

"That's reaching. He chose his own way. It'll be up to him if he wants to do better."

She nods. "I think he's ready. He agreed to go to rehab."

"Best place for him."

"He's going to be okay. My boy is a fighter."

"Like his momma."

Her brows scrunch. "I'm trying to do better—to be braver."

"One day at a time."

"You know," Rhiannon says, a soft smile on her lips, "you're good for my sister. She's not so cold and distant. I know you've helped her a lot. And Kaden thinks the world of you."

"Your kid is cool as shit. As far as Sloane, she helps me too. We're good for each other."

Rhiannon's expression turns wistful. "Sometimes I wonder what finding true, healthy love would feel like. Sometimes I don't think it's in the cards for me. Hell, look at my track record so far. The first man I loved abandoned me and our kids. The second one abused me. I'm a magnet for disaster."

"You just haven't found the right one yet. He's out there. Don't give up hope." I turn to look at Sloane's beautiful sleeping form. "I have loved your sister for as long as I can remember. Now look at us. Imagine if I'd given up."

Rhiannon sighs and then parrots my words, "Don't give up hope."

"Never." I bring Sloane's hand to my lips and kiss her again. "Never ever."

EPILOGUE

Sloane
Several months later…

"CAN I HAVE HIM?" TATE ASKS, GIVING ME HIS SADDEST face. "I'll be the best daddy to her in the whole world."

Jude grunts nearby and I can't smother the giggle that erupts from me.

"Didn't you guys just get two more dogs?" I ask, amused by my friend.

"But we don't have this one." Tate snuggles Dempsey's and my new pup. "See, she loves me."

Dempsey saunters over and holds out his hands. "Mine."

Tate rolls his eyes playfully at me before passing the sleeping puppy to his real daddy. Dempsey hugs Beauty to his chest and kisses her golden, fuzzy head. I rescued her earlier this week from a dumpster. Her mother was nowhere to be found. Beauty and her siblings were malnourished, cold, and on the brink of death. The other four pups were quickly rehomed to Tara, Aisha, and Tanaka of all people, who took two. Beauty was mine the second I laid eyes on her. Bringing her home to Dempsey and seeing his overjoyed look was one of the best sights I'd ever seen.

We're a family now with a little furbaby.

Dempsey, seeing my dopey smile, leans in and kisses my cheek. "You're mine too. Don't be jealous, babe."

He leaves my side with Beauty to go sit by Spencer, who's trying to corral Rex. Kaden, who came with me for this week's family dinner, is helping Jamie and Gemma in the kitchen. I actually look forward to the Park Sunday meal with this chaotic group.

"How are you doing?" Tate asks, slipping into therapist mode. "You're awfully quiet today."

"I'm just happy. Enjoying life."

He hooks his arm in mine and leans his head on my shoulder. "Good. I knew we'd get there eventually."

When Dempsey told me he'd set me up an appointment with a therapist, I felt betrayed and pissed. I was defensive, thinking something was wrong with me he wanted to fix. Yes, I went through a traumatic experience with the bikers, but I was fine. We fought about it for a straight week where I did my best to ice him out, but eventually, I gave in.

It probably would've helped if he'd told me the therapist was Tate. At first, when I'd met with Tate, I was guarded and quite bitchy, to be honest. But Tate has a way of getting you to spill your guts. We talked about the shooting and then the assault. Eventually, we started digging into my past and childhood. I didn't realize how much I needed to talk through all of that stuff until we got into it. Now I look forward to my weekly meeting with Tate. And since he just opened up his own practice near the station, it's been easier to get by to see him during lunch or right after work.

I was able to give Tate some closure too, at least. His stalker and Bishop were friends. Bishop abused his police power to help him find Tate. This was all uncovered after Bishop was arrested. Knowing we got that rat out is relieving to everyone. I'd even pushed Tanaka on Oliver, my dud of a date who was involved in the Ghirard case, thinking maybe he could've been an accomplice, but he was cleared of any wrongdoing. Since I know Tanaka is a good guy now, I was able to let it go, trusting my chief's judgment.

I've certainly come a long way in the trust department. My therapist would be proud.

My phone buzzes in my pocket. I pull it out to find a text from Nevaeh.

Nev: Mom wants us all to get together for Christmas. What does your schedule look like? Also, can we do it at your place since you have more room?

In the past, this would have caused me great anxiety, but since I've been working on forgiving my family and myself, it's easier to take this stuff one day at a time rather than stewing on any tension between us.

Me: I'm happy to host. Ask Mom if she'll cook her famous mac and cheese. Dempsey got a new smoker he's been practicing with. I bet he could make the ham.

Nev: Sweet. Thanks, sis. The kids have been dying to go over to your house again. Plus, they want to see your new puppy.

This makes me smile. Mom is still cantankerous, but my sisters are warming back up to me, Rhiannon more so than Nevaeh. I've been inviting them over weekly once life went back to normal. And though it feels anything but normal to have my family in my house, I enjoy it nonetheless.

Nathan, who'd been talking to Hugo, excuses himself and saunters my way. Tate allows Jude to tug him away from me over to the dining room table. Normally, I'd brace myself for a conversation with Nathan, but things are different between us now.

"Sloane," he says, offering his hand to shake. "I wanted to congratulate you on making detective."

Pride thumps in my chest as I shake Nathan's hand. "Well, they had an opening, so…"

He smirks. "They don't just fill it with anyone. You deserve to be in that position."

"Thank you." Nathan doesn't typically praise me, so this feels strange.

"Hiroshi tells me you're doing well. I'm pleased the two of you were able to work things out."

Once I learned that Tanaka was actually a good guy, it was easier to get to know him. I was also shocked to learn his wealthy wife was the Seattle gallery owner who hired Dempsey for commission work. Small world. Because of this, we've gone to dinner on a double date with them a few times now. Mona and Dempsey nerd out over art, while me and Tanaka talk about work, mostly to discuss updates on how Bishop and the mayor are faring in prison. I even talked Tanaka into buying the station a badass coffee machine when I got a few drinks in him one night.

"Me too," I agree with a smile. "And Mona just found a buyer for a piece Dempsey is working on. Did he tell you? They're from New York and offered him fifty thousand."

Nathan nods, pleasure gleaming in his eyes. "He's well worth it. Does this mean he's going to pay off that ridiculous car now?"

The pearl-white Dodge Hellcat Redeye, the Widebody Jailbreak edition, purchase was another source of contention between Nathan and Dempsey. I'd cosigned on it for Dempsey since his credit's still new, which didn't earn me any brownie points from his father. Nathan thought Dempsey would choose something more practical or affordable. But my man prefers 807 horsepower over practicality. The girlfriend in me thinks he's hot driving the thing. The cop in me nearly has a shit fit whenever he exceeds the speed limit.

"Doubtful," I tell him honestly. "He wants to remodel the kitchen."

Nathan narrows his eyes for a moment, considers my answer, and then nods. "Your kitchen does need updating."

I flip him off. "I know, I know. My oven sucks and it drives Dempsey insane. You two are cut from the same cloth."

Nathan claps me on the shoulder and then leaves me be. I find my seat beside Dempsey as Jamie starts bringing out casserole dishes. Beauty is asleep in Dempsey's lap, so his hand is free to take mine and he threads our fingers together.

I'm happy—really happy—with him.

Rex, who's now in a highchair between Spencer and Dempsey, tries to make a grab for the puppy. Luckily, his arms aren't long enough. He settles for throwing his sippy cup instead. Dempsey deflects it with his elbow and then playfully tickles Rex until he squeals. Then Dempsey turns to me and mouths, "Thank God you don't want kids."

I burst out laughing. It's a conversation we've had many times over. I wanted to make sure he was okay with the fact I never plan to get pregnant. He's young and I didn't want him to be held back if that's what he wanted. Thankfully, we were on the same page. Sure, he'd make a great dad, but he's a fantastic uncle not just to the kids in his family, but to those in mine.

I'm okay with being Aunt Sloane and Uncle Dempsey over Mom and Dad.

My phone buzzes again. When I pull it out to peek at it, it's my other sister this time.

Rhiannon: Trevor got the job! He's going to be a mechanic's apprentice at the garage. They're paying him fifteen dollars an hour with no experience and working around his school schedule. I'm so proud of him!

I send her back a bunch of hearts and clapping emojis. I show Dempsey and he grins. Jamie lent me the money and we were able to get Trevor into a fantastic rehab facility. Not only did he get sober and proper mental health treatment while there, but they also enrolled him in a tech program for him to continue now that he's out of rehab.

Rhiannon: I think we should celebrate. Mom says everyone should meet up at Nadine's for supper one day this week. Can you and Dempsey make it? I know it'd mean a lot to Trevor.

Me: Absolutely. We'll be there.

Rhiannon: Yay! I'll start making plans and let you know the exact date.

I put my phone away as soon as the table is set with mountains of food. Jamie sits beside me and we chat about Kaden while food is passed around. I tell her the good news about Trevor and she's just as thrilled as I am. The dynamics of our friendship have changed since I'm with her son, but we're finding new ground and I'm grateful to have her back in my life.

Dinner is the usual whirlwind with everyone talking over each other, babies crying, and more food than we could ever eat. Tate and Jude steal Beauty, but we'll steal her back before we leave.

Dempsey stands, grabs his butter knife, and loudly clanks his glass. "Yo! Listen up, fam!"

I look up at him, wondering what in the world he's going to tell them. With Dempsey, you never know what'll come out of his mouth. Sometimes he blurts out exactly what's on his mind. That can be both a good thing and a bad thing.

"So I know we're planning a spring wedding for Tate and Jude," he says, grinning at the recently engaged couple, "but I was wondering how you all also thought about having a wedding this summer."

I blink at him in confusion. "What are you saying?"

He fishes a box out of his pocket and sits back down, facing me. "I'm saying let's make us official, babe. I love you. I want to be with you forever. Say yes."

Heat floods my cheeks. I can feel everyone's eyes on me. This is wild and reckless, and most assuredly way too soon.

"Yes, of course," I rush out because despite those things, life's too short to let opportunities pass you by. "I love you too, honey."

Dempsey fist pumps the air and then pulls me to him for a filthy kiss that has no business being shown to the whole damn family. When he pulls away, I'm breathless and dizzy. He slides on a simple rose gold band with a few tiny diamonds embedded in it. I love how simple and me the ring is. It'll be easy to work in too. Just goes to show that even when he appears to be spontaneous, Dempsey puts a lot of thought into pleasing the ones he loves.

The whole family talks over each other after that. Callum thinks it's hysterical and won't stop laughing. Hugo seems embarrassed on our behalf. Spencer has a lot to say but mostly inappropriate stuff that has Aubrey trying to cover his mouth with her hand. Tate wears a cheesy grin, whereas Jude scowls at Dempsey, probably for overshadowing their own engagement. Nathan shakes his head with a mix of irritation and amusement. Gemma and Jamie both keep saying, "Oh my God." Kaden babbles about how he should get to be the best man and lists all the reasons why.

It's absolute madness, but I love it.

I love him.

Dempsey tugs me out of the chair and away from the noise of his family. I giggle as he all but drags me upstairs. He pulls me into his childhood bedroom that Jamie hasn't touched since he left.

"Finally," Dempsey growls, tugging at the button on my jeans. "We can celebrate."

We get our clothes off in record time and then he drags us over to his bed. I yelp when he tosses me onto it. He pounces on me, ravaging me with soul-stealing kisses. Being in his bedroom feels extremely inappropriate and naughty, but I'm totally into it.

He slips a finger inside me and hums with appreciation. "Detective Do-Good is hot for the bad boy."

I groan, threading my fingers in his hair as he fingerfucks me. "Maybe I'm not so good."

His grin is devilish as he strums my G-spot so perfectly I come quickly with a strangled cry. Then he replaces his finger with his gorgeous, pierced cock and thrusts hard into me.

"I'm going to fuck you fast, babe, before my parents come looking for us," he says, breathing heavily against my lips. "Just so you know, this fantasy that's coming to life is something I've beat off to more than I will ever admit."

"Stop talking, troublemaker, and fuck me like you always dreamed of doing."

He turns feral after that and I get to orgasm once more before someone knocks on the bedroom door. While I squeal with embarrassment and he hollers for them to go away, we finish with a grand finale that has Dempsey pulling out to paint my stomach with his cum.

"Mom sent me to come get you," Gemma huffs from the other side of the door. "You two are so gross. I can't believe you're having sex right now!"

"Already finished, sis. Tell Mom I'm showing her where the bathroom is. We'll be down in five."

"She knows Sloane knows where the bathroom is, dumbass. Just hurry before Mom decides to come up here herself!"

She storms off and we both crack up laughing. Dempsey brings out a playful side of me I never knew existed. I'm going to die of humiliation when I have to do the walk of shame in a few minutes, but it'll be worth this stolen moment with my fiancé.

Holy shit.

I'm getting married.

"I love you, Dempsey Park," I blurt out, suddenly overcome with emotion.

He gently brushes some of my hair out of my eyes and gives me a tender smile. "I love you too, wifey. Always have. Always will."

I hope you enjoyed Dempsey and Sloane's story!
Want to read about the alluring Gemma Park?
The Torment of Two is next!

If you're curious about Callum and Willa's story, check out The
Teacher of Nothing!

*Or, if you're dying to read about Spencer, Hugo, and Aubrey,
check out The Tangle of Awful!*

*Wondering about the mysterious Jude and his therapist, Tate,
check out The Heart of Smoke!*

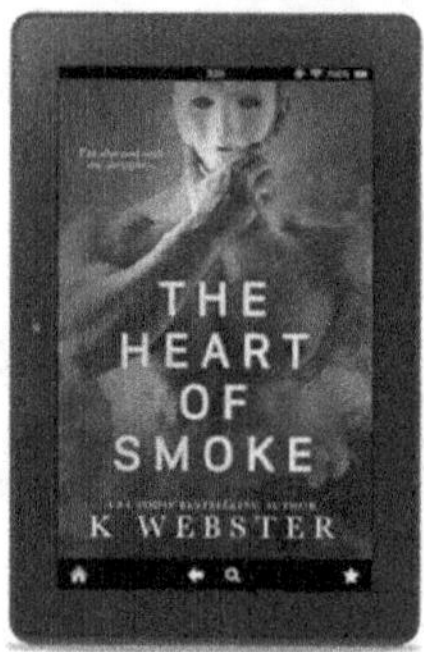

ABOUT THE AUTHOR

K Webster is a *USA Today* Bestselling author. Her titles have claimed many bestseller tags in numerous categories, are translated in multiple languages, and have been adapted into audiobooks. She lives in "Tornado Alley" with her husband, two children, and her baby dog named Blue. When she's not writing, she's reading, drinking copious amounts of coffee, and researching aliens.

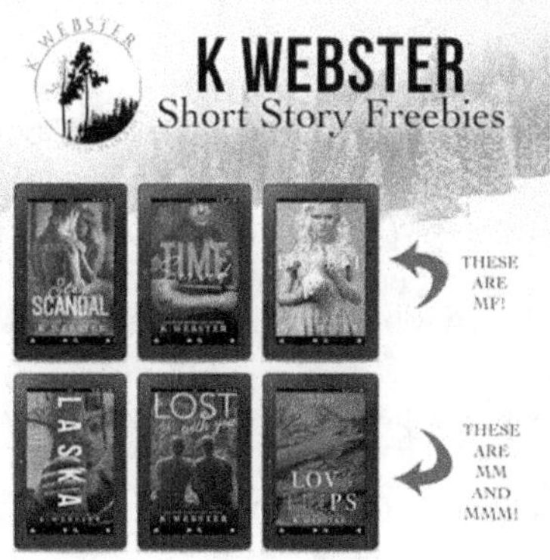

Download at
books.bookfunnel.com/k_webster_short_story_bundle

JOIN MY NEWSLETTER
at authorkwebster.com/newsletter

JOIN MY PRIVATE GROUP
at reamstories.com/authorkwebster

Follow K Webster here!

Facebook: www.facebook.com/authorkwebster

Readers Group:
www.facebook.com/groups/krazyforkwebstersbooks

Patreon: patreon.com/authorkwebster

Twitter: twitter.com/KristiWebster

Goodreads:
www.goodreads.com/author/show/7741564.K_Webster

Instagram: www.instagram.com/authorkwebster

BookBub: www.bookbub.com/authors/k-webster

Wattpad: www.wattpad.com/user/kwebster-wildromance

TikTok: www.tiktok.com/@authorkwebster

Pinterest: www.pinterest.com/kwebsterwildromance

LinkedIn: www.linkedin.com/in/k-webster-396b7021

THE TORMENT OF TWO

Gemma

KNOW I'M A JOKE TO MY FAMILY.

They think my job as an influencer is made up and silly. Dad is convinced it's dangerous and not something I should do long-term, often lecturing me on putting my focus on school rather than my platform.

For me, though, it's something I'm proud of. I built it from nothing and shaped it into something that not only awards me a viable income but also gives me a voice to help other people.

Sure, sometimes that help is showing my followers what moisturizer I use or my favorite lip gloss, but it feels bigger than that. One day, I hope to use it in a way that's more impactful.

One day.

I'm not really sure how I'll turn my content around without some blowback, but I'll figure it out. It's why I'm majoring in marketing at PMU.

What my family and followers don't see is all that goes into maintaining and growing my audience. Each day, I spend hours strategizing content, researching what others are doing, and replying to my followers to cultivate and build solid relationships. So many girls my age and younger have reached out to me to let me know they aspire to be like me. It makes me feel good that I'm inspiring them, even if it's just to feel better about their outward appearance.

I'm making my way through my messages when I come to a strange one.

@TwoCanPlayThisGame.

The username sends a chill down my spine.
I read the message, trying to make sense of it.

I see you. The real you. The you no one else but me sees.

I click on their profile to see what sort of person is sending me this message. From another girl like myself, it could mean something totally different than some random weird man. The profile, though, has nothing to offer. It's a new account. They're not following anyone but me and they have no posts. The picture is a screenshot of my profile page.

This is the kind of stuff Dad is worried about, but thankfully, I know how to handle it. It's not the first weirdo to message me and it certainly won't be the last. I quickly block the person and delete the message without giving it another thought.

I move on to more sweet messages about how my recommendation for an acne treatment helped one girl's skin clear up and now she's feeling more confident. As I read through them all—each one kind and uplifting—I can't help but keep thinking back to the creepy message.

I see you. The real you. The you no one else but me sees.

It's a scary thought. The real me, the girl buried deep

beneath the perfect makeup, style, and smile, is insecure, feels smothered by her father wanting to keep her safe, and wants to be seen for more than a trophy. That girl isn't as confident as the one she outwardly portrays for the internet. Knowing someone else might see her leaves me feeling exposed and raw.

I suck in a deep breath and exhale heavily. My nerves are brittle, making me feel slightly nauseous. Imposter syndrome claws its way up inside me, mocking me.

Who do I think I am?

Maybe I am just a joke.

I give my head a sharp shake and look at my follower count that's recently surpassed a million. I'm doing something right or these people wouldn't be here.

With a quick check of my makeup, I turn the camera on me and push the live button. My smile is wide and bright—you can't even tell it's fake.

"Hey, Gems," I say, waving at the camera. "If you're new here, I'm @GemmaLovesUx2 and I'm dying to tell you about this new primer I just got. Your makeup will look as flawless when you go to bed as when you applied it in the morning. I'm telling you guys you're going to freak out at how amazing this product is."

The hearts and comments start flooding in, reminding me I *am* good at this.

I won't let some creep torment me and throw me off my game.

I'm Gemma freaking Park.

I *invented* the game.

Read *The Torment of Two*, the final book in the series, up next!